Nekkid Lake

a novel by Noah Bond

NEKKID LAKE

A NOVEL BY NOAH BOND

First Edition. Published at Fort Lauderdale, Florida, by Mission Investments, Inc. Cover design by CityStreetz, Hollywood, Florida. Printed by BookMasters, Inc., Mansfield, Ohio.

Library of Congress Control Number: 2014913807.

ISBN 978-0-9673551-4-6.

Dedications and Expressions of Gratitude

This novel is dedicated to my wife Susan.

Thanks to:

Vera K. Randall, my senior English teacher.

My musical accomplices Kathleen Patricia, Nicholas Coppola, Chris Capozza and Bryan Wilson.

Copyright attorney, Barry L. Haley.

The good people who proof-read the manuscript and hopefully made it a better story, including Susan Agee, novelist Ben Hopkin, screenwriter Michael de Silva, and Lucille Haynes

Most of all, I thank He who made this book possible.

NOAH BOND

Nekkid Lake

A GOTHIC MYSTERY

Nekkid Lake

a novel by Noah Bond

Secluded Necklan's Lake is the idyllic spot for a picnic or skinny-dipping. Hence the nickname *Nekkid Lake.* But, according to local lore, never be there after darkness falls.

God made the wild animals according to their kinds, the livestock according to their kinds, and all the creatures that move along the ground according to their kinds. And God saw that it was good.

--- Genesis 1:25

PROLOGUE

Necklan's Lake, Vermont
Friday, May 16, 2014, 11:09 PM EDT

The Senior Class had not been deceived by the crepe paper which the Future Teachers of America had applied to the gym, although the scented candles had admittedly reduced the odors that haunted the gym from previous athletic endeavors. The Seniors were too high on graduation to care. They were in that place where they were invincible and immortal --- even though not one of them could imagine being thirty. Their anticipation of the future was unchecked by reality. Tonight was the night they had dreamed about for years. And it was about to get even better.

In tuxedos and prom gowns, they exploded from

the high school into the clear moonlit night. The boys discarded their bow ties and gave their jackets to the girls to cover their bare shoulders. Car doors slammed. Windows were rolled down. Despite the crisp weather, convertible tops were lowered. Horns were honked relentlessly. The Seniors shouted to each other from car to car. Some back seats contained two couples, squeezed in or simply heaped upon each other. Pickup truck beds were packed with overdressed students. Laughing and hollering, they set off, tires spraying gravel. Country music blasted:

O.K., cowboy. Let's push our luck.
Show me the stars in your pickup truck.©

They planned to party all night. Nekkid Lake beckoned.

Few of them noticed that the Moon had turned a reddish color while they had been inside celebrating. Those that did had more important things on their minds. At least they thought they did.

Deep into the forest they drove, swigging Genessee

and hard lemonade from long necks. Flask bottles of vodka appeared as the road became a track. The sound of daddy's Mercury Marquis scraping bottom blended with the chaotic melody. It was all part of the ritual, this rite of passage.

At last a clearing appeared. Just beyond lay a narrow strand which gave way to a pristine body of water, shimmering under the full red Moon.

The cars parked randomly and the Seniors bailed out. A few more-prepared girls had changed into shorts and sweatshirts somehow along the way. Ice chests were carried into the clearing. Blankets were laid out. A boom box split the air. A bonfire was lit by impatient young woodsmen using copious amounts of charcoal lighter. Shoes and socks disappeared. The girls began to laugh nervously as the moment of truth neared. A few boys tested the water and pronounced it to be warm enough to swim — after a few more drinks. This gave rise to chug-a-lug contests, at first just the boys. Then the girls joined in. Some danced in the sand. Tequila appeared, and with it shooters. The noise increased, but who could hear?

Back lakeside, the "shoot and plunge" had started: shoot tequila and then strip naked and plunge into the frigid waters of the lake. The guys had gone first and were pleading with their dates to join them. Most of the girls were being coy, but nobody doubted the outcome. It was, after all, a hallowed ritual. One by one, they doffed their gowns and raced into the water, doing their best to cover themselves with their hands --- screaming from the cold. Their dates embraced them, which didn't help from a thermal perspective, but it undoubtedly gave them something else to think about.

Not all couples were exploring each other. Some had been there before. Others still had inhibitions. The ritual didn't necessarily include touching.

Off in deeper water, massive rocks broke the surface. In their shadows, a couple was kissing.

One girl remained in her gown on shore. She had accepted the date with Harvey, the class nerd, solely because she didn't want to attend the prom alone. She sipped a diet Coke sullenly. She was thoroughly disgusted to think he had expected her to skinny-dip. He actually hadn't, and was handling her hostility by getting plastered on beer. When nature inevitably called, he went into the woods to relieve himself. She became uncomfortable being alone, even more so when she heard what just might have been his scream over the pounding music.

Having experienced the thrill, a few girls saw no further benefit from being in the chilly lake. They began to straggle ashore. Two bolder ones warmed themselves before the bonfire wearing only their dates' tuxedo jackets. Some donned the shorts and sweatshirts they'd thought to bring. The remainder retrieved their gowns and disappeared into the woods. The process continued, with the boys coming out as well. The first boys to exit the lake received some taunts from the others, of course, but they were half-hearted. That water was *really* cold. Most of the boys went straight to the fire to warm themselves before completely dressing. A bottle of vodka was passed around the bonfire. A couple the girls by the fire began to dance slowly, driving the boys happily insane.

The only girl who hadn't gone swimming went down to dip her toes in the lake. When she returned to the fire, someone asked her where Harvey was.

"He went into the woods," she replied casually. "Been gone ten minutes."

"Maybe he found a computer!" a male voice ventured, causing a small outbreak of drunken laughter.

"Give him five more minutes," another voice chimed in. "Then we'll send in a search team."

The couple kissing behind the rocks remained in the lake, oblivious to the scene on the beach.

A scream penetrated the night. The dancing stopped. A girl raced from the woods clutching her gown. She fell forward into the clearing and was dragged back by forces unseen. Suddenly the forest was alive with the sounds of terror. Several boys sprinted into the woods — and disappeared forever.

Those by the bonfire scrambled to regain their clothes in response to the unwritten rule that fear is inversely proportional to clothing. When mostly dressed, they peered uncertainly into the woods. A girl by the fire began to cry softly. Someone turned off the boom box. The screams had stopped. The Seniors began calling out for their dates and friends. There was no answer.

"Who has a cell phone?" a boy asked.

"I do," replied one of the girls. "No reception out here." Several others tried to use their phones with similar results.

It was the quarterback who assumed control. "Stay here by the fire! Stay together! Go back into the water if you feel safer. But keep away from the woods! I'll try to get my car and go for help."

"My car's closer," another volunteered. "Let's take that. Follow me."

Just beyond the edge of the clearing sat a shiny silver convertible with the top down. The two boys leapt over the doors into the front seat. The engine started. The wheels spun.

The group by the bonfire cheered as the car charged down the road.

Until it crashed into a tree and the screams began again.

The couple in the lake had become aware of the

scene in the clearing. They parted. "Stay here as long as you can. Don't try to look. Don't make a sound!" he said to her. "I'm going ashore."

"Don't! It's not safe."

"I know my way around here. I'll be all right. So will you if you stay put. Whatever you do, don't let anyone on shore see you."

With that, he left her alone --- naked in the cold lake.

He swam off silently.

She never saw him again.

A motorcycle roared to life and drove away. Then the beach came alive with the sounds of terror. She covered her ears and began to pray.

The sounds of slaughter were heard a half mile away by the men tied to stakes and the men who had tied the knots. Both groups were terrified. Silent prayers were made to the same God in a least four different languages.

The human noises soon stopped for good. They

were replaced by a prehistoric keening that blended with the wind. Patty shivered uncontrollably. Her teeth chattered. Unable to bear the cold any longer, she peered toward shore when silence finally returned. But there was still activity. She knew it couldn't be the Seniors. Any who had somehow survived would have left immediately.

No. This activity was silent and furtive. And she wasn't close enough to really see what was going on. Patty resolved to stay in the water until she was the last person at at the lake.

Two hours later, she staggered onto the deserted beach. The beach blankets and towels had disappeared. She got as close as she could to the embers of the bonfire. She stared at the abandoned automobiles in disbelief. There was no sign of anyone else, not even discarded clothing. She cried, prayed and shivered until she passed out.

Patty was the only person the Sheriff found that morning, which didn't make sense considering all the vehicles parked nearby — including the bloody convertible smashed into a large oak tree. He'd recognized her. She was Patty something, who lived with her parents on the next street over from his house. One of the high school cheerleaders, he'd thought. Firm young body. He'd noticed when they'd removed the blanket. He'd also noticed that there were no other blankets, towels or clothing to be seen.

She was suffering from exposure and severe hypothermia, unable to communicate. Sheriff Roy figured she could tell him what had happened at the hospital later.

He was wrong.

CHAPTER 1

Cobbler's Knob, Vermont
Monday, April 3, 2017, 7:56 AM EDT

Cobbler's Knob was the shire town, or county seat, of Allen County. The county had been named after Ethan Allen, a cabinet maker turned revolutionary. Allen had been the leader of the Green Mountain Boys war militia that took on the British garrisons in that part of the colonies. The stately county courthouse had been erected more than a century before, facing the Commons, a large square which had once served as the protected common grazing area for the villagers' cattle. In the intervening years, the livestock had yielded to monuments, park benches and, in the center, a substantial gazebo where brass ensembles had played in a calmer era before the proliferation of recorded music. The courthouse now sported two wings for administrative functions like the land registry, the license bureau and the building department. Below the flags of the United States and the State of Vermont flew a flag of green and blue horizontal stripes with white stars on a field of blue in the upper left hand corner, the banner of the Green Mountain Boys. The former stable behind it all had been converted into the law enforcement offices.

Within these converted stables, Sheriff Roy was regaling his deputy with the story of how he caught the largest bass ever taken from Necklan's Lake. Deputy Lucas had heard it before, but didn't bother to say so. He was less than inspired by paperwork, and it was easier to listen than to work. In fact, they both considered it too early to work. Nothing much happened this early in Cobbler's Knob anyway.

So they were surprised when a young woman presented herself at the front door to the Sheriff's Office at that hour. Lucas sized her up. She stood about five feet, eight inches, sported a tan, wore her jet black hair in a pony tail that went past her shoulders, and her legs were muscular. Sheriff Roy simply said "Good morning. What can we do for you?"

"Good morning. I'm Tess Chandler, from Dartmouth."

Silence greeted her.

"I'm here to intern for a month," she explained. "I'm majoring in Forensic Science."

Deputy Lucas groaned softly.

"Pay no attention to Deputy Lucas. He has an aversion to formal education. I'm Sheriff Leroy Hughes. Just call me Sheriff Roy. Everyone else does. I have your paperwork here somewhere. Guess I'll have to find it later. Have a seat and tell us about yourself."

When she finished twelve minutes later, all that the deputy had learned was that she had no idea how real policemen worked. For some reason, he thought of himself as a real policeman. Maybe it was the badge.

On the other hand, Sheriff Roy was welcoming her as if she was the solution to all their law enforcement problems --- if only they'd had any. But, maybe the Sheriff had a plan for handling this unwelcome intrusion.

Stranger things had happened.

"Because I'm the Sheriff, and older than dirt according to my faithful deputy here, I get to ask uncomfortable questions...."

She had known it would come; just not this soon. "Fire away, Sheriff."

"Is there any genetic basis for that lovely tan of yours, Tess?"

"I don't have any tan lines, if that's what you mean."

The mention of tan lines was enough to bring Deputy Lucas to a state of alertness unusual for the early hour. It had been a long winter of heavy, shape-concealing clothing.

"Well parried, Miss Chandler," the Sheriff admitted. "But I'd still like an answer. We're a bit insular up here in the north woods. Slow to adapt. Still getting used to the Irish who came over during the Potato Famine."

"Well then, you'll be relieved to hear that my ancestors arrived before the Mayflower."

"Indians?" Sheriff Roy paused. "Guess they're called Native Americans now."

"And English. As you probably know, the Pilgrims brought indentured servants with them. Those servants were mostly male, and not well regarded by the Pilgrims."

"In other words, the Pilgrim girls were off limits to them."

"Exactly. So the indentured servants intermarried with the local tribes to start families. Over the years, the Indian genes have been diluted. But some obvious aspects remain."

"I've always liked high cheek bones, myself," the Sheriff commented. "Gives a woman a feline look. How about you, deputy?"

He appraised her face with a long green-eyed gaze, then said "I suppose so."

"Is he always this talkative?"

"No. You caught him on a good day," Sheriff Roy admitted. "Do I detect an accent?"

"Wetback. Northern branch."

"Canadian?"

"Guilty. Toronto."

"Fine city, Toronto," Sheriff Roy observed. "Citizenship?"

"Dual. U.S. and Canadian."

"Best of both worlds, eh?"

"Gets complicated at times, but yes. By the way, nice try with the 'eh,' but you need to begin hard and then draw it out a bit."

"I appreciate your coaching, Tess," the Sheriff replied. "Since we don't have to pay you, I guess I don't need your social security number."

"Let me know if you ever do."

"Do you have a place to stay?"

"I'm boarding with Hazel Daniels in town. She has a mother-in-law suite."

"Hazel's a good person. Had those rooms added on for her father, but he never made it out of the hospital. This could be the first time she's let them out. If so, she might be a bit skittish."

"Well, I brought my VW Beetle."

"As opposed to?"

"I didn't bring my Harley."

"Ah! That was a good call!"

"You've got a Harley?" Deputy Lucas was re-evaluating the intern.

"Red 1990 Super Glide with under fifty thousand on the clock. Rebuilt it last summer. Went up to Gaspé on a shakedown last autumn."

"Awesome."

"You have a bike?"

"I'm between bikes now."

"That means he crashed the last one," the Sheriff explained. "Wasn't even drunk. Just reckless."

"I like to go fast on curves," Deputy Lucas admitted.

Noting the *double entendre*, she warned him. "Get you into trouble every time."

"Why don't you go on into town and get yourself organized, Tess. Report back here about this time tomorrow and we'll start you off."

"That would be great. I look forward to working with you — both."

As she drove away, Sheriff Roy decided to torture his deputy. "Bet she's quite a sight, roaring down the highway on her Harley, that long black hair blowing straight back, wearing a tank top, short shorts--- nothing else but her boots...."

Deputy Lucas groaned.

CHAPTER 2

Cobbler's Knob, Vermont
Tuesday, April 4, 2017, 7:51 AM EDT

"Let's start with the basics, Deputy Tess. Can you make a decent cup of coffee? 'Cause neither of us can."

She laughed. "Normal or strong?"

"Me, I like my coffee strong. Deputy Lucas, he *needs* it that way."

"Like reanimating the dead?"

"Pretty much so, yes."

"Espresso?"

"That would do it. Where would you get it?"

"I have a machine in my car. Didn't see any reason to leave it at school. Want me to get it?"

"I'll help."

Deputy Lucas pulled in as they were carrying the

espresso-making paraphernalia. He followed them inside.

"The girl's a marvel!" the Sheriff told his deputy.

The Sheriff sat at his large wooden desk, enjoying his espresso. Tess was seated in front of the desk, ready for her first assignment. Deputy Lucas was at his slightly smaller desk nearby — close enough to be part of any conversation if he so chose. The vintage computers at each desk had yet to be turned on.

"We don't have anything interesting pending right now; so I thought I'd give you a cold case to review."

Her heart sank, but her face didn't reveal it. "Felony?"

"Multiple homicide, about three years ago." She perked up. "Only one we've ever had in these parts. The state sent in a pack of crime scene investigators. They examined and processed up a storm. About a week later we got the results, all bound up neatly and tagged."

"Not enough to solve the case, though?"

"Not by a long shot. You see, more than a dozen teenagers disappeared that night. We're pretty certain they were all at the crime scene just before they vanished. But not one body was found. Not even a body part — unless you count blood. One of the forensics team said the scene was incredibly clean. Even the blood --- definitely human --- resisted DNA testing. Contaminated, I think they said."

"Does this case have a reference name?"

"*The Burlington Free Press* called it the 'Necklan's Lake Massacre.'"

"It caught on," Deputy Lucas observed.

"I remember hearing about it, but I really don't know anything. I was up to my eyes in classes and tests."

"Good. You can start with a fresh perspective."

"Where do I begin?"

"Did you notice the high school on the way into town?"

"Hard to miss, Sheriff."

"Drop by there and speak with the principal, Lucy Thornton. Ask her about it."

"Was she a witness?"

"No. She can fill you in on the local rite of passage

that preceded the incident. Give you a feel for it. I'll call to tell her you're coming."

"If you think that's best."

"I do."

CHAPTER 3

Cobbler's Knob, Vermont

Tuesday, April 4, 2017, 10:02 AM EDT

Allen County Consolidated was the only secondary school in the county. It was a federal style red brick structure to which a more modern brick wing had been added. The attempt to match the old brick had been less than a rousing success, but at least they were both red. The original building had been an imposing, fortress-like building with a flight of stone steps at the entrance. The more accessible addition reflected the passage of the Americans with Disabilities Act. As Tess drove into the parking lot, she noticed the gargoyles on the roof. *Notre Dame de Cobblers' Knob?*

"Welcome to the madhouse, Miss Chandler. I'm Lucy Thornton, the principal." She wore a conservative gray suit with a bright yellow scarf to break the monotony. "That's what the students call it. I hope it refers to the building, not the curriculum."

Tess laughed. "Well, it's not exactly a welcoming façade."

"And the gargoyles don't help...."

"Yes. I noticed. I never saw them on a school before."

"It's our dubious distinction, I fear. Seems this part of Vermont was considered haunted or something. The gargoyles were meant to protect the children. They were apparently quite serious about this."

"Do people still feel that way?"

"The local folks are no more superstitious than other parts of the country these days." She cracked a small smile, then continued "But that still leaves some room, doesn't it?"

"I guess it does, Tess admitted. "Vampires and werewolves are all over the television and movies."

"The local legends here seem to favor the latter —
at least it's some creature that is considerate enough to
not leave any bodies around that reanimate and then bite
your neck." She became serious. "Actually, the Algonquin
tribe in this area believed in shape shifters."

"Shape shifters?"

"Humans that turn into animals --- or other
species. Confined to the Animal Kingdom, I suspect. I
never heard of a were-maple...."

"Ware?"

"W E R E." The principal spelled it. "It's an old
English word for human. It's still used today to designate
humans who turn into wolves, should that ever become
necessary."

"Let's hope not."

"Amen to that."

"Are you from here?" Tess ventured.

"Born and bred, as they say. But I was married to
a career soldier; so I've been around. Lived in Germany
four years, two in the Phillippines. When my husband was
killed, I came back here to close up the family house. I

decided to stay a while to recharge my batteries. Took a teaching job and ended up running the place." She shook her head in wonder. "Never saw *that* coming." She paused. "So what did Sheriff Roy think I could help you with — no apology for the dangling participle."

"Winston Churchill said 'That is the type of nonsense up with which I shall not put.'"

"Indeed he did. Smart man. How can I assist your inquiry?"

"Sheriff Roy thought you could tell me about the traditions of the Seniors."

Principal Thornton thought a moment, then asked "What is it you're investigating?"

"The Necklan's Lake Massacre."

"Oh." It was clearly not her favorite topic.

"Happened about three years ago...," Tess prompted.

"Yes. I remember it. Everyone in town does, I guess. It was my first year as principal. Only a handful of students lived to graduate. And one of them couldn't attend."

"Was she ill?"

The principal considered her answer for a moment. "In the hospital at the time."

"That's tough, to miss your graduation ceremony."

"More like a funeral service really. It wasn't like we could just ignore what had happened."

"No. I imagine you couldn't," Tess agreed. "Can you explain why they were all at Necklan's Lake that night?"

"First of all, you need to know that the kids call it Nekkid Lake."

"Nekkid?"

"As in buck nekkid."

"Got it now."

"It is a firmly established — nay, *sacred*— ritual for the Seniors to go out to Necklan's Lake after the Senior Prom. Once there, they build a bonfire and get drunk enough to go skinny-dipping."

"Must be cold."

"The Senior Prom is usually held in April, at least a month before the final exams. Removes the distraction from a time when they need to be studying. At that time of year, Necklan's Lake can still have patches of ice in the shaded inlets. You can count on it being no warmer than 35 degrees."

"I don't think I've ever been that drunk."

"Me neither!" Principal Thornton agreed."Makes me cold just thinking about it. But it *is* a time-honored ritual. The boys have to go in to prove that they're macho. The reasons for the girls are more complex. It is part of the implied contract for a date to the prom. Of course, some of the girls have been looking for an excuse to take their clothes off with their boyfriends anyway. The others are talked into it by the other girls. Alcohol lubricates the process. Probably some pot, as well."

"Why do you allow them to go?"

The principal sighed. "The Board of Education has no jurisdiction outside school property. But we couldn't stop them anyway. And it could be worse...."

"Skinny-dipping is relatively harmless."

"They can only stay in the frigid water for a few minutes. Then they all race back to warm themselves by the bonfire. The conditions are not conducive to seduction."

"They could sneak back to the cars."

"You must have been a fun date in high school."

Tess blushed until the principal laughed. Then Tess joined her. When the laughter subsided, Tess asked "Have you been to Necklan's Lake?"

"Never at night. But I think it would be a pretty spooky place without other people around — at least two carloads of them. You should check it out."

"I plan to."

"At night."

"I was afraid you meant that."

Bells sounded, followed by the sounds of students in the hallways. "And they're off!" Lucy commented.

CHAPTER 4

Cobbler's Knob, Vermont
Tuesday, April 4, 2017, 11:22 AM EDT

There was only one law enforcement vehicle parked in front of the office. Deputy Lucas was on patrol. This knowledge did not instill any assurance of public safety in Deputy Tess.

"Principal Lucy set you straight?" greeted her at the door.

"And then some, Sheriff. Nice lady. Known her long?"

"Took her to the Senior Prom — a few years back, mind you."

"Were you going steady?"

"Yeah, I guess so. Known each other most of our lives and all that. Then she went off to college and married her soldier. I stayed here to pursue a promising career in law enforcement. They didn't teach it in college in those days; it was strictly on-the-job training."

She sensed that it was time to be diplomatic. "I think that's probably still the best, but the courses do help us catch up with all the technology that's been developed in the last twenty years."

"Congratulations, you're the new IT department," Sheriff Roy commented wryly.

"This conversation just took a nasty turn," she noted. "But I may be able to help out with that. I've had a computer since I could crawl."

"You should see me with a chisel and a slab of rock."

She could almost picture it. He interrupted this thought.

"Lucy give you any advice?"

"She said I should see Necklan's Lake — or Nekkid Lake --- for myself."

"Already got the name right, I see," he remarked. "That's what they call it."

"Do you think I should go there?"

"Not alone. I'll drive you there myself. Let's see....
How about after lunch?"

"Shouldn't I read the file first?" she inquired.

"It'll be easier to picture it in your mind while
you're reading."

"That makes sense."

"Happens every so often," he observed.

CHAPTER 5

Necklan's Lake, Vermont

Tuesday, April 4, 2017, 1:42 PM EDT

The Sheriff drove his official Jeep to the high school first. It was on the way. He stopped in the parking lot, pointed to the entrances to the gymnasium. "Picture more than a dozen high school Seniors, high on life. They've just completed a twelve-year sentence in the name of education. Now finally, they're as free as they've ever been. And more than a few suspect they will never be this free again. Their parents are proud of them. Even their teachers are proud --- and more than a little relieved. This is heady stuff! And they are basking in it. Do you see it?"

"I can feel it!" she admitted. "That how it was for you?"

"Absolutely. And that night I wanted it to last forever. But it never does, of course." The Sheriff pulled back onto the road.

"Did you go to the lake?"

"No. Didn't do that then. There was a church camp down there at the time; so it was off limits to randy teenagers."

"Did the camp close?"

"Burnt to the ground years ago. Nothing left. They never reopened it."

"How'd that happen?"

"One cold case isn't enough?"

"Might help with the one I've already got...."

Sheriff Roy looked doubtful. "It was September. It was a summer camp. The counselors were having a wrap-up party. There was no fuel for the generator; so they used candles to light the lodge. There was drinking. That's all we know for sure."

"Anyone hurt?"

"Doubt it."

"You doubt it? Don't you know?"

"Not really. You see, the fire wasn't reported right away. In any event, it would have been futile to attempt to extinguish a burning wooden building in the middle of the woods at night. There wasn't a pumper truck to shoot the lake water on the fire. The camp counselors weren't from around here. They apparently just went home. No bodies were found."

"That's it?"

"Well," he continued reluctantly, "we thought it was. Later a family came from out of town looking for their daughter who had worked at the camp. She still hadn't shown up at home. They were worried she might have run off with one of the boys. After talking to them for an hour, I was convinced that she would have run of with the village idiot rather than return home."

"Unstable?"

"Unbalanced is more like it. Rip-roaring religious fanatics. The kind that do more harm to Christianity than good."

"I know the type," she agreed.

Sheriff Roy slowed, then turned into a gravel road

bursting forth with weeds and grass. They passed two fieldstone columns about three feet high, one on either side of the road. He pointed them out to her. "Those are all that's left of the entrance sign to Camp Bethany — named after the village where Lazarus and his sister Mary lived."

"Is there anyone still around who might know about the camp?"

The Sheriff frowned. "I don't think you need to be that thorough, but you might speak with the minister. There's only one church in town, in case you haven't noticed yet. It's a community church, which boils down to the fact that there are a lot of generalities and very little doctrine."

"I can see how that could work," she said. "What about baptism?"

"You can be immersed or sprinkled, as a baby or an adult — or not at all. No pressure there."

"That seems to cover all the bases. What about communion?"

"Offered for those who wish after the regular

services." He added "You're pretty good at identifying flashpoints."

"Sounds like the minister is pretty good at dealing with them. What about gays?"

"We're ready for that one. We have a lay minister. He's not ordained or recognized by the State; so he can't perform marriages. Besides, the building is somewhat cozy; so the weddings are held elsewhere. Makes it all kind of moot."

"Tell me there's a cross."

"Yes there is. One atop the bell tower and another above the altar. There's even a stained glass window of Jesus driving out the demons."

"Into some pigs that had the misfortune of being nearby." Tess thought for a moment. "Does it show the pigs drowning themselves?"

"Shows 'em headed toward the water. You have to figure out on your own that they aren't going to be doing laps."

She laughed. "Well put, Sheriff!"

"It's a nice friendly congregation. As one of the

deacons, I invite you to attend services Sunday morning at 10:00. If it doesn't suit you, then drive about seventy miles to the church in Cambridge — but you won't see a world of difference."

"I look forward to it."

The dirt road opened onto a clearing which was bordered by a lake. Sheriff Roy stopped the car. "Last stop Necklan's Lake," he announced in the manner of an old time train conductor.

CHAPTER 6

Necklan's Lake, Vermont
Tuesday, April 4, 2017, 2:33 PM EDT

They left the Jeep at the entrance to the clearing. What remained of the road turned back into the woods. The Sheriff noticed her looking that direction and explained "It continues to the site of the lodge. Nothing left but parts of the stone foundation mixed in with the new growth trees." He kept walking toward the lake. "This is where it happened."

The clearing was almost the size of a baseball infield, but crescent shaped. It dropped off abruptly a few feet to a coarse sand beach. This strand was several yards at its widest point. The waters of Lake Necklan were rippling gently in the Spring breeze. Across the lake was unbroken forest. She could imagine this being an idyllic retreat from the heat of August, but she shivered when she stood before it that afternoon.

Sheriff Roy interrupted her thoughts. "Over there," he said, pointing in the water to the left, "are the rocks we think the survivor may have hidden behind." She saw three granite boulders rising from the water, the nearest being twenty feet from the shore. "But that's just speculation to explain her survival. We really don't know what happened here that night. Probably never will --- unless you figure it out."

"This survivor...." Tess left it hanging.

"Found her lying just up from the beach, about there. That's where the bonfire was. It had burnt out long before we discovered her, wrapped in a blanket, shivering and incoherent."

"Hypothermia?"

"One of the worst cases Doc McAdams had ever seen. Thought she might lose her toes, but he saved them. Said her youth made the difference."

"How cold was it that night?"

"Temperature dipped into the forties, as I recall."

"Brrr. Who was she?"

"Patty Martin. Pretty girl. On the cheerleading squad. You know, peppy type."

"Is she still around?"

Some time passed before the Sheriff answered. "Maybe you could talk to her after you've reviewed the evidence file."

Tess recognized an order, even if it was wrapped in a suggestion. "O.K. What else is out here to see?"

"The cars were parked about where we parked."

"What kind of cars?"

The Sheriff thought a moment. "About half were parents' cars, on loan for the big night. A vintage Mercury Marquis, big old Buick, that sort. Then there were the students' cars. PT Cruiser in mint condition, Jeep Cherokee, couple worn out pickup trucks."

"No vans, motorcycles or ATVs?"

"None. There was a Mustang convertible just off the road that had run headlong into an oak tree. The top was down. Probably had been since they left the prom. From the tire marks, it was clear that the driver had floored it and headed back toward town. Didn't get very far. Windshield fractures indicate both the driver and a front-seat passenger collided with it. That's consistent with the unused seatbelts --- and the blood on the dashboard. Like I said, they were in a hurry."

"Were their necks broken?"

"We'll never know. Their bodies weren't found."

Tess considered that for a moment. "What about the others?"

Sheriff Roy just shook his head.

Wordlessly, they returned to the Jeep.

CHAPTER 7

Cobbler's Knob, Vermont

Wednesday, April 5, 2017, 7:47 AM EDT

The sun was bright, as Tess lugged the file from her car up the steps to the Sheriff's office.

Sheriff Roy greeted her. "Beautiful morning, Deputy Tess! The sun is chirping, the birds are shining."

"And you could use some strong coffee."

"Smart *and* sassy this time of day. You're a marvel, all right" he noted. "Get a chance to look at the file?"

"Yes. It was like putting my brain in a blender."

"If it were simple, anyone could figure it out. You just need more time."

The espresso machine began to whir. She asked "Do you have any other unsolved disappearances besides the Seniors and the Camp Bethany counselors?"

"No. We thought those were enough."

"Well, I'm not much of fan of coincidence. They both happened at the lake. They could be related."

"Crossed my mind too, but we had even less evidence from the Camp — what with the fire and the passage of time before it was discovered. Besides, we had no victims. Wasn't any point pursuing it. It sure looked like an accident."

She brought him a cup of espresso. "Is there a file on Camp Bethany?"

"Just a couple pages. You can have a look. Should be under B."

Tess went to the file cabinets and extracted a thin file, peeked inside it. "I've seen bumper stickers with more information."

"That investigation — to the extent it can be called one — occurred before my time in office. If you want to know more, ask the minister. He was affiliated with Camp Bethany."

"I'll do that."

"It wouldn't surprise me if there was a connection

or commonality, but nobody's found it yet. If it doesn't leap out at you, don't waste time looking for it. There's not enough evidence and you don't have forever."

"Good advice, Sheriff. Do you have the minister's number?"

Sheriff Roy turned on his computer.

"I'll acquaint myself with the facts while you're calling him." It took two minutes to digest the entire file.

CHAPTER 8

Cobbler's Knob, Vermont
Wednesday, April 5, 2017, 10:30 AM EDT

The minister lived in yet another of the red brick houses that flourished in Cobbler's Knob. Tess ascended the stone steps, where she was met on the front porch by a tall man in his early fifties. He had the rangy aspect of an old cowboy, but without the weathered face.

"Good morning. I'm what passes for an emissary of the Lord in Allen County. Call me Matt. At least the name sounds right."

"It's a pleasure. I'm Tess," she said as she entered the front door ahead of him.

"My office is a rat's nest. Take a chair here in the living room. Coffee?"

"Not unless you're having some. I've had my wake-up cup already."

"I don't seem to need one any more. Seems strange after all those years of running on caffeine...." Matt returned to the subject. "I was a counselor at Camp Bethany during the final year — when it burnt down. I understand you have some inquiries about it."

"Yes, just a few. Were you there the day it burned?"

"Yes. The campers — that is, the kids — had all left several days before. The counselors had stayed on to clean up and lock the camp down for the winter. The cabins were already closed up. Only the lodge itself was still in use. Everyone had their duffle bags and suitcases stacked up there. There was to be a party that night. With no fuel for the generator, it looked like it would just be couples cuddling in front of the fireplace. Nothing wrong with that, but the rest of us weren't couples. So we left that afternoon, before it got dark."

"How many stayed for the party?"

"I can only remember four couples. I'm pretty sure about that number. It was a small camp. I may even have their names somewhere."

"Maybe later," Tess said, not wanting him to stop now. "Where did you go?'

"Here. Right here. This is the family home."

"Did you ever go back to Camp Bethany?"

"Yes. About a week after the fire. To describe the camp to the fire department, mainly tell them what was the function of each destroyed building."

"Please tell me what you saw."

Matt paused to summon up his memory of the event. "The lodge, the garage and tool shed were burnt to the ground. None of the buildings had a basement or concrete pad; so nothing was left but burnt wood, stone steps, the great fireplace, and some twisted pieces of metal. The rest was just ashes. One of the nearby cabins was also gone, but the others were intact — still locked up for winter as we had left them."

"Why were they spared?"

"The buildings that burned were all in the same clearing, close to each other. The fire didn't spread beyond the clearing. It was assumed that the fire started in the lodge, which was in use — fireplace and candles, maybe cooking on the propane stove. That's where the activity would have been that night. As the county fire chief said, 'Most fires are started by people.' Made sense. And there were no lightning storms that night. There may have been some oil in the garage or the tool shed, but nobody should have been there.   At some point the propane tank exploded. It was just outside the kitchen, which was part of the lodge. But they don't explode out of the blue. The fire chief thought the source of the fire was elsewhere, that it ignited the tank when it reached it."

"How difficult would it have been to escape the fire?"

"Should have been simple. That's what's puzzling. The lodge had several doors and big glass windows which could be opened or broken out. There was lots of heavy wood furniture you could use to break a window."

"You think that's what happened?"

"The fire chief did." Then he added "Except for one thing."

"What was that?"

"The fire had melted the glass in the windows. But

no glass --- melted or intact ---was found outside the lodge, like you'd expect if they broke the windows out."

"Then they probably used the doors," Tess replied.

Matt was not so sure. "But there *was* melted glass — window glass — inside the lodge. As if the windows had broken inward."

She paused to consider that, then said "Someone who got outside first could have done that to help the people trapped inside...."

"But why break most of the windows in?"

"Damned if I know.... Oh! I'm sorry. I shouldn't have said that."

Matt smiled. "Don't worry. I'm not authorized to send your soul to Hell. Above my pay grade."

Comforted by this revelation, Tess continued. "What happened then?"

"Starting with the fact that none of the counselors who stayed were ever heard from again, could be that no one escaped."

"Maybe one or two escaped, but disappeared to avoid prosecution for the fire that killed the others," she suggested.

"But there were no human remains found. And they looked all around the site."

"So they were completely burned up?"

"The fire chief said it would take temperatures of 400 degrees, sustained over more than an hour, to consume all traces of adult human bones. I've since confirmed that independently," Matt told her. Then he added "I read up on it." Just in case she thought he'd tried it.

"Do we know for sure that the counselors were still there when the fire began?"

"No way of knowing, but both cars they were intending to leave in were still there after the fire. Undamaged by the fire, by the way."

"Maybe they just left them."

"Well, one was an old Chevy, pretty much used up. Might not have started. But the Mustang was relatively new."

"So, how did they leave?" she wondered.

"Maybe someone came to pick one of them up and

they all ended up leaving in that car...."

"I'm going off on a wild tangent here, but what if some of the counselors were killed and their bodies dumped elsewhere...."

Matt smiled. Wild tangents were part and parcel of his job. "Making the fire a way to cover up the evidence."

"Or simply a distraction," she suggested. "Where would you dump bodies?"

"There is a real big lake handy...."

"I assume there were boats."

"Two speedboats, lots of canoes."

"I favor the speedboats. Where were they?"

"Locked up in the garage, which burned to the ground.'

"Evidence destroyed effectively," she observed.

"Still doesn't explain why the windows were broken inward," Matt reminded her.

"Right. Let's back up a step. Do you have any reason to believe there might have been a fight after you left?"

"These were four couples who hung around

together, got along. I didn't see any signs of tension between them."

"What about jealousy?"

"Well, you never know, do you? Each of them seemed more than satisfied with his or her partner. These were relationships that had probably advanced to some stage involving consensual sex." He noted her surprise. "Yes, in a church camp. The counselors didn't think *all* the rules applied to them. In fact, there was this feeling that a counselor had more latitude than a camper, because of his position and experience."

"But you'd think that they'd be more devout."

"Ah. That's part of the problem. The New Testament doesn't outright condemn sex between people who aren't married to each other. True, it has negative pronouncements about marital infidelity and the taking of virgins, but mainly because females were chattels, possessions. It was less about sex than theft."

"That's harsh."

"But pretty accurate. And the counselors knew this. So hormones trumped the rules. And that's another point. This was a church camp. The counselors gave religious instruction and enforced those rules. All in all, we were a mild bunch."

"Not given to drinking or fighting?"

"An occasional beer was all. Wasn't much available out there to tempt us. No drunks among us. No brawlers. Gosh, none of us even smoked."

"Gosh?"

Matt blushed slightly. "See what I mean. Real Puritans."

"Let's go back to the windows, then."

"Fine by me," Matt said.

"Could an animal have broken a window?"

"Have to be a large animal, like a moose. But why would it do it?"

"What about a bear or a wolf?"

"Certainly possible, but unlikely."

"Rabid?"

"More likely," he conceded. "Not sure if bears get rabies, but I think wolves do."

"If large flesh-eating animals attacked through the

windows, that could explain the absence of bodies — and the fire could have been caused by overturned candles in the panic that would have ensued."

"You're talking about a hunting pack. That's wolves," Matt pointed out. "But even individual wolf sightings were pretty rare back then."

"Unlikely as it may be, it's the only scenario yet that supports all the facts as we know them. Indulge me a bit longer."

Matt sighed. "That's unheard of — at least around here. There must be another explanation."

"What about the Necklan's Lake Massacre?"

Matt couldn't deflect that one. It had happened on the Camp Bethany grounds — just down the road from the lodge.

"It *might* explain ...," he ventured. Then he shook his head, as if to clear it. "You're an interesting person, Tess. I think I need to let this stimulating conversation of ours percolate for a few days." He was wary. She sensed it and backed off.

"You're not the only one, Matt. Thank you for your

insights. I'm not sure where they got me, but I'm not convinced that four couples died in an accidental fire at Camp Bethany. It's not that simple."

"I've never been able to completely believe it — but I've sure tried to." Matt rose from his chair. Tess followed suit. "You let me know of any developments."

"I shall. Let me know if you think of anything else. I'll see you Sunday."

"I promise not to give a tedious sermon."

"Fire and brimstone?"

He smiled. "Not likely. Once you get your mind around the fact that you can't earn your way into Heaven, that sort of thing loses its relevancy."

That stopped her. She didn't know how to respond.

He explained. "We focus on the benefits of belief during our time on Earth."

"I'll be up front."

CHAPTER 9

Cobbler's Knob, Vermont

Wednesday, April 5, 2017, 6:15 PM EDT

"Nice of you to take me to dinner, Tess. What's it going to cost me?"

Lucy was seated across from Tess in the Ethan Allen Inn, an old coaching house right downtown.

"We need drinks first," Tess responded.

"Are we old enough?"

"We can prove it."

"I guess that's all that counts, then," the principal conceded. "The house red is quite passable here."

"Then it's settled."

When they had each taken some wine, Tess said "I was fascinated about shape shifters. Tell me more."

"Oh dear. It's just folklore."

"I like folklore."

"I don't know where to start...."

"How about vampires?"

"Vampires." Lucy thought a moment, sipped some wine. "The vampire of tradition is not a shape shifter. He maintains the same form all the time, which is humanoid. He drinks blood for his sustenance, usually from a human or another mammal because they are practical sources of supply."

"I recall that Igor ate bugs...."

"He was imprisoned at the time. Took what was available. Besides, he wasn't a full-fledged vampire — more of an apprentice."

"Duly noted. Sorry I interrupted. Please continue."

Lucy took a leisurely drink from her glass, as if deciding whether she should go on. "I'm not sure that a human could actually live long on such a diet, but I suppose blood from a healthy human or animal could be an excellent source of nutrients — as would be human flesh. Are you sure we should be discussing this at the dinner table?"

"I've already decided to order the eggplant Parmesan."

"Good decision. I may opt for the vegetarian lasagna." Lucy paused, then continued. "This vampire business seems to go back to the days when warlords would taunt their enemies by threatening to drink their blood and eat their flesh."

"Not unlike the threats professional wrestlers make today."

"True enough, but more often than not, that's exactly what they did — if they won. Then the Ottoman Turks invaded Europe and were approaching the gates of Budapest when a warlord called Vlad the Impaler stopped them, drank their blood, ate their flesh and impaled their warriors along the sides of the road for miles and miles. It was said that his vanquished enemies were so numerous, that he required no other food or drink. He certainly had an ample supply, which would have been maintained alive in some dungeon until the master became thirsty." She stopped to drive the point home.

"Yet another benefit of modern refrigeration." Tess

got it, but was ready to move on.

"I dare say," Lucy agreed. "In any event, the story gets twisted around until he's a creature who survives *only* on blood. Never touches regular food. Mind you, he would have done nothing to discourage these rumors. It was an image builder. Hunts for it at night, of course. The darkness held all sorts of terrors back then. After hunting all night, he would sleep much of the day. So he was seldom seen during daylight — which prompted the embellishment that he must hide during the day. That, of course, raised the questions of the where and why of his hiding. Pretty soon the speculation was rampant, and the legend of the human vampire who can't tolerate daylight was created. Then Bram Stoker happened along and consolidated the various local traditions into one coherent gothic tale, transforming Vlad into Dracula — the misspelled name of another person altogether."

"You took a course in gothic literature at college!" Tess accused.

"And you just listened to my theme paper," Lucy admitted.

"To tell the truth, I quite enjoyed it."

"Thank you. My professor told me I had overthought it."

"Bastard."

"Oh well. Makes graduation so much more rewarding, leaving them behind."

"So Dracula didn't turn into a bat?"

"No. Dracula was always what he was. His dining habits might have resembled the vampire bat, but his body did not. The idea that he could turn into a bat having about Two Percent of his body mass was an invention of film makers to make him appear more frightening than he was."

"Actually, the human Dracula is scary enough for me.

"Me too," Lucy agreed. "Let's just say the bat transformation made him more...."

"Portable?"

"Not the word I would have chosen."

"I didn't choose it. It just popped out."

"Well, it may be technically accurate, but it doesn't

convey the menace of being able to travel rapidly, unseen."

"How about 'dangerous' or 'threatening' instead?

"Not to mention 'terrifying.'"

"Could we be overthinking it now?" Tess asked.

"Yes, my impertinent little friend. We certainly could," Lucy admitted. "Time to change the subject."

"So I should ask about werewolves?"

Lucy sighed deeply before responding. "I think you just did. But we need to discuss shape shifters in general first. For example, do they actually turn into animals?"

"I'm sensing a trick question, but I'm guessing they don't because they retain human intelligence."

"Exactly. Even when the beast takes over, the human usually remembers it."

"Not always right away, though. Often he thinks it was a dream at first."

"That's Hollywood again. Not part of the tradition. The tradition ignores the psyche of the beast. However, twentieth century film censorship required that the beast have regrets about his conduct. You're too young to remember, but — if I may digress — the original King Kong motion picture was made before this censorship was imposed. As a result, King Kong was an oversexed son of a bitch, not a misunderstood gorilla on steroids."

"So forget the conscience, but still not a complete transformation."

"Right. Usually the shape shifter is described as taking on some *aspects* of an animal, not becoming one. Think of Lon Chaney, Jr. with fur sprouting all over him. He didn't actually become a wolf."

"O.K. I've got that. In order to become more dangerous than either the man or the beast, the result had to be a combination of the two. What else?"

"The tradition isn't limited to animals. Ancient Greek shape shifters included Arachne, who was turned into a spider as punishment for her pride in weaving."

"Spider?" Tess did not like the thought.

"It is more difficult to imagine, but it would fit if spiders actually wove their webs. But that was more of a morality tale than a tradition."

"So, they're mostly animals?"

"Seem to be, mostly indigenous species."

"Hard to describe a creature you'd never seen in those days," Tess offered. "Next question."

"Is the change voluntary?" Lucy asked her.

"Never thought of that," Tess admitted. "The Wolfman had to have a full Moon, as I recall. And he didn't seem to have much choice in the matter."

"True. But other portrayals have the shape shifting triggered by stress or entirely voluntary, with or without the Moon. The full Moon could simply be the time when they were best seen and reported. Anyway, these reported triggers are mostly literary. The folklore doesn't refer to them — indicating that the transition is voluntary. Although sometimes the transition into a fearsome beast has been described as coinciding with a need to protect or feed itself."

"You've given this some serious thought."

"When you work in a place guarded by gargoyles, you develop certain thought patterns."

"Apparently. So, do you know what variety of shape shifter you are being protected from here in Cobbler's

Knob?"

Lucy became quite calm. "There is no doubt. They are reputed to be wolf-like creatures that — unlike the film versions — hunt together, in packs. According to the legends, the full Moon may be a trigger, but the reaction to the Moon could to be voluntary --- in that it might depend upon their needs at the time."

"You're serious."

"Never more so."

"The source of the legends would be?"

"The oldest ones come from the Algonquin tribes who inhabited the area, but early settlers provided corroboration. The stories were remarkably similar, despite having come from different civilizations, different perspectives. Even called them the same thing, more or less."

"Really?"

"Indeed. The Indians called them *Karoo*. The settlers called them *Coriloo*. For a long time, people looking into the matter thought the settlers' version was a corruption of the Indian word. They had it backwards.

The original term came from the French settlers. It was *Corps Loup.*"

"*Loup*, as in wolf?"

"Wolf bodies."

Tess took a minute to digest this.

"What does that reveal? I mean the agreement on reports."

"The significance is that separate sources agreed on important facts. I'll bet that doesn't happen often in your line of work."

"I had a professor, a former Boston detective, who insisted that you could rob any bank and not get caught if you just painted each side of the getaway car a different color."

Lucy laughed. "Certainly makes the point about conflicting witness testimony. Did he have any suggestions regarding the pigments?"

"Actually, he did. Suggested avoiding primary colors that everyone could agree upon. His preferences were chartreuse and mauve — colors that straight men would never be able to describe accurately."

"And women?"

"Experience had taught him that women never agree on colors."

"That man might be brilliant!"

Tess nodded in agreement, as she took a few minutes to finish eating. Then she asked "Where did they hunt?"

"Back to that, are we?" Lucy observed. "In the wild. There may be ancestral hunting grounds. The Indians certainly had them; so why not? They shun civilization, but have been reported to approach outposts where their numbers favor them."

"Like a summer camp after the kids have left?"

"That would fit the description. There are none around here."

"Probably a good thing." Tess was thinking about Camp Bethany.

"I suppose." Lucy wasn't.

"Room for dessert?"

"Always," Lucy answered. "As long as we change the subject."

"Just a couple more questions."

Lucy sighed deeply, theatrically.

"How did shape shifters come about?"

"Oh, I suppose some DNA strand mutated — or whatever they do. We are supposed to have bits of animal DNA in us. That's a bit out of my depth, though."

"Then it might be possible for that mutation to be passed on," Tess pondered.

"You mean, be hereditary?"

"That's the term."

"Well, the literature would support that."

"Like in *Teen Wolf*, Michael J. Fox's father was a werewolf too," Tess teased.

"Perfect example," Lucy replied with sarcasm. "Not exactly scholarly, though."

But Tess was undaunted. "If a person had the normal human abilities plus the ability to shift his shape into a hunting animal, wouldn't that person be superior to a normal human?"

"You have phrased the question so that only one answer is possible, but I'll play along. Of course they would."

"Then why haven't they replaced humans?"

"Your mind has a grisly bent," Lucy observed.

"That's not an answer."

"Well, they're vastly outnumbered by normal humans; so confrontation is out of the question. And maybe they have no such ambitions."

"We're talking about natural selection, survival of the fittest. Not ambition."

Smugness overcame Lucy's face. "Besides...."

Tess became wary, but ventured "Besides what?"

"What would they eat after they'd wiped out the humans?"

Tess was stumped, but gamely offered "Dessert?"

"Thought you'd never ask."

"Good. You can tell me all about Sheriff Roy."

"Not a chance, my young friend."

CHAPTER 10

Cobbler's Knob, Vermont

Thursday, April 6, 2017, 8:30 AM EDT

Tess was reviewing the case with the Sheriff. She read from a checklist she had made. "Autopsies?"

"No bodies recovered --- only blood."

"DNA?"

"Inconclusive."

Tess just looked at him.

"Contaminated mostly. Crime scene guys didn't arrive until around Noon."

"Footprints?"

"None that didn't belong to me and the other responders."

"What about Patty Martin's? She didn't fly out of the lake."

"Apparently she did."

"Weapons?"

"None found," he replied. "No bullets or bullet holes either."

"Dogs?"

"No packs of dogs, rabid or otherwise, in the area at the time."

"Wild animals?"

"Ruled out —but there were beavers at the lake."

Deputy Lucas had come through the front door in time to add "But they all had alibis."

The Sheriff shot him a stern look.

"Sorry," he said with a total lack of sincerity.

Tess consulted her notes. "What did the survivor say?"

"You should talk to her yourself," advised Sheriff Roy. "She's in a nursing home up in Wellston. Wellston Care or something along those lines."

CHAPTER 11

Wellston, Vermont

Thursday, April 6, 2017, 3:46 PM EDT

Tess watched while the lone survivor of the Necklan's Lake Massacre was wheeled into the day room. Patty Martin's eyes were unfocused, like she was unaware of her surroundings. She didn't respond when the attendant said good-bye. Tess sat before her and introduced herself. There was no reaction, although Patty did seem to see her, to be aware of her presence.

After a few futile attempts at conversation, Tess slipped into a narrative, slowly describing that night as she understood it. She attempted to determine by Patty's eyes when she had guessed wrong. But Patty didn't appear to recall anything about that night. No part of the story provoked a reaction.

But the subject clearly disturbed Patty. The interview was over. Patty was now frantically looking for the attendant to take her away.

"Relax. I'm leaving now. Sorry if I upset you, Patty."

Moving slowly, Tess rose and walked to the door. She nodded to the attendant as she left.

On the way out, Tess stopped at the front desk to ask the receptionist why Patty was in a wheelchair. "Why can't she walk?"

The answer shocked her.

"According to the doctors, she can walk. She just doesn't. That's probably one of the reasons she's in the psychiatric ward."

"What are the others?"

"You'd have to ask the doctor. But he probably can't tell you anything. You know, patient confidentiality."

"What about you?"

"I've already said too much."

"I have a poor memory." Tess winked.

"Glad to hear it," she replied as Tess went out the door.

CHAPTER 12

Cobbler's Knob, Vermont

Thursday, April 7, 2017, 8:51 AM EDT

Tess greeted the Sheriff, then sat down in front of Lucas, addressing him.

"Did you know Patty Martin?"

Sheriff Roy turned to face them.

"She was a cheerleader. Hard not to notice them, what with the bouncing around at the pep rallies and football games," Lucas observed. "It was a small school; so yes. I saw her in the hallways. She was kinda cute. But she was a couple grades below me. We didn't have any classes together. Don't recall running into her after I graduated."

Sheriff Roy intervened. "I believe my deputy here was trying his luck in the big city at the time. All those people working so hard to get ahead. Guess it didn't agree with Lucas, 'cause here he is."

"That true?"

"Close enough," admitted Lucas with a grin.

"You know anything about that night?" she persisted.

"No. I'd already had my night of debauchery at Necklan's Lake." He smiled at the recollection. "And you're too young to hear about it, Miss Tess."

"Like I'd want to," she replied. She dropped a pen into her shoulder bag, and headed for the door.

In the school library. Tess perused the 2014 Allen County Hawks high school year book, making notes. She soon discovered that Patty had been in the Drama Club and the French Club. Not bad looking, Patty was no shrinking violet before that night. So what had happened to her?

With help of Janet, the school librarian, Tess made two copies of a photo of Patty in the year book. It showed her on stage in a play, a speaking part.

CHAPTER 13

Wellston, Vermont
Thursday, April 7, 2017, 1:26 PM EDT

Back at Wellston Care, Tess studied the Drama Club photo she had copied. Patty was wheeled in. Tess ignored her, continuing to stare at the photo until Patty was overcome with curiosity. Then Tess casually turned it around, in front of Patty's face. At first, Patty seemed to be startled. Then she began to whimper. It was the first sound she had made.

Tess spoke calmly but firmly. "You're still that person --- if you want to be."

Patty looked at her and slowly shook her head to indicate "no." Then she grabbed the photo and ripped it up, scattering the pieces on the floor.

Tess pretended to ignore the theatrics. "Then again,

perhaps not."

Tess stood to leave.

Patty moved the wheelchair to block her exit. Although she could have outmaneuvered her, Tess sat back down. After a minute of silent eye contact, Tess suggested that something happened in the water that upset her. Maybe the boy she was with did something to her. Patty burst into tears.

"You were with a date."

Patty responded by cutting off eye contact and rolling her wheelchair out of the way.

"Bonjour," Tess casually said as she exited the sun room. Patty was not the only one who'd taken French in high school.

"A bientôt."

Tess whirled around, catching Patty with a mischievous look on her face.

"A la prochaine, OK?" Tess indicated she would be back.

"Tres bien," Patty answered, looking away, trying to act blasé.

Happy but confused, Tess left. She'd found an opening. But she didn't want to push too hard. Not yet.

On the way out, the receptionist asked Tess to come back when she could. She explained "Patty gets no visitors except her mother, once a month, and Pastor Matt from the church every now and then. Neither of them stays long."

"I'll try to do that."

"You stimulate her. The minister just quotes the Bible to her."

"What about her mother?"

"You didn't hear this from me, but she's usually drunk."

"When she visits?"

"Pretty much all the time, I hear."

"I'll be back."

CHAPTER 14

Cobbler's Knob, Vermont

Thursday, April 7, 2017, 2:41 PM EDT

Back at the office, Sheriff Roy asked Tess "She tell you anything?"

"Nothing resembling English," she lied truthfully."

"Damn shame."

"Sheriff Roy, who were the kids who disappeared?"

"It's in the file. I recollect they were all Seniors, straight from the prom."

Frustrated, she began to re-examine the file. The Sheriff and Deputy Lucas ignored her. Then something struck her as odd. "Why 14?" she suddenly asked.

"She's gonna drive us crazy with that damn file," Lucas complained.

"Why not 14?" Sheriff Roy responded.

"Because they were couples! Since Patty survived, there would have been 15 students there."

"So what?" Lucas wondered aloud.

But the Sheriff pointed out that "Math never was Lucas' strong suit." He was finally interested. "Best we could determine was that they were all couples...."

"Then there was someone else there. Unaccounted for."

"You may be onto something, Deputy Tess," the Sheriff admitted.

"Doesn't necessarily mean he got away," Lucas added.

"So you agree it was a boy," she pointed out.

"Fits your theory," he grumbled.

"If Patty was with a boy who wasn't a student, he might not have been missed. At least not by the people at school."

CHAPTER 15

Cobbler's Knob, Vermont
Friday, April 8, 2017, 10:12 PM EDT

Back at the school library, Tess located photos of the 2014 Senior Prom and tried to match them up with the year book. Janet, the librarian, helped her, having been drawn into the mystery. As she explained "I'm a school librarian in the deep north woods. I could perish from lack of excitement."

Janet brought the graduation records to eliminate those who did not survive. There was no discrepancy there. Patty could be seen dancing with several of the boys, including some who had disappeared that night. They confirmed that seven boys were missing, and seven girls, plus Patty. So there must have been another boy at the lake. But it is strict policy that only Seniors can attend the Senior Prom, rigidly enforced by the teachers who act as chaperones. Not difficult with a Senior class of fewer than two dozen.

"Are any of these boys dancing with Patty still around?"

After a moment of scrutiny, Janet identified one. "Pretty sure that's Earl Robinson. He still lives in town. Works at the hardware store. That's where they sell electronics and cell phones around here. He's their resident genius."

Tess glanced at the photo. "Still the nerd?"

"That's kind of harsh."

"But accurate?"

"Dead on."

After inquiring at George's True Value, Tess found Earl in the Commons. He was sitting alone on a wooden bench, eating a homemade ham and cheese sandwich from a bag. Yellow mustard had taken up residence on his chin. After cursory introductions, she plunged right into it.

"I saw a photograph of you dancing with Patty Martin at the Senior Prom. Was she your date?"

"Hardly," he responded dully. "That was a mercy dance, my one chance in a lifetime to dance with a popular girl. I made sure my friend in the Photography Club got the shot."

"Who was that?"

"Fred Sawyer, President of the club."

"Patty wasn't your date then?"

"I didn't have a date." Earl felt the need to explain. "Attendance at the Senior Prom is pretty much compulsory from a social point of view. So dates aren't that important."

"So you danced with Patty, but she left with her date...."

"It was only one dance."

"Got it. Anything else you can tell me about that night?"

"No. My buddies and I went back to Fred's house to develop the photos and drink beer."

"Not too exciting, huh?"

"Well...." Earl looked sly. It was not a good look for him.

"Well, what?"

"Is this off the record?"

"Depends. Does it involve a crime?"

Earl gave it some thought before answering. "Doubt it."

"Let's hear it then. If I don't read you your Miranda rights first, a confession wouldn't be admissible."

"No. It's nothing that serious."

"Glad to hear it." Tess couldn't imagine Earl intentionally breaking the law.

"O.K. Fred lived right behind Patty's house. He had taken some photos of her and her friends sunbathing in her back yard. He slipped those negatives into the batch from the prom — to liven things up."

"I'm betting they did."

"Did they ever," he admitted with gusto. "I mean, it was still a bunch of guys drinking beer. But now we were hooting and shouting."

"I wonder if that's where the word hooters comes from?"

"Could be," he said.

"I was kidding."

"I wasn't."

Tess sighed. "So Fred was Patty's neighbor. Were they friendly to each other?"

"Oh, yes. They'd been playmates when they were little. Knew each other forever. But she, uh, evolved faster."

"I get your drift. It happens. So they never dated?"

"No. She was out of his league."He hesitated. "But...."

"But what?"

"Well, Patty had been seeing someone outside the school."

Tess understood the implication. "Someone who wouldn't be allowed to take her to the prom?"

"Yeah." Thoughts did not come fast to Earl. "Now that I think about it, Fred was her date! She asked him, because she knew he wouldn't raise a fuss about her leaving with someone else."

Tess tried to contain her excitement. "Did she?"

"We wouldn't have been at Fred's house, drinking beer if she hadn't left with someone else."

"You make a good point, Earl. Any idea who she left with?"

"No, but he was riding an old Harley Duo-Glide with straight pipes."

"Straight pipes? As in no muffler?"

"Exactly. Had a great sound. Rumbled."

"Rumbled," she repeated. "You ever see that bike around afterward?"

"No. I'd have noticed, unless he put a muffler on it," he admitted. "Any of this help you?"

"I sure hope so. Thanks." Then she thought of another question. "Do you know where Fred is?"

Earl's face clouded. "Cemetery. Killed in Iraq."

"Sorry to hear it."

"It's O.K. Been a long time."

"Did you ever see Patty again?"

"I went out to that hospital once, but she couldn't

talk. Didn't seem to care that I was there. So I never went back." Earl paused. "Sad to see her like that."

"I know what you mean. I've seen her too," Tess agreed.

"She doing any better?"

Ignoring the obvious fact that she hadn't seen her before, Tess replied "She's got a long way to go." Tess did not want Earl to blunder into Patty's life just when there might be a breakthrough; so she added. "Still unresponsive."

It was her first job-related lie. She knew there would be more. It came with police work.

But she still didn't like it.

Earl had a question. "Am I in the clear?"

"What?" Her thoughts were elsewhere.

"The photos," he reminded her. He seemed concerned.

"Oh, yes." She needed to assure him that he was not in trouble. "You didn't participate in taking these pictures, right?"

"No."

"And Fred isn't around anymore?'

"That's right."

"Don't see any problem, then."

"Good." Earl looked satisfied with her assessment.

"Thank you for your cooperation, Earl. Nice to meet you."

"Same here."

Tess rose to leave. "See you around town."

"Do you need to see them?"

"See what?"

"The photos."

She sat down again. Abruptly. "You have them?"

"Fred gave them to me to hold before he deployed."

"Might be useful, but probably not. I guess I need to find out though."

"I'll find them, then give you a call at the Sheriff's Office."

"No. Just use my cell phone. No sense making it official business. Might be nothing." Tess wrote her cell phone number on his extra paper napkin. Next to the mustard.

She was wondering why she wanted to see the photos. Could this be her very first police hunch?

CHAPTER 16

Cobbler's Knob, Vermont
Friday, April 8, 2017, 3:03 PM EDT

In the Sheriff's office, Tess complained. "Dead ends, literally dead in some cases."

Sheriff Roy asked "Have you visited the scene of the crime lately, now that you have more information?" She blushed when she realized she had overlooked the first rule of crime investigation. "Take that as a no. Bring Lucas along for protection if you're going at night."

"Why would I go at night?"

"That's when the crime occurred," Sheriff Roy explained. "Did you ever see the movie *Fate Is the Hunter?* Glenn Ford, I think. Rod Taylor. Maybe Suzanne Pleshette. About a twin engine commercial aircraft that crashed due to multiple engine failure. The pilots and almost everyone else died, except a stewardess. When they investigated, they discovered that one of the engines still worked fine, but it had been manually turned off. To figure out why, they went up in a similar plane and recreated the conditions. Damn near crashed themselves, but they found out what happened. Turned out that the cup of coffee the stewardess --- it *was* Suzanne Pleshette — brought to the pilot caused the whole problem when it spilled."

Tess and Lucas exchanged furtive glances indicating neither had any idea who Suzanne Pleshette might be.

The Sheriff, lost in his story, continued. "They'd have never figured it out if Glenn Ford hadn't insisted on recreating every little detail." His summation complete, he smiled at them.

"Who's Glenn Ford?" Deputy Lucas inquired solely to remind the Sheriff how old he was.

Sheriff Roy ignored him. "When you go out there, that's what you do. Recreate the scene, close as you can. Use every detail you know about."

"Maybe we should ask some rowdy teenagers to accompany us," Lucas mused aloud.

"He means nubile," Sheriff Roy suggested. "Can't see that as being helpful to the investigation."

"O.K. We'll go alone then," Lucas conceded. "Get's dark around 7:15 now. Maybe we should get there before dark to have a good look, then stick around. Build a fire. Have a beer."

"It's not a date," Tess reminded him.

"Wasn't lookin' to get lucky." Deputy Lucas added "Can't do it tonight anyway. Band practice."

"You're in a band?"

"You should see us in our uniforms, marching down Broad Street on the Fourth of July," Lucas lied with a grin. "I play the glockenspiel."

Sheriff Roy intervened. "It seems that Deputy Lucas actually does have some talent. Plays guitar and sings a bit, too. You should come by the community center tomorrow night and see for yourself. Good way to meet more of the local folk, as well."

"Cobblers' Knob has a community center?" Tess

hadn't seen one.

"Just past the Irving gas station." The Sheriff smiled. "It's actually a roadhouse."

"Oh. *Rachel's?*"

"The very same," he confirmed. "Tomorrow night about 9:00 PM."

"I'll be there."

"Dress is casual."

"Now there's a surprise."

"Stiletto heels tend to sink into the mud parking lot," Lucas observed drily. "But if you intend to wear some, let me know."

"So you can rescue me?"

He considered this. "Maybe. After I take a picture of you stuck in the mud."

The image formed in her mind. "You've convinced me."

CHAPTER 17

Wellston, Vermont

Saturday, April 9, 2017, 10:30 AM EDT

As an intern, Tess didn't have to work on Saturdays, but she had nothing else to do. And visiting Patty Martin again might not result in any progress on her assignment anyway. At the very least, it had been a beautiful ride from Cobblers' Knob.

Tess had decided to start slowly, greeting Patty with *"Bonjour."* She did this solely because it had worked before. She had no idea where it would lead.

"Bonne journée à vous aussi."

"Parlez-vous anglais?" Tess asked.

Patty stared at Tess for nearly a minute, then replied cautiously *"Oui."*

"That's a relief," Tess admitted. "I was running out

of words."

Patty was apparently deciding whether to converse in English --- something she had not done in four years. Finally, she said *"Je parle anglais, mais suelement un peu."* Patty had a mischievous smile.

She had said she only spoke a little English. This wasn't going to be easy. Tess sighed deeply. *"Je suis Tess. Souvenez-vous?"*

"Bien sûr, Tess. Je me souviens."

So Patty remembered her. And was willing to talk to her. Tess decided to keep her going — as long as her French held out. *"Comment vous appelez-vous?"* Maybe she could get Patty to say her name aloud. Her name was English. It would be a start.

"Je m'appelle Patricia Martín," she said, proudly using the French pronunciation. Then she added *"Un truc, n'est-ce pas?"*

"Ouí. Touché!" Tess acknowledged that she had tried to trick Patty into speaking English, and had failed. Discouraged, Tess started to rise. *"Adieu, Patricia Martín."* She was surprised to hear Patty respond.

"Did you actually pass French?"

Tess sat back down. "Came away with a B. The curve was involved," she admitted. "I take it you aced it."

"Top of the class. I wanted to go to Paris. Still do."

Tess wanted to tell her that Paris was a great city to walk around in, but she decided that might not play well to a girl in a wheelchair. "So you remember who I am?"

"You're the girl cop who speaks French — not real well."

Tess considered her words. "Close enough."

"What are you doing here?"

"Trying to solve a crime, a cold case."

"No, I mean how did you get here in the north woods?"

"Oh. I'm in college. My major is criminology. I'm here on an apprenticeship. It's part of the course. I get graded."

"Has Cobblers' Knob become a hotbed of crime?"

"Hardly. But I wanted a small department, where I might be able to do something besides bring coffee to the officers."

"Still, Cobbler's Knob?"

"It is possible that I erred some in the degree of smallness desired." She sighed. "But here I am."

"Here you are," Patty echoed flatly.

Continuing the conversation was clearly Tess' job. "I heard a story about Albert Einstein. He kept a sailboat, but he didn't take it out when the weather was perfect. Instead, he sailed when there was almost no wind. His explanation was that it was easier to study the dynamics when there weren't a lot of things going on."

"In other words, anyone can sail when it's windy?"

Tess laughed. "Not exactly the way he phrased it, but I think that's in there somewhere."

"I'm not stupid," she replied. "Just ... disconnected."

Tess considered this. "How's that been working out for you?"

For a moment, Tess thought she'd lost her. But Patty decided to take the question at face value. "Could be better."

"Ready to re-connect yet?"

"I don't think so. It's overwhelming."

"Maybe you could ease your way back. Deal with the basics first."

"Maybe," she responded without conviction.

"Care to discuss it?"

"Not now." Patty was backing off.

"O.K., then. Perhaps, next time." Tess was not going to push her any more today.

"Maybe." Patty wasn't making any promises, but clearly wanted Tess to return.

Tess stood to leave. *"Au revoir."*

"Au revoir." French was almost like a secret handshake between them. Tess resigned herself to a quick refresher course in the language, maybe something online.

On the way out, the receptionist said "Thank you for visiting her."

Tess stopped, turned to the desk. "Patty's an interesting person. What does she do with herself here."

"Well, for one thing, she keeps the librarian busy."

"She reads?"

"Goes through at least one book a week."

"What kind?"

"Michael Connelly, James Patterson, Edna Buchanan, Carolyn McCray. Let's see.... Oh, Carl Hiaasen and Dave Barry. I can't remember all of them. Whatever Patty liked was added to the library. The staff could use the library; so we all benefitted. I started reading more. The librarian finally got her a Kindle reader; so we can't keep track any more."

"What else does she do with her time?"

"Well, she swims."

"You have a pool?"

"Big one, indoors."

"Wow. Does the staff get to use it?"

"Yes, indeed. But only between 8:00 PM and 10:00 PM weekdays."

"Do you use it?"

"Not as often as I'd like to, because of the hours. But on Wednesday nights, a small group of us get together to swim. It's really great when the snow is two feet deep outside. There's a picture window."

Tess wanted to ask if she could get a job there, but instead asked "So Patty swims a lot?"

"Does fifty laps every day, religiously. Says she does it to build up her leg muscles; so she can walk again some day. She must be planning to climb Mount Everest."

"That explains why she looks so fit for someone confined to a wheelchair."

"She's not exactly confined."

Tess gave her a seriously inquiring look.

"I mean, she can transfer by herself."

"Transfer?"

"Transfer. Go from her wheelchair to another chair or to her bed. That sort of thing."

"Does she need assistance getting into or out of the pool?"

"I'm not sure."

"Why?"

"There's always someone with her at the pool. That's a rule here. So they help her. That way she doesn't slip."

"Hard to argue with that. Have you ever seen her

-101-

swimming her laps?"

"Oh, yes. The break room is right next to the pool. We sometimes go into there just to breathe in the humidity ---- especially in the winter when the air is dry."

"Patty's a good swimmer?"

"I'm not an expert, but she's the best I've ever seen. Cuts through the water like a knife."

"Good exercise. I appreciate learning this. Makes it easier to talk to her when I know what she likes to do."

Nobody's going to leave her behind in the water again.

"Glad I could help out."

"Me too. See you next time."

Outside, Tess looked at her watch. She had enough time for a quick trip to Hanover. And a faster one back.

CHAPTER 18

Cobblers' Knob, Vermont

Saturday, April 9, 2017, 8:30 PM EDT

Rachel's parking lot was already crowded when she pulled her red Harley off the road. Tess pulled over to a lamp post and attached the bike's frame to it with a length of heavy chain and combination lock. She removed her helmet and shook out her long hair. She wore new jeans — not too tight — and a pale blue turtle neck sweater under her leather jacket. No purse, just the red helmet dangling from her elbow.

A sign on the massive oak door advised "No Smoking before Midnight." Tess guessed that must be when they stopped serving food.

She crossed the dirt parking area confidently in motorcycle boots, and strode into the roadhouse for the first time. Even though it was dusk outside, the darker interior required a moment of ocular adjustment. She closed her eyes to speed up the process. She heard her name.

"Tess! Over here!"

The place wasn't that large, and she could see clearly thanks to the lack of smoke. It was Lucy Thornton. Tess looked towards the sound, saw the Principal waving to her from atop a high stool at a high-top table in the rear. She waved back and began making her way through the jumble of chairs, tables, waitresses and customers. It seemed that everyone was wearing blue jeans, except the few older women who wore long skirts that Tess associated with the country. Inevitably, there were a few younger girls who had shorter skirts for dancing, or just showing off their legs by the makeshift stage.

Not surprisingly, that's where Deputy Lucas was meticulously tuning his guitar as though it were rocket science.

"You alone?" Tess asked, wondering which chair to take.

"Not any more. Sit here where you can see the stage."

A waitress appeared instantly. She had followed Tess to the table. "Good evening. Something to drink?"

Tess cast a quick look at the table, seeing a pint of something amber in front of Lucy. The glass was frosted.

"Cider. Neat," Lucy explained.

"Same for me, thanks."

"Not good for the schoolmarm to pass out in a bar."

"Nor the young deputy," Tess agreed.

"Did I hear a motorcycle?"

"You sure did. Weather's too good. I retrieved it from college this afternoon."

"Give me ride sometime?"

"Tomorrow?"

"Well, not to church," Lucy said. "But afterwards would be good if the weather cooperates."

"Maybe we should ask Pastor Matt...."

"So I'll see you in church?"

"Wouldn't miss it for the world. Pastor Matt seems like an interesting guy."

"That he is."

Her pint of cider arrived. It was ice cold and delicious.

"Cuts the dust, doesn't it?" asked the Sheriff, who had appeared from nowhere. "Mind if I join you for the first set?"

"Only if you promise not to get fresh with us," Lucy responded by way of convoluted invitation.

"Yes, ma'am. It will be difficult, but I will put my whole mind to it." He sat beside Tess to demonstrate his determination to avoid Lucy's charms. "Would it be inappropriate to mention that you both look lovely this evening?"

"Not at all, since it's the indisputable truth," Lucy replied.

"Why, thank you, Sheriff," Tess added. "You're looking pretty dapper yourself."

Sheriff Roy gave them his best smile.

"Don't encourage him," Lucy advised.

"Lucy's madly in love with me," he confided to Tess.

"Too late," Lucy muttered.

Then, to Tess' astonishment, Lucy reached out and took his left hand in hers. 'Your first beer's on me, you smooth talker."

"She's an angel," he explained to Tess.

"It's what you are that's in question," Lucy said. Then she shouted to the waitress "We need a draft beer over here for local law enforcement!"

"What a woman!" he observed.

"What a pair!" Tess decided aloud.

The musicians began to wander out onto the small wooden platform that served as the stage. Others hung around near the stage. Four was evidently a quorum. There were a fiddle, a guitar, a banjo and a bass guitar. Deputy Lucas held the guitar. No drums, but the fiddler had a homemade contraption that held a wood block and a cow bell on a stand. Interesting, if not downright ominous.

Nothing really happened until the banjo guy brought a big, old fashioned microphone with stand to the front of the stage. He adjusted the height to just below his chin, so it could pick up his voice and his banjo — if he had bothered to plug it in.

To Tess' surprise, the group gathered round the unplugged microphone and immediately launched into *Countin' Flowers on the Wall*. After a moment, she realized they each had portable mikes. The big old microphone was just a prop. The next surprise was that they were actually pretty good. And Deputy Lucas had a fine baritone voice. She had underestimated him. That would not do.

When the set was finished, Lucas dropped by the table to pay his respects before being led outside by a young girl, who was obviously thrilled to be in his company.

"Heartbreaker," Lucy commented to no one in particular.

CHAPTER 19

Cobblers' Knob, Vermont
Sunday, April 10, 2017, 9:30 AM EDT

"Is the Bible the word of God?" Pastor Matt asked rhetorically. "There are people who insist that it is. Like the televangelist I watched briefly on some obscure cable channel last night." He paused for effect. "The only explanation for this I have come up with is that they haven't read it! So, let's break it down. The Old Testament starts with the Hebrew version of the *Gilgamesh,* the ancient creation myth that predates the Bible. By the way, the use of the word 'myth' is not intended to question the veracity of the story. A myth is simply an old story that has been passed down for generations --- usually by word of mouth prior to being written down. This, of course, renders the story subject to the memories, embellishments and prejudices of the storytellers."

"The Book of Genesis then moves onto other myths, including the Garden of Eden and the Flood, which secular scholars confirm actually occurred --- but covered only a large portion of the land, which was translated as covering the earth. Then someone decided it was the Earth, with a capital E — meaning the planet. And away we went!" He paused to let that sink in.

"The Book of Exodus is primarily the story of the Jewish people leaving bondage in Egypt to wander through the Wilderness, receiving the Ten Commandments along the way, until they reach the Promised Land. This is the *Cliff's Notes* version. It covers a lot of history. Then the Book of Leviticus presents us with a shorter version, which provides considerable corroboration." Pastor Matt scanned the congregation. "Why would the word of God have two versions?" he thundered rhetorically. "Why would it need corroboration?"

"So the Old Testament is a historical record. It

includes the religious laws, such as the famously misunderstood 'An eye for an eye,' which was a punishment only applied in certain unusual circumstances. It is a catchy phrase though," he admitted. "With the notable exception of the Ten Commandments and a few conversations between God and Abraham, the Bible does not ever purport to be the word of God."

"If you are not yet convinced, consider this. The Old Testament contains an account of a wrestling match between God and Abraham. For those of the congregation keeping score, Abraham lost." He paused. "But the point here is that an account of a wrestling match is unlikely to be the word of God. Just picture Howard Cosell doing the commentary, if that helps." A scattering of laughs followed.

"Embedded in this historical record is the story of man seeking independence from God, turning away from Him in the Garden of Eden. It is the story of man beseeching God for assistance with mostly inconsistent results: decisive victory at Jericho and enslavement in Egypt. And at the end, there is the vital prophecy that a man of God will come to reconcile with mankind."

"That's where the New Testament picks up the story of this reconciliation, with the Books of Matthew, Mark, Luke and John — four frequently conflicting accounts of the life of Jesus, the Christ, all written more than half a century after His death. Following these first books are accounts of His apostles and their missionary work, including Paul's unauthorized insertion of celibacy into the message. In fact, the New Testament tells us that Paul's embellishments to Christ's message were so upsetting that he was recalled to Jerusalem to stand trial for heresy. Again, for those keeping score, Paul escaped by invoking his right to be tried in Rome as a Roman citizen. He wound up being the co-founder of the Roman Catholic Church. Plucky guy, Paul."

"Then, at the end, comes the zinger: the Book of the Revelations of St. John the Divine, an obscure mystic who relayed his dreams to a long-forgotten scribe." The pastor cleared his throat. "It has no connection to the remainder of the New Testament, but it makes for a dramatic ending." He cleared his throat. "So much so that some scholars have suggested that the Book of Revelations was included primarily for its entertainment value." He let the congregation chew on that while he shuffled his notes.

"To return to the point, if the Bible was the word of God, why did man undertake to decide what books should be included--- excluding the Book of Thomas, who was Jesus' own brother?"

"Then, the very essence of Jesus was edited to make Him fit into the Roman Pantheon. The result of this was to recast Jesus as one of the lesser gods under Sol Invictus, the Invincible Sun. This was the price of admission, of legitimacy under Roman law. It's why the Sabbath came to be celebrated on the Day of the Sun, or Sunday. It's why we celebrate Jesus' birth on the date of the Winter Solstice instead of in early January as the Eastern Orthodox Church still does. It is even why many worship Jesus instead of the Lord God Jehovah."

"You see, until the introduction into the Roman Pantheon, Jesus was not considered to be a god himself. Rather, he was described as the human son of God ---

God's representative on Earth. So the act of subordinating Christianity to the Sun God had the unexpected effect of elevating Jesus to the status of a god himself. Like most negotiated compromises, not everyone was happy with this result at the time. But it endured because it worked."

"And to further appease the Romans, the fact that Jesus was executed for the crime of treason by the Romans because he claimed to be the King of the Jews was twisted to indicate that the Jewish high priests had demanded his execution. Contrary to this revised scenario, the Jewish High Priests could have executed Him themselves by stoning. They did not need the Romans' involvement. But Jesus was crucified by the Romans --- which was the very specific manner of death reserved under Roman law for traitors to Rome."

"And the Roman gods did not have wives — at least not in the way we perceive a husband and wife relationship. So there is no mention of Him being married. Yet, He is referred to as Rabbi scores of times. And it is clear to religious scholars that He had formal religious training." Pastor Matt paused. "Yes, he was possibly a carpenter as well, but he would probably be described as a building contractor today. Being a rabbi was not a paid position for most of them."

"But one essential prerequisite to becoming a rabbi was marriage. So let's look at the situation with fresh eyes. Unlike today, when it is not unusual to still be in school in one's mid-twenties, in biblical times people were usually married in their teens. And in the dark days before online dating services, men often married the sisters of their friends — like Lazarus' sister Mary of Bethany. I mention her because in the story of Lazarus, as told in the Book of John, Chapter 11, Jesus orders Mary to stop sitting *shiva* for her deceased brother. And she immediately stops. But under Jewish law, only certain male relatives or a husband could do this. Jesus was not a relative. Was He married to Lazarus' sister Mary?"

"I don't know. Some scholars think so."

"But we digress!" he announced. "And that's the royal we, meaning I digress and include you in the blame for not stopping me. If we're trying to figure out to whom Jesus was married, then we have at least entertained the possibility that He was married," he concluded triumphantly. But he wasn't done.

"Another point is this. If it was His wedding, it would explain why it was up to Jesus to provide more wine at the wedding feast." Pastor Matt assumed a conspiratorial tone. "Imagine the discussions that must have taken place over that one. There's this irresistible event of turning water into wine — and not just swill, but excellent wine, according to the account. And there were many witnesses present. But these editors of the Bible can't say it was Jesus' wedding. So the only wedding celebration to receive any description in the entire New Testament doesn't identify the bride, the groom, their families, their tribes, or even the location. It became a generic wedding --- its only purpose as a backdrop for the miracle."

"So there is no specific mention of Jesus' marriage in the Bible. It was not god-like." Pastor Matt put his hands in the air and shrugged, as if to indicate that it was a significant omission.

"As most of you know, and probably fear, I could

continue in this vein all day. You may relax. I won't."

There were some chuckles, which the Pastor had anticipated and paused for.

"No, the Bible is not the word of God. It is the word of men, subject to their misconceptions, prejudices and caprices." He made a gesture, holding both palms up to indicate confusion. "So where does that leave us?"

"On top of all the editing and omissions, we are still left with the Bible, which must be read with care and understanding, not with misplaced faith that it is the word of God. One must continually put it into context. Even the quotations of Jesus may in fact be misquotations, considering the decades which passed before they were reduced to writing. To add to the confusion, the books of the Bible were not all written in the same language. Most were translated into Greek, then Latin, then a version of English that renders it nearly incomprehensible to modern English speakers. Errors were certainly made with each translation. Not always the fault of the translator since languages tend to be uncooperative in these matters. For example, there are six different Greek words that all translate into the single English word 'love,' causing the nuances of each version to be lost." He paused and looked around.

"And then there's the loss of context. We simply don't understand references to a society that existed two thousand years ago, half a world away. In other words, we can't relate to a society that didn't have apps for their smart phones. While that may be obvious to you, I have an example anyway. You have all heard that it is more difficult for a rich man to enter the Kingdom of Heaven than for a camel to pass through the eye of a needle. Well, those of you who are rich — or who aspire to be rich — take heart! A khan in Nazareth had a walled enclosure around his home and business --- sort of a private gated community. The main entrance to his compound was a splendid arched gateway with ample clearance for caravans, which were conveyed by domesticated dromedaries. We refer to them as camels. When not in use, this arch was sealed by a pair of stout wooden doors. Opening and closing these huge doors was not a simple matter. The act itself probably required at least several strong men. Rather than open these large doors for the occasional human foot traffic, a small door was cut into one of the large ones for this purpose. This small door was known throughout the land as the Eye of a Needle. So we are not talking about a real needle. More importantly, a camel on its knees *could* fit through it — but neither the camel, nor the people pulling in front and pushing behind, were likely to recall the experience as being pleasurable. I speculate that such activity would only have been undertaken in response to a wager."

"And that is why you should *study* the Bible, not just read it." Pastor Matt sharply slapped one hand against the other, and rolled up his sleeves in the manner of a carnival huckster. "Now here's the pitch. We have several Bible study groups who meet right here on Sunday evenings. I suggest you come by at 7:00 PM to meet with one of them."

The remainder of the service was more conventional.

"Wow!" Tess exclaimed in a stage whisper when

she and Lucy reached the steps.

"Tells it like he sees it," Lucy responded.

"You ever go to Bible study?"

"I will if you will."

"I may just take you up on that."

"But first, we hit the road," Lucy reminded her.

"Pick you up in forty-five minutes?"

"I'll be ready."

CHAPTER 20

Cobblers' Knob, Vermont
Sunday, April 10, 2017, 11:22 AM EDT

"Glorious day for a ride, don't you think?" Lucy, now wearing tight blue jeans and an oversized sweater, was pumped. She threw her left leg over the saddle and dropped into the buddy seat. "What's that written on the back of your jacket?"

**IYCRT
TBFO**

"Oh, just some motorcycle lore." Tess replied. But she was smiling.

"Come on! What does it mean?"

"If you can read this, the bitch fell off."

"What?" Then Lucy howled with delight.

"Like I said: lore."

"Well, since you've brought the subject up — so humorously — how do I avoid that fate?"

"Keep your legs tight against the bike and hold onto the metal bars just under your seat. Lean back against that chrome thing. It'll seem awkward at first, but it works."

"I'll try, but I warn you that I'm one of those tenderfoots who grabs the saddle horn if the horse scares me."

"Well, try not to choke me. It doesn't improve my driving. And one more thing, Whatever you do, don't try to help me drive by leaning on the curves. It's not like sailing."

"Tenderfeet," Lucy corrected herself.

"Whatever you say, schoolmarm." Tess pulled out slowly, but then accelerated to fifty in the space of a block."

"Whoo-ee!"

The roar of the engine, combined with the wind, discouraged further conversation.

By the time they turned at the two field stone columns that had served as the entrance to the camp, it was clear to Lucy that they were going to Necklan's Lake. So she waited until Tess pulled up to the shore before speaking.

"Why are we here?"

Tess looked out across the calm blue water. "Good place for a picnic."

"That usually involves food," Lucy pointed out.

"And ants," Tess responded cheerily. "I hope you brought the ants. All I have is sandwiches and soft drinks."

Lucy was nothing if not flexible. "What kind of sandwiches?"

"Ham and cheese. Homemade!"

"Bless your heart." Then she added with a smile, " That ride made me hungry as a ... shape shifter."

Tess gave her a startled look.

"Don't worry. I only intend to make my stomach a bit larger right now."

"Just took me by surprise."

"Get used to it. I can't stand being predictable."

"Maybe I should have brought something less predictable, like onion sandwiches."

"I'll manage fine with the ham and cheese, thanks."

Tess chose a spot on the grass, just above the pebbly strand at water's edge. "No blanket."

Lucy crossed her ankles and lowered herself to the grass in one graceful move that left her seated with her legs crossed. Tess observed, then copied the maneuver as best she could. She hit harder and fell backward upon landing. "You made it look easy," she commented as she arranged herself in a sitting position.

"Practice. Also yoga."

"Guess I'd better practice."

"Aging really is a use-it-or-lose-it proposition."

"Well, you're not that old."

"That fact that you brought it up says volumes," Lucy accused. "But, you're right. If you take reasonable care of your body, the symptoms of old age can be put off until you're in your eighties. Luck is also a big factor. I've been lucky."

"I've read that more people are living to one hundred. A lot more."

"Actually nobody dies anymore, except for homicides and accidents," Lucy opined. "At least not publicly."

"How do you figure?"

"These days, when people no longer function in some significant regard, they get shipped off to a facility, where they're warehoused until the scale finally tips in favor of death. By that time, they've been long forgotten. Former associates read the obituaries and say to themselves 'I thought she died years ago.'"

"You make it sound Orwellian."

"It is, except the government is not doing it to its citizens. The other citizens are."

"But some people receive special treatment...."

"Some people are more equal than others. *Animal Farm.*"

"Orwell nailed that one, all right." Tess took a bite of her sandwich. "So you don't care much for the current procedures?"

"I have no fear of death, when it comes. I'm reaching the age when I can't be cut down in my prime. Dodged that bullet, so to speak."

"Hadn't thought of it that way," Tess admitted.

"Hopefully, you will have the opportunity. But you see, it's the manner of death that terrifies people."

"People are afraid of dying, but not necessarily of being dead?" Tess suggested.

"It's not the *prospect* of death that troubles people, so much as the *process* of death. I think a lot of people feel that way. Especially people over sixty. They've accepted the fact of eventual death, because it comes to everyone. They've seen that first hand by that age. But they do worry about the disabilities and discomfort that often precede it. Those are not inevitable. Naturally they would like to avoid them." Lucy then polished off the remainder of her sandwich with the gusto of one who intended to live forever.

"What about belief in an afterlife?" Tess asked.

"Probably helps dealing with death itself more than with the dying process," she replied casually. "This whole excursion going to be this morbid?"

"Oh, yeah." Tess leaned forward and rose unsteadily by scissoring her legs. Then she stared at Lucy.

""You don't think I can do that!" Lucy arose in the same manner, but with considerably more grace. "Ha!"

Tess acknowledged her superior performance in this feat with an elaborate bow, of the exaggerated variety rarely seen outside *The Three Musketeers* films.

"What now, young Tess?"

"An experiment!" With that cryptic reply, Tess took leave of her loafers, kicking them in the general direction of Lucy, but without putting her in any danger. A few steps and a slight jump conveyed Tess to the water's edge. Pausing a few moments to steel herself to the task, she then determinedly clomped into the frigid lake. "Aaaagh!"

"Should be about thirty-three degrees by this time of year," Lucy reflected.

"Any colder and I could walk on it."

"Well, did your nipples get hard or not. I assume that was the experiment."

"No, that was not the experiment," Tess replied.

"But my feet are getting numb. That's an improvement, by the way."

"But you'd tell me if...."

"No they didn't, damn it!"

Lucy began to laugh so hard she bent double. Tess threw up her arms in frustration. "Some people just have no scientific bent." But by then she was laughing too.

Lucy got her laughter under control just long enough to inquire "Why are you still in the water?"

Tess regarded her submerged ankles and admitted "Darned if I know." Then she retreated clumsily to the shore, where she unceremoniously plopped down and began to message her toes. "Wanted to see how cold it was for myself," she explained. "Empirical knowledge."

"Thirty-three sound about right?"

"Might even be on the high side."

Lucy's face took on a thoughtful aspect, as though she had just been struck by an idea. "Is this what they call bonding?"

"No. This is me making a fool of myself and you being the amused spectator."

"So, it's more of an entertainment thing?"

Tess shot her a dirty look before both were overtaken by laughter again.

Lucy recovered first. "I just had...." She tried again. "I just had this picture of you standing in the lake up to your ankles ... singing *Let Me Entertain You.*"

Tess acknowledged the humor, but turned serious. "I have no idea how I'll make myself go in any deeper. My ankles are blue."

"Why on earth would you want to?"

"Sheriff Roy thinks I should re-create the crime scene."

"Oh." Lucy gazed over the icy water. "Maybe you should insist he come in with you to provide the benefit of his expertise, and all."

"He's appointed Deputy Lucas to fill that position."

"Smarter than he looks, our Sheriff." Then Lucy added "I don't suppose you could do what the kids do...."

"Get drunk first?"

"I hadn't thought it through," Lucy admitted.

"Actually, the idea has some merit, but I don't

think so."

"I'm not suggesting you get smashed, just a quick bracer or two."

"A dozen might do the trick," Tess speculated. "Of course, I think Deputy Lucas would be all for it."

"Drinking too much...." Lucy could envision it.

"Then removing my clothes."

"Oh my. The imagination just boggled."

"I had rather hoped that the crime scene re-creation would stop short of me being found naked on the beach with acute hypothermia."

"Yes. I suppose that would be taking it too far."

"Thank you for your support," Tess replied wryly.

"You're welcome. But seriously, what do you plan to do?"

"I wouldn't call it a plan, but I do have to cover several matters...."

"Besides your butt," Lucy observed. "So you have a locus?"

It took a moment for her to recognize the term from a high school geometry class. "Spoken like a teacher.

You've still got the knack."

"So what are your loci?"

Tess shook her head. She raised her right hand with the fingers closed. She raised one finger theatrically. "First, light a fire there." Second finger raised. "Then drink some beer by said fire." Third finger raised. "Then disrobe over there." Fourth finger. "Plunge into the ice water." Last finger. "Investigate rocky formations near shore."

"And then?"

"Get as close as I can to the fire."

"Before you get dressed?"

"Probably. Depends on the amount of wind."

"Taking a towel?"

"And a bathrobe. Big fuzzy one."

"Thermos of hot coffee?"

"I knew there was a reason I brought you along," Tess confided.

"About the disrobing...."

"I've got a wet suit."

"That should do it," Lucy agreed.

"I doubt it. It would send the wrong message."

"Clever, but not ... macho?"

"Yeah. That pretty much covers it."

"Must be difficult being a woman in the police world," Lucy observed.

"Getting better, but it's still a boy's club."

"So, you're opting for stark naked?"

"It's the most accurate re-creation of the scene...."

"True. But Deputy Lucas is not a shy high school Senior," Lucy reminded her.

"I'll just have to handle it — somehow."

"Get the Sheriff to issue some ground rules; so Lucas has to obey orders."

Tess nodded slowly. "If I'd known you were going to be this helpful, I'd have brought dessert."

Lucy gazed out over the lake. "So tell me about the rocks."

"We think Patty Martin escaped the fate of her fellow Seniors by hiding behind one of those three rocky formations. I'd like to test that theory. And thanks for changing the subject."

"Where was she found?"

"Next to the smoldering ashes of the bonfire. Up over there."

"Yes, the fire pit someone dug decades ago. Most likely the counselors when this was Camp Bethany."

"Sheriff Roy told me the state investigators removed everything in the pit to search for clues."

"Must have been a truckload of ash," Lucy assumed aloud. "Find anything?"

"Bottle caps and lot of those pull rings they used to have on cans."

"I remember those. Razor sharp bits of aluminum to be discarded wherever. I may still have one embedded in my foot. Brilliant concept."

"You're like living history."

"Something I always aspired to."

"I could tell."

"Whippersnapper."

"What does that mean?"

"Literally?"

"Sure."

"Someone whose unsolicited opinion doesn't count for anything."

"Old fashioned term for a smart-ass, then," Tess concluded.

"If the shoe fits...."

"And here I thought I was engaged in witty banter and sharp repartee."

"Must be a fine line somewhere."

"Ready to move on?"

"Need to spend a minute at the site of the lodge before we go."

"Count me in."

The walk to the lodge took about four minutes. After observing Tess clawing at the dirt, Lucy ventured "I see you've heard about the lost treasure."

"Looking for glass," Tess explained.

"If you need some stemware, I've got plenty."

"No, this kind." Tess held up a smooth blob of melted glass she had just discovered inside the foundation. "I need to find some outside the old foundation."

"I'll participate if you explain while we're doing it."

"Deal." And she did.

But after about fifteen minutes where the largest windows had been, they heard thunder — not too distant. Lucy suggested they leave.

"I'd like to beat the rain, especially since our chariot is topless."

"Good point. I've only got one set of rain gear with me."

"Then you could get soaked."

Just then the breeze picked up. There was moisture in it.

They moved briskly toward the Harley.

By the time they'd returned to town, it had been agreed that Bible study could continue another week without them. But they did agree to meet for dinner some evening. Lucy offered to pay. In return, she expected the lurid details of the re-creation of the skinny-dipping at Necklan's Lake.

Tess was hoping there would be nothing lurid to

report.

CHAPTER 21

Cobblers' Knob, Vermont
Monday, April 11, 2017, 9:32 AM EDT

Sheriff Roy finished his first cup of coffee and looked over the office at Tess. "Making any progress on your cold case, Deputy Tess?"

"Absolutely, Sheriff."

Deputy Lucas indicated interest by his inquisitive glance.

"I have investigated the scene of the crime, interviewed several people who have knowledge about it, and accumulated a notebook of facts and opinions."

"And?"

"I have reached some tentative conclusions. For one, I believe that the Camp Bethany fire was a similar incident. It appears that the fire was collateral damage from another event involving the counselors who stayed that last night for a farewell party."

Both men gave her their full attention.

"Start with that party then," the Sheriff instructed.

"You both know the basic story. Only a handful of counselors remained. No gas for the generator; so candles provided the light. There was propane for the stove. Either heat source could have ignited the fire. But a candle is more likely, I think."

"Why is that?" the Sheriff wondered. "Seems to me that a fire from a candle would be easily extinguished."

"True," she conceded. "Assuming that someone was nearby — and paying attention. Not otherwise engaged. But let me offer some more before we go there. The propane tank was permanently installed. It had at least two cutoff valves, one inside and one out. In addition, it had controls and safety features. In contrast, the candles would have been set out that night. More thought was probably given to creating a mood than to safety. These were young couples, after all."

"Ah. So it all comes down to hormones...." Deputy

Lucas smiled broadly at his witticism.

"Ignore him," the Sheriff instructed. "Let's assume a candle started the fire. Why didn't someone put it out?"

Tess paused before responding. "For one thing, it is likely that alcohol was being consumed. Can't be proved, but I can't imagine it being absent from this type of gathering. And Pastor Matt said that some of the counselors drank beer. Maybe marijuana too. Their senses could have been dulled."

"I'm afraid I can see it. Gazing into a roaring fire in the fireplace, not noticing a candle igniting a curtain behind them."

"You didn't mention heavy petting," Lucas observed. "That fits your 'otherwise engaged' hypothesis."

If he was trying to embarrass her, Tess wasn't having it. "It's a given that sexual activity would have been involved. The only questions are what forms it took and how far it had progressed. The answers are irrelevant. Whatever the case, that would be a big distraction."

"What other distractions have you postulated?" asked the Sheriff.

"That's where it gets interesting,'" Tess answered. "I think there was an event outside the building which drew their attention."

"What type of event?"

"It could have just been that some of the other counselors returned to the camp that night to harass them. They could have been drunk. Maybe jealous." She let it dangle.

"And it got out of hand?"

"Could be someone got injured or killed accidently, and it escalated," she posited.

"And then, being inebriated, these attackers concluded that they had to finish off the others in order to save themselves."

"Sounds like a *Billy Jack* movie," Deputy Lucas observed.

"What's a *Billy Jack* movie?" Tess wondered aloud.

"Shut up, Lucas. Ignore him, Tess. Besides, it's more like *Straw Dogs.*" Sheriff Roy stood and walked to her desk. "Is there any evidence to support this?

"Yes, there is. It's the windows."

"What about them?"

"An explosion would have blown them out. Same thing if the counselors had broken through them to evacuate the building."

"Sounds right," the Sheriff admitted. "Proceed."

"Now the heat of the fire melted the glass. But it left a residue, and that residue is all inside the foundation of the building. I dug around the outside looking for some."

"You didn't find any?"

"None."

"But you found some inside?"

"Lots of it. I think that indicates the windows were broken inward — like someone was trying to get inside."

"You're sure of this?"

"I can show you."

"O.K. You may be on to something. We'll make some time to take a look. Maybe later today. What about the case involving the Senior Class?"

Tess shot a quick glance at Lucas before responding. "There is at least one survivor, Patty Martin. But no other Seniors were missing. So, we have to accept the possibility that Patty was there with someone who was not a classmate. Her date for the prom was her neighbor, another Senior. Only Seniors could attend. A friend of hers told me that Patty left with someone else, someone he didn't know."

"Can this witness account for his own whereabouts?" asked the Sheriff.

"I haven't checked his alibi, but he says he was with some of his other friends — guys like him. Fellow nerds, to use his terminology. One of the friends he was with after the prom was Patty's date, Fred Sawyer."

"Where is he?"

"Killed in Iraq." That terminated that line of investigation.

"So Patty may have been at the lake with a fellow we haven't accounted for?"

"Who may have survived, since no one else was reported missing."

"Might not have been a local boy." Deputy Lucas suggested.

"Either that or he's still walking around," said Tess.

"Have you tried to find out who this mystery boy

might be?" asked the Sheriff.

"I've visited Patty Martin twice, but she doesn't remember anything. Haven't given up yet, though."

"She still up at Wellston?"

"Yes, she is."

"Poor kid." That seemed to be all, but Sheriff Roy surprised her. "Have you re-created the scene yet?"

"You mean gone swimming there at night?"

Deputy Lucas perked up. The Sheriff nodded.

"Not yet," Tess admitted.

"That lake was scraped out by a glacier. It's several hundred feet deep. The water never warms up. Won't help to put it off. Do it tonight or tomorrow. Might learn something."

Tess caught Lucas' eye.

"I can make it tonight," he volunteered. "I'll bring some firewood."

"Great."

"And just enough beer to make it authentic," Lucas ventured. "Or does our college girl prefer wine?"

"Beer's just fine," she replied in what she hoped was a casual manner. Deputy Lucas was annoying her, as was his intention.

Sheriff Roy intervened. "Neither of you has to drink anything. I deem it irrelevant to the investigation. Although you might want one to brave that cold water."

"There is another aspect of authenticity that could be a problem...."

The puzzled look quickly left the Sheriff's face. "Ah, yes. The tuxedo and prom gown. Not necessary either. Irrelevant. Wear whatever you like. It will be chilly out — even if Deputy Scoutmaster here makes good on his promise of a fire."

Tess gave the Sheriff a look that clearly indicated he had not covered all the ground.

He got it. "And if either of you opts to wear revealing swimming attire, I remind you both that this is an official investigation of the Allen County Sheriff's Department. You are to conduct yourselves as officers on duty at all times."

Tess felt some relief.

Deputy Lucas asked "The beer?"

"Undercover duty occasionally requires deviations from the norm." Sheriff Roy was on top of the situation this morning.

"Thank you for the clarification, Sheriff," Tess said.

"Want to ride out there together?" Deputy Lucas inquired.

"Not necessary, thanks. I'll take my bike. Weather looks great."

"Suit yourself. I'll start the fire about 6:30. Give it five minutes to get toasty."

"Toasty?" she countered. "Really?"

Sheriff Roy said "You kids play pretty now, and don't fight." Then he laughed.

Tess was still at the office when her cell phone rang. It was Earl, from the hardware store.

"Found 'em," he announced after introducing himself.

"Oh. Are you at the store?"

CHAPTER 22

Wellston, Vermont
Monday, April 11, 2017, 10:49 AM EDT

Tess was on her way back to Wellston. She'd obtained the photographs from Earl, who told her she could keep them. That convinced her that he still had the negatives. The pictures were clearly not posed, but were excellent close-ups. Along with the best equipment, nerds would have a decent zoom lens. The photos were hardly shocking. Just three young girls sunning themselves in modest bikinis on beach towels in a back yard. They were all lying face down with their top straps undone. Nothing to see really, but she could imagine the teenage boys fantasizing about them rolling over onto their backs. Nerds!

But, how would Patty react to the photos?

Not how she had thought.

"Glad to see they turned out. Poor Fred was making a such a determined effort."

"You knew?"

"That's why we undid our straps," Patty sort of explained.

"You what?"

"It was exciting for us too. Boys aren't the only teenagers with hormones, you know. We felt like models."

"Erotic?"

"That's it. Harmlessly erotic."

"Teasing the poor kid. Hardly harmless," Tess opined.

"Are you kidding? Bikini photos of the cheerleaders. Probably made Fred a rock star among his friends."

She was right. "Actually, it did. Earl told me."

"See? No harm. No foul."

"And you all had plausible deniability."

"Cop talk," Patty reminded her.

"How did you know?"

"Fred's dad had one of those old 35 millimeter

cameras. The kind with an automatic film advance. Made a distinctive clicking sound. Couldn't miss it. I told the other girls; so we decided to give him a show."

"I notice you've kept your tan." It was an implied question.

"I use the tanning bed." When Tess looked confused, Patty added "This is a high class facility. Not just any naked teenager with amnesia can get in. Of course, there's something in the family genes that contributes as well."

"Family jeans?"

With conspiratorial whisper Patty disclosed the family secret. "Martin used to be Martino, until the old ancestors hit Ellis Island."

"Ah." Tess was up to speed again, and ready to continue. "What was your relationship with Fred?"

"He was my neighbor for most of my life. We grew up together. We were friends. Our families went to each other's barbeques. He taught me how to work the computer and play video games, although I never got into the games like he did. And when my father gave me an iPhone, Fred had to teach me how to use it. Dad had no clue at all. I love Fred, and he knows it. We just weren't romantically involved in any way."

"But you went to the Senior Prom with him."

"So we're back to that again...."

"It does have a way of coming up," Tess admitted.

"I don't remember. But it's possible. He could have been my official date, but the Senior Prom isn't like that. The *school* isn't like that. No girl thinks she's going to find the love of her life among a dozen or so random choices her age. Of course, there were some regular couples, but mostly it's about sitting around big community tables and talking as friends. We'd be celebrating our impending graduation, of course, but we'd also be saying good-bye to those who were leaving the area." She looked accusingly at Tess. "How would you know who I went to the prom with?"

"That's what I heard."

"Who's your source? And don't tell me you have to protect your sources."

"Well, I did talk to Earl."

"Figures. Fred's best friend. Still in town?"

"Works at George's Hardware."

"And Fred?"

"Went into the army, I hear."

"He talked about that. Wanted Uncle Sam to pay for his education."

"Uncle can afford it," Tess replied. "But you didn't leave the prom with Fred."

"I didn't?"

Patty's frank response caught Tess by surprise, but she soldiered on. "Word is that you went out to Necklan's Lake afterwards with someone else."

"It's called Nekkid Lake. Some cop you are."

"Why?" Tess was playing dumb.

Patty sighed deeply before answering. "Kids go skinny-dipping there."

"After the Senior Prom?"

"That's the tradition."

"Did you?"

"Evidently. They told me I was found wet and naked, wrapped in a blanket on the beach."

"Do you believe that?"

Patty looked startled. "Why? Shouldn't I?"

"If that's how you were found, it's a fair assumption

that you were skinny-dipping," Tess agreed. "Like you said, it fits with the tradition. Did you consume any alcohol that night?"

"I think that's a given. The punch was spiked. Vodka, probably. The jocks kept adding it, even as the punch ran out. It was pretty lethal by the end of the evening."

"Do I detect that you may have been personally involved?"

Patty smiled slyly. "One of the many responsibilities of a cheerleader. Distract the chaperones while the punch is being fortified. Easy to do when you're wearing a low-cut prom gown."

"What about the female chaperones?"

"They're always watching the male chaperones to avoid any appearance of impropriety."

"So, no one watches the punch bowl."

"Not when the mighty Hawks cheerleaders are on the job." Patty delivered this line with an equal mix of pride and sarcasm.

Eager to keep her talking, Tess decided to continue on the subject. "Did the cheerleaders have other, uh, unexpected duties?"

"Oh yes. Like the topless cheer in the locker room after winning the conference football championship." Patty watched Tess closely for her reaction.

"You did that?"

Patty laughed. "The Hawks haven't won the championship in decades. Wasn't much to worry about there, but who knows?"

"But you would have done it?"

"It's part of the deal. Part of the tradition, *supposedly*. According to the football jocks. So, I just might have. If the other girls did, of course."

"Well, I feel better now about not making the cheerleading squad."

"Big school?'

"Hundreds in my class." Then she confided "Told me I wasn't springy enough."

Patty laughed. "What's that supposed to mean?"

"Never asked, but I've always wondered."

"I imagine so," she agreed. Then Patty unexpectedly added "By the way, I was putting you on about the whole topless cheer thing. See if you'd buy it."

"Hook, line and sinker."

"And then some," Patty observed. "In reality, we talked like the tough city girls we saw on television, but we were just of bunch of bouncing virgins."

"You're just full of surprises today."

"It's going to get worse," she predicted.

"Why?"

"Old age," she responded glumly.

Perplexed, Tess asked "You?"

"I'll be twenty-one in October."

"So you'll be able to drink alcohol that's not in a punch bowl?"

"Clever, but you don't get it."

"Why don't you try telling me then?"

"They kick me out of here then. This place is not for adults. I'm already the oldest inmate. Or is it patient?"

"What?"

"I have no money. Insurance pays for everything now, but not if I'm discharged."

"That doesn't seem right."

"No argument there," Patty agreed. "Why do you think I've kept using this wheelchair when I can walk just fine?"

"Oh." Tess' head stopped spinning long enough to say "I'm going to pretend I didn't hear that."

"I'd need a place to stay. Can't go home."

Tess recalled that Patty's mother had been described as an alcoholic. "Something could be arranged," she mumbled unconvincingly.

"They already threw me out of one place when I didn't recover fast enough for them."

This bit of news hit Tess like a hammer to the forehead. But she managed to ask "How old were you when you graduated?"

"Seventeen. Why?"

"Could be important. Not sure." She needed information. Now! But she looked Patty in the eye and said "We can work on your situation together. There's a solution. We'll find it and make it work for you."

A glimmer of hope shown in Patty's eyes. "You think so?"

"I know so. But I have to digest this first. And I've got to be somewhere." Tess stood to leave. *"Au revoir, Patty."*

"Au revoir, Tess."

CHAPTER 23

Wellston, Vermont
Monday, April 11, 2017, 11:58 AM EDT

For the first time ever, Tess had her badge out. But she didn't take time to reflect on the event. They already knew she was a deputy, but she figured it wouldn't hurt to display the evidence. But she kept it far enough away from the receptionist that it was hard to see that Tess was out of her jurisdiction. It seemed to be working. It probably helped that she liked Tess.

"Don't have much for you, I'm afraid. Patty wasn't there long. And they only forward an abstract of the records, since they have to keep the originals." She held out a thin blue file folder. "Says here that this can't leave the building without a court order. Maybe you could read it here."

"Works for me." Tess took the folder and opened it. "Maybe you can help me with some of the medical terms."

"I'll try."

"Like the diagnosis. It says severe PTSD. I'm venturing that means post-traumatic stress disorder?"

"Just like the soldiers coming back from Afghanistan."

"Right."

Tess collapsed into the nearest chair. It took about a minute to get her eyes to focus on the contents of the file, but after that she didn't look away.

Patient in shock from exposure. Witness to multiple deaths. 17 years old at admission. Events memory loss - possibly permanent. Patient unresponsive at discharge. Transfer to Wellston.

Tess wanted to cry, but that wouldn't help Patty or solve the case. So she returned the file to the receptionist. "Keep it handy."

"Are you O.K.?"

"I will be. Thanks."

CHAPTER 24

Necklan's Lake, Vermont

Monday, April 11, 2017, 6:41 PM EDT

Tess rolled her Harley into the clearing. It was already dusk. Deputy Lucas was feeding an enormous bonfire, which she approached slowly.

"You planning to stay late, Lucas? Because that's a four-hour fire if I ever saw one."

"Yeah. I may have outdone myself. Thinking too much about how cold it's gonna be when we come back out."

"Oh, crap!" Her brain had been so consumed by Patty that she had forgotten her robe. And something else. Oh, yes. Her bathing suit was in her VW --- not the motorcycle saddlebags. Just dandy.

"You sure this isn't a date? I don't go skinny-dipping at the drop of a hat. Got my standards."

"You keep your standard the Hell away from me, you hear?"

"If you say so." It was clear that he considered this to be an incomprehensible decision on her part.

"Tess, you are the dumbest bitch on the planet." Tess muttered to herself as she walked into the woods to distance herself from Lucas. But the cold and dark turned her back toward the fire. "Any bears around here?"

"Not in my lifetime."

"Wolves?"

"Not unless they escaped from a zoo."

From the warmth of the blaze, they watched the sun sink into the lake. Then Tess walked down to the shore, removed her shoes, stepped into the water, jumped back out.

"Colder than you expected?"

"Any colder and we could skate on it."

"So, you're chickening out on the swim?"

"What do you think, Deputy Macho?"

"Don't get all hostile now. Look. Here's how you do it. You sit next to the fire until you need to cool off. You have a beer or two to take the edge off."

"You've done this before."

They sat next to the fire on beach blankets. "Could say that." He opened two longnecks, put the bottle caps in his shirt pocket. Mr. Environment, now.

After sipping a few minutes in silence, she said "I'm shy."

"I'm not."

"That doesn't help."

"When you're ready, I'll walk into the woods --- with my night vision binoculars."

She punched him in the arm, hard. "I'm serious!"

"And I don't have any damn binoculars. Lighten up!"

"Sorry. I'm a bit tense."

"Finish your beer. I'm not trying to get you drunk, just a trifle numb is all."

"This won't do it." Tess stood and walked to her bike. She produced a bottle of Irish whiskey from the saddlebag. "I was saving this for the recovery. But I think we could use some now."

"Now who's trying to get whom drunk?"

"Want some or not?"

"Talked me into it." Lucas took the bottle from her and had a double swig.

"Hey, save some for later."

"That's all I need for now. I'm as ready as I'll ever be. How about you?"

She had one more taste, then capped the bottle.

Deputy Lucas was already on his way to the trees. There was no evidence that he had any swimming attire.

Tess rose slowly. This was a fitting ending to a day of surprises, was it not?   "You don't come out until I call you."

"Agreed. And you can watch me or turn your head. Makes no difference to me."

She considered this. "O.K." She chugged the remainder of her beer. "Let's do this." She started disrobing as he made it to the woods. But she stopped after removing her bra. She could cover her breasts with her hands. *Authenticity has its limits.* Tess dashed into the lake in a blur.

So cold it hurts!

"You'd better hurry before I freeze!"

She was surprised to see Lucas to jog out of the woods full frontal naked, no attempt to conceal anything. She promptly averted her gaze. She heard him splashing toward her. "Not too close!"

"See anything you like, Deputy Tess?"

"Nope."

"It's catch and release."

Despite herself, she found this amusing. "Never doubted it."

"Y'know, you look good all wet."

"And half-naked."

"That helps. For sure. Too bad I didn't bring my flashlight."

Tess laughed, then swam over to the rocks about twenty-five feet from shore, realizing there wasn't much she could do about her bottom sticking out of the water. *Should have learned to swim underwater.* Sand had accumulated around the boulders, making it possible to stand. This might have been where Patty was. Had she been alone? Or had she been there with a mystery man? She couldn't deal with these images right then. "Do wolves swim?"

"Only if they fall in the water. And then not for long."

"So if Patty was out here, a wolf wouldn't have come after her."

"No. And I told you there weren't any wolves in these parts."

"Just a thought." She took another look around and said "I'm ready to get back to the fire."

"After you."

Tess tensed immediately. "That wasn't the deal."

"I don't remember discussing any exit plan." But Lucas started toward the shore. She felt relieved until he called back. "This afternoon, I finally learned how to work the camera in my cell phone. So, don't forget to smile."

He went straight into the woods and she watched him go. The man had a nice build. *Like Adonis.* To her relief, he stayed there until she was dressed again. Then they sat very near to the fire and passed the Jameson bottle between them until it was half empty. "I'm warm enough," she declared as she capped it. "And thanks for the bonfire. Feels good."

"Almost hate to leave it...."

"Stay if you want. I'm hitting the trail."

"I'll wait until it burns down some more. Study the sky. Listen to the owls."

"Finish the beers," Tess interrupted.

"Strum my guitar," he continued as if she hadn't spoken.

"That ought to keep the wolves away," she predicted as she rose from the blanket.

"Now that hurt — even if it is true."

"You're a handful."

"You peeked!"

"Not what I meant, Lucas."

"It's O.K. So did I."

Yeah. That was absolutely the right note to end her weird day.

She drove up the drive on the Harley. She'd reached the road when it started to rain. Buckets of cold rain. By the time she'd put on her rain gear, she was soaked.

And she had to pretend it was just a minor

inconvenience to a hardy sheriff's deputy like her.

"Right!" she sputtered into the deluge.

CHAPTER 25

Cobbler's Knob, Vermont
Tuesday, April 12, 2017, 8:57 AM EDT

Tess appeared at the office looking like she'd spent the previous day being pampered in a spa. It was her way of coping. After what she had come to regard as the Coffee Ceremony, she stepped outside to make a cell phone call to Wellston. The rain had passed in the night, leaving a few puddles to dry in the bright sunlight.

"I wanted to thank you again for the information yesterday. I had one more question, but it didn't come to me until I was halfway back to the office." The reference to "the office" was a premeditated reminder of Tess' official status as a deputy. This casual call had been scripted and rehearsed. "Could I impose on you to check one little item for me? It would save me a trip back."

Tess held her breath.

"I'd really appreciate it. And you don't need to do it right now if you're real busy."

Tess had her.

"I forgot to get the name of the insurance company or agency that's paying for Patty's care. Yes. That's all. Well, I guess I should have the address and other contact information. Maybe her patient or policy file number, if you have it. Could simplify any inquiries I might have. Yes, I can hold."

It was amazing how casual contact trumped official channels.

"Professional Case Management, LLC. Yes. A Nevada limited liability company. Got it. What's next? 7423 North Walker River Avenue. Suite 63141. Yes. Carson City, Nevada 89604. Yes, I have it all so far. Telephone? None listed?"

She waited.

"Isn't that unusual? Oh. So it's probably an independent healthcare accounting firm that handles the disbursements for the insurance company. Not that unusual? I can see why they wouldn't want to give out their number. Anything else? File number? Please. Account No. CWP643W0015. No dashes. O.K. then. Thanks a lot. See you soon."

Tess disconnected. This was unexpected. Not ominous or even suspicious, but unexpected. She went back inside.

"Gonna tell us about your phone call?" Deputy Lucas asked.

"Oh. I just told my boyfriend about last night."

"Nothing happened last night."

"I told him that, too."

"So no big deal...."

"He's bringing the rest of the lacrosse team to teach you a lesson."

"What?"

Sheriff Roy cracked up laughing. "Good one, Tess!" he managed.

Lucas realized he'd been had. "Smart-ass college girl." He started to get up, but the Sheriff stopped him.

"Hang on, Deputy. Let's see if the cold lake revealed any new information on her cold case." Sheriff Roy looked inquiringly at Tess. He was all smiles.

"Well, the investigative pursuits of last evening revealed the following. Deputy Lucas builds a mean bonfire. And, you have to be under orders or drunk to enter Necklan's Lake at this time of year."

"We weren't drunk, Sheriff," Lucas interjected.

"True. Not even close," Tess confirmed. "And, the water is shallow enough around the boulders for a person five feet tall to stand; so Patty Martin could have been behind one of them that night. And, last but not least, surprisingly, Deputy Lucas is a gentleman — even if he is somewhat of a rascal." She bowed to the deputy.

Lucas nodded back, beaming.

"Not much else came to light last night, I'm afraid."

"And the phone call?" the Sheriff reminded her.

"Not sure if it leads anywhere. It was a follow-up to my visit to Wellston yesterday."

"Been busy," the Sheriff commented absently. When he did that, he was usually listening very carefully to what was being said.

"Patty told me the other day that she was worried about being discharged from Wellston when she turns twenty-one in a few months."

"She's talking?" Sheriff Roy asked.

"To me, at least." Both men were sitting forward in their chairs as if they were straining to hear. "No. Don't get your hopes up. She doesn't remember anything about the Senior Prom or Necklan's Lake. Doesn't remember who took her to the prom. Doesn't even remember the hypothermia or the treatment she received. Just remembers being in a rehab center. Everything else is a total blank."

Sheriff Roy looked disappointed. It was hard to read Deputy Lucas, but it occurred to her that he appeared to be relieved at this news.

"I read the file. The medical opinion is that Patty will never recover those memories. They even tried hypnosis, more than once."

"So we're not going to learn anything from the only survivor," the Sheriff declared.

"Only known survivor," she added.

Deputy Lucas rolled his green eyes. She ignored the gesture.

"However, I did find out that Patty went to another medical facility before Wellston. That's where the testing took place."

"After the hospital?" The Sheriff sought clarification.

"Yes. Wasn't there long. The transfer to Wellston occurred before a year had elapsed. No reason was given other than the first facility did not handle long-term patients. I checked on the internet. The website for the facility confirmed that to be the case. So that part fits."

"That what the call was about?" Lucas casually asked. His speech pattern did not indicate stress. She began to question her initial suspicions about Lucas and Patty being a couple.

"No. I wondered what company was paying Patty's bills at Wellston. Thought I might be able to find out if they're going to continue payments after her birthday."

"Not exactly part of the investigation," Sheriff Roy observed. "But what did you find out, now that we've come this far?"

"The payments come from a company in Nevada." Tess consulted her notes. "Carson City. Hmm. Must have tall buildings there...."

"Now why would you say that?"

"The office is in Suite 63141. At 7423 North Walker River Avenue."

"Why don't you check it out with the GPS program?"

"Really?"

"Indulge an old man, Deputy."

Tess set to work while the men did nothing but watch her. After 110 seconds she announced "It's a shopping plaza. A really small one. With a gas station. I've got the bird's eye view on."

"Look like a place where you'd find a big insurance company?" Sheriff Roy raised one eyebrow.

"No. Not really. Looks kind of seedy for anything like that," she admitted.

"Then I'm guessing that it's one of those places that rents cheap, unofficial mail boxes. Check it out."

"Checking now."

Deputy Lucas was impressed. "O.K. What made you think that?"

"It was the comment about the tall buildings that got me started. I've never been to Carson City, but I don't picture a lot of high-rise buildings --- even if it is the capital of Nevada. And the address didn't sound like it was anywhere near downtown. So I figured someone wanted an address that indicated there was an office suite where there might be only a mail drop."

"You're right," Tess announced. "It's a copy and office supply shop that rents boxes for mail delivery. 'One-Stop Office Supply.'"

"You must have really attended those criminology seminars in Boston," Deputy Lucas concluded. The Sheriff wasn't sure that was a compliment. He wondered what the deputy thought he might have been doing instead. Red Sox games?

"So now what?" Tess asked.

"Check out the Nevada company records. And if you have to hack, I don't want to know."

"Got it."

About fifteen minutes later, Tess exclaimed "It's nothing but a shell!"

Sheriff Roy wasn't surprised. "Fits with the address."

"I can't find the person who formed it, the owners,

the officers. No one. It doesn't even have a taxpayer identification number. There's no website, no phone number, no fax. Zip!"

"No taxpayer number? That's a nice touch." Lucas was impressed.

"Doesn't sound like an insurance company to me. They're highly regulated, even in places like Nevada."

"The lady at Wellston said it could be an independent accounting firm that had a contract to deliver and document the payments."

"Possible," conceded the Sheriff, "but that doesn't fit all the facts either. No it's some kind of scam."

"But they've been paying out benefits for years."

"Gives them credibility. Could be a long con, but I can't see how they'd ever even get their money back."

Deputy Lucas had an idea. "Maybe Patty's one of the few real cases?"

"That's good," admitted the Sheriff. "I may have underestimated your criminal mind."

That comment confused Lucas.

"Uh-oh." Tess was staring at her notes.

"What is it?"

"The account number. Didn't notice when I was writing it down."

"Well?"

"It's CWP643W0015."

"CWP could stand for anything, but...." It hit the Sheriff. "It ends in 15?"

"Yes," she whispered, as if that would diminish its impact.

"What?" Deputy Lucas hadn't arrived yet.

Tess was apparently unable to speak; so Sheriff Roy explained. "Fourteen missing and one survivor. Patty was the fifteenth person."

"Could be a coincidence," Tess suggested, totally without conviction.

"A coincidence is just a connection that we don't yet understand," Lucas said, to their utter astonishment.

"He's right," Tess agreed. "The account number has to be related to the massacre. It's not an insurance or patient file number at all."

"Now we have to completely revise our approach, the Sheriff decided. "Tess, can you search common usages of initials by government agencies?"

"Don't know, Sheriff. But I can't wait to try."

"Don't let us stop you."

CHAPTER 26

Cobbler's Knob, Vermont
Tuesday, April 12, 2017, 12:06 PM EDT

Tess had worked through lunch. She placed the sandwich the Sheriff had brought her to the side of her desk. 'This is what I've got so far. May be nothing. The letter 'c' at the beginning of a string often means 'confidential,' 'classified,' or 'clandestine.' If it is any of these, it probably doesn't matter which one. They all mean pretty much the same thing. The letter often means 'civil' or 'civilian,' too." Not to mention 'client' and 'compromise."

"What about 'computer?'" Lucas wondered.

"For reasons I don't understand, 'computer' is usually abbreviated with a 'k.' But unless it's a specific name or place, the first letter is probably not going to hold the key. The first letter is usually an adjective."

"Interesting observation, Deputy. Please continue."

"I'm skipping to the final letter for the moment. The letter 'p.' At the end of a string, it usually denotes, 'program,' 'project,' 'policy,' 'protection,''protocol' or 'plan.' So that's the noun. But again, this type of noun doesn't reveal much either."

"So we focus on the middle letter."

"Exactly, Sheriff. The letter 'w' probably describes the program or plan."

"And 'w' is not the first letter of that many significant words. Could be worse."

"But if the 'w' stands for a place or thing that isn't local, we're probably not going to figure it out."

"Correct. So do you have any local places or things that begin with that letter? Especially any that might relate to Necklan's Lake or the massacre."

A pause, then "Wellston?" Lucas offered.

"I'll write it down." And she did.

"Maybe we'd better move on to other words,' Sheriff Roy suggested.

"There's a whole chapter of the dictionary devoted

to the letter, but the ones that stand out in governmental use are these." She read her list slowly.

"Wall, War, Warp, Wasp, Waste, Water, Wave, Wealth, Weapon, Weather, Web, Welcome, Well, West, White, Wide, Will, Win, Wind, Wing, Winter, Witness, Wizard, Woman, Word, Work and World. These words may also be plural or be just the first part of a word, like Wavelength or Worldwide. There are more, of course, but let's try these out first."

Silence.

"I'll start then. It's probably best if we take the 'w' words in order. So Confidential Wall Plan."

"Let's skip Wall for now." the Sheriff suggested.

"O.K. then. Confidential War Plan."

"Seems a bit out of proportion to the problem," Lucas noted.

"Could be Client Welcome Policy. Or Welfare Plan," volunteered the Sheriff. "But we're pretty sure it's not, aren't we?"

"Maybe we should look at the most negative possibilities first," she conceded. "Like Classified Weapons Program. That certainly raises the speculative bar a few notches."

Apparently it did, because there was an intense quality to the silence that followed.

"Hold it! No more. Just stop. I need a minute to think." The Sheriff was shouting.

The deputies fell silent. No sound except breathing. And Tess substituting words with her pen. She wrote Classified Weapons Program on her tablet. Then she set the pen down. No need to continue.

It was possible that Patty Martin was File No. 15 of a Classified Weapons Program, whatever that might be.

Tess shuddered as the possibilities flew unbidden from their dark places into her mind.

Sheriff Roy looked up from his desk. He stared at them for a moment, then forged ahead. He tried to keep it light. "The possibility has arisen that, somewhere along the line, we have stumbled across a government project of which we were unaware. If so, we don't know what may be involved. What we must do now is to stop dead in our tracks and stumble no further." He raised his voice to discourage interruption. "Specifically, this means the investigation into the events at Necklan's Lake ceases completely as of right now. There are no exceptions. Tess, you need to turn over every note and item you have now, without comment. Both of you are sworn to silence about everything you've heard or learned. Don't even speak to each other about it. Neither of you is to go near Necklan's Lake."

"And, Deputies, I will make it my personal quest to see that you never work for any law enforcement organization in the world if you don't follow these simple instructions. And no more communications of any type with Patty Martin or Wellston." He was speaking directly to Tess.

Tears had formed in Tess' eyes, but she didn't speak.

"I know this sounds harsh. And it is. No doubt about it. But you will have other cases that don't put you in conflict with what may be a federal agency project. I am taking this action in order to remove us all from unknown potential harm. A cold case is not worth the risk. I just hope we're backing off in time."

Sheriff Roy marched over to Tess' desk and removed every piece of paper from the top, taking it to his own desk. He returned to make sure she turned over the contents of the desk drawers. She couldn't meet his gaze.

Then she threw the sandwich in the trash, and stalked out. Neither one tried to stop her. Her motorcycle roared away.

"She'll get over it, Sheriff."

"I won't!" he shot back. "Shouldn't you be on patrol?"

"Just on my way out, Sheriff."

CHAPTER 27

Northern Vermont
Tuesday, April 12, 2017, 1:35 PM EDT

Tess had a sunny day and the afternoon off. At least she'd taken it off. She needed to think. But she had no place to go. So she drove back to Dartmouth on the pretext that she would need her Beetle.

"Too late for the swim suit," she reminded herself.

As she drove the back roads, she came to understand Sheriff Roy's decision. She even conceded that he had no other choice. But she was not ready to abandon Patty, whom she had recently and recklessly assured that all would fine.

Big mouth!

And if her investigation had inadvertently terminated the program that supported Patty, where did that leave Patty? Unsupported, probably. Terminated? Maybe.

How did things go so badly so fast?

Time to review.

If there was a government program, what government? From the Sheriff's reaction, he must believe it was federal. That made the most sense. So it was the executive branch of the federal government. Hardly narrowed it down.

Ah! Weapons. Classified weapons, yet. Some branch of the military? That didn't seem right. "Close --- but no cigar." The armed forces ordered weapons and used them, but she didn't think they designed and tested them first. Pretty sure.

No. That wasn't true. The Air Force actively participated in the development of aircraft with selected contractors. That meant the Navy might also. But aircraft didn't fit with Necklan's Lake. The topography was wrong. And it wasn't *that* remote. Not like Area 51 or that place they'd tested the atomic bomb in New Mexico.

Ruling out aircraft, ships and nuclear devices, that left the private contractors that designed and built the other classified weapons. For that matter, who declared them classified? Had to be some agency. Maybe the Pentagon. But that was a building, not an agency. Then she had it.

"Department of Defense." Just saying it out loud frightened her. "Nice work, Deputy. Provoked the wrath of the DoD --- without even trying."

"But wait! I didn't see any weapons at the lake. And none were reported after the massacre by the state forensic teams. Where were these weapons? What were they?"

Maybe Sheriff Roy was wrong, had gone off the deep end. He'd realize his mistake soon enough. Not to worry.

She took the next mountain curve aggressively and encountered a bull moose standing directly in her path. Tess desperately cut to the right shoulder and managed to sail past it with only inches to spare, thankful for the size and maneuverability of her Harley. There was no way she could have avoided the giant moose in her Volkswagen.

"Now those would make great weapons!" she reflected. "If you could control them."

She pulled over at the next scenic stop. She needed to get off the bike and rest. Get her pulse down after her near collision with two tons of moose. She recalled how she had regarded the moose as a potential weapon. "Maybe the Department of Defense was studying the moose at Necklan's Lake," she conjectured playfully. Didn't matter that she had never actually seen one at the lake. It was easy to picture.

That was when she made the breakthrough.

They weren't studying moose. They were studying whatever attacked the Seniors!

As potential weapons!

Then they had removed the evidence before the scene was discovered. In order to keep the project secret.

"And I have officially crossed the line into madness," she rebuked herself.

"But, damn!" She thought a bit more.

I hate it when crazy and real fit together like that!

CHAPTER 28

Cobbler's Knob, Vermont
Wednesday, April 13, 2017, 8:26 AM EDT

Sheriff Roy pulled in to the office parking lot beside Tess' Beetle. He'd never owned one, but recalled that Lucy had one in high school that she'd driven aggressively. It had started every time, even on the coldest days. Of course, it spun out on the ice. But so did the big American cars. It was more fun in the Beetle though. Like bumper cars.

Opening the door to the office transported his olfactory sense to an imaginary coffee plantation. Colombia, maybe. Was that Juan Valdez in the mist? It takes Juan to know Juan, he decided.

He'd let her go first.

"Good morning, Sheriff. Coffee's just ready."

Not a bad start, he conceded. "Same to you, Deputy. At least about the morning."

"Your headache any better?" Tess asked.

"Headache?"

"The one you got yesterday afternoon."

"Oh, that one." He groped for the right word and found it. "Persistent."

"Sorry to hear it, but understandable," she sympathized. "In fact, after you gave me the afternoon off...."

"Did I catch that right?"

"Well then, after you drove me away."

He nodded. "Sounds more like it. Please continue."

"I had to re-boot my brain, at least as far as the Necklan's Lake investigation. I mean, I sensed that you had jumped to the right conclusion. But I had to see if I could make it fit with what I had already learned."

"And you've done that?"

"Either that or I should be locked up for my own good."

"Always that fine line...."

"You've noticed?"

"Comes with the territory," he advised amiably.

"Anyhow, I see that your tentative conclusion about stumbling, unwanted, into the middle of Department of Defense Classified Weapons Program No. 643W would...."

"I don't recall saying anything about the DoD."

"Well, as I said, I gave it some serious thought, and decided that the DoD was a neat fit for an agency that would cause your reaction. And since we're speculating, why not speculate big?"

"Hmm. Interesting approach. Give the unseen enemy a face, so to speak."

"That wasn't exactly what I was trying to do, but perhaps I did."

"And the 643W?"

"It's the part of the file number that precedes the 0015."

"643 Whiskey, in military speak?"

"Yes."

"A reasonable assumption. Not that it gets us anywhere. Any other insights?"

"There was no evidence of weapons found," Tess

ventured.

"True," he admitted. "Where are you going with this?"

"If a secret DoD project was involved, it follows that the evidence would have been removed."

"Like policing your brass?"

"Exactly, but on a grander scale."

"O.K. But what type of weapons were they testing? And how on earth did the Seniors get in the line of fire?"

"One of my instructors told us that a terrorist views people outside his family as having only three possible roles: obstacles, targets and collateral damage. That thinking might apply here."

"The DoD as terrorists?" Sheriff Roy was not ready to accept that. At least not out loud.

"Just the mind set. Perhaps the Seniors showed up unexpectedly at the wrong time, unwittingly becoming obstacles or collateral damage."

"Maybe both, in that order," he conceded the possibility. "Could have been too late to stop a test that was already in motion." He could envision the horror of the project managers when the Seniors rolled in, whooping and drinking. "Everybody lost that round, then."

"Murphy's Law, squared."

He thought about it, weighed it, found it more than adequate. "Yeah. That sums it up."

"Without using the word 'cluster,'" Tess added quietly.

He smiled. "There's that, too."

"So they would have had to clean it up before anyone happened by. And given the large number of casualties, it was clear that someone would come looking."

"By morning, at the latest. They did a Hell of a job, then."

"On short notice," Tess observed. "Unless they had a crew standing by for that purpose."

"I think we can assume a DoD team would be prepared for just about anything. And probably this test was going to require cleanup in any event. Couldn't just leave expended ammunition or ordnance lying around."

"But why choose Necklan's Lake? Don't they have regular testing sites in New England or upstate New York?"

"I'm sure they do." Sheriff Roy was puzzled. "So, why would they favor Necklan's Lake over a place that already had infrastructure for weapons testing?"

"Not to mention convenience, and privacy."

"I have a feeling that the answer to that holds the key to the mystery."

"Well put, Holmes," she chided.

He grinned. "That was a bit fusty, wasn't it? Must be a side effect of the job."

"Let's assume you're right. There has to be something that makes Necklan's Lake more suitable for the testing."

"Can't be the terrain. It's fairly typical. And there are lakes like that everywhere in New England."

"You're from these parts, Sheriff. What makes Necklan's Lake different — even if it doesn't seem important?"

"Well, it was a church camp. Before that, I've been told that there were some independent logging operations that never amounted to much."

"Before that?"

"Nothing. Not even any French trapper cabins or

Indian settlements."

"Seems like an ideal spot for an Indian village," Tess observed.

"That's not the way Algonquin tribes looked at land. Access to water was most important, but not much of a challenge in these parts. The second priority was good hunting grounds. Necklan's Lake was known to be one of them. The tribes never settled close to the hunting grounds for fear of driving the game away."

"Hard to argue with that."

"See how your perspective changes when you eliminate grocery stores from the equation?"

"So what does an Indian hunting ground have in common with a DoD testing site?"

"Hunting involves weapons," he observed.

"Oh my, yes." It was easy to overlook flint-tipped arrows and obsidian knives when mentally dealing with advanced weaponry.

"And something else...." The Sheriff spoke as if it had just occurred to him.

"What?"

"Prey," he said flatly. "Or targets--- going back to

your terrorist mind set."

"Are you suggesting that the Seniors were...." Tess stopped cold. "I can't even finish that sentence!"

"I'm just saying it's a possibility, that's all. Unless there's some evidence to rule it out."

Tess looked more like a deer in the headlights than any deer the Sheriff had ever seen. She shook her head to clear it. "I can't think of any. Sheriff. None at all."

"Me neither. Can't rule it in or rule it out at this point."

"More coffee?" Tess forced herself to move.

"Can't hurt," he answered without conviction.

They sipped their coffees in silence. They did nothing else.

Sheriff Roy had been correct. The coffee didn't hurt. But it sure didn't help any.

CHAPTER 29

Cobbler's Knob, Vermont
Wednesday, April 13, 2017, 9:14 AM EDT

It was the telephone that startled them both back to the present. Sheriff Roy answered it. He still wasn't used to having someone else who would answer it. Or perhaps he had a need to know what was going on.

"It's for you."

Tess nodded to him by way of acknowledgment, and picked up her receiver. It was the receptionist at Wellston.

"The insurance man just left. He wanted to know who you were and why you were visiting Patty Martin."

"What insurance man?"

"The man who comes by every now and then to read Patty's chart," she explained.

Tess signaled to the Sheriff to pick up his receiver again, quietly. He did.

"I didn't know about him. How long has he been dropping by?"

"Ever since Patty got here. He comes by every few months. Same middle-aged guy. Doesn't seem to be on a regular schedule, you know?"

"Well, it must be part of his job to keep track of the patients they pay for." She was winging it. "How many others does he check on?"

"Oh, just Patty."

"I hope you didn't tell him I ride a motorcycle," she said in a conspiratorial tone.

"No. It didn't come up."

Tess out-waited her. Most people would keep talking if you just waited.

"I told him you had met Patty and become friends. That you were about the same age, and both pretty smart. Not really any other people Patty's age here, mostly a lot younger. And they're all quite intimidated by Patty's maturity and good looks."

"Did the insurance man want to know anything else

about me?"

"Yes. He asked what you did together. I said I really didn't know, but that I'd heard you speaking French or Spanish. I wasn't sure which."

"It was French."

"I *thought* it was," she said proudly. "That might have confused him. The French, I mean."

"Maybe he though I was a spy," Tess suggested.

"Oh no! At least I don't think so," the receptionist replied. Tess could picture her eyes wide at the thought.

"Did you tell him I was a deputy?"

"No. Didn't come up either. But it's probably in the file."

Time to change the subject. "How's Patty doing?'

"She's fine, but I know she'd like a visitor," she said with a complete absence of subtlety.

"I'll try to get by soon. I miss her too."

After they disconnected, the Sheriff asked "What do you make of that?"

"That the DoD is keeping tabs on her."

"Think they might be worried that she'll remember what happened?"

"Sounds like it." She had an unpleasant thought. "I almost hate to ask, but why didn't they just remove her during the cleanup?"

"They could have overlooked her, if she was hiding in the water. If not, maybe they're not as heartless as we first thought."

"That would be a relief."

"Or maybe they thought she would die of exposure anyway. So they left her to confuse the investigation. If true, it was brilliant. The survival of Patty Martin, unable to explain what happened, provided a huge distraction."

"Along with the possibility that she might recover her memory at any time and simply tell the investigators what had happened."

Sheriff Roy told Tess "I can say for a fact that that very possibility significantly reduced the incentive to investigate further at the time."

"Wait."

"Yes?"

"But where then did Patty get the blanket?"

"Good question." he admitted. "Either she already had it or someone wrapped it around her."

"What about the emergency rescue people?"

"Weren't any there."

"Who was there first?"

"Just me. Spotted Patty Martin right away, lying next to the fire pit. I verified she had a pulse before making any calls. Temperature outside must have been in low 'fifties by then. I called Doctor McAdams from the car phone. He warned me not to move her in case she had any severe injuries. So I got the fire going again to warm her up. Pulled a blanket from the back of my car and spread that over her too. Doctor was there within twenty minutes. Said he thought she'd make it."

"Did she look like someone had wrapped her up?"

A blank stare from the Sheriff.

"Like someone had rolled her up in the blanket?"

"I was looking for signs of injury when she was unwrapped, not really thinking about the blanket itself. But, now that you mention it, she sort of rolled out."

"Like Cleopatra?"

"What? Oh yeah. Like that I suppose," he supposed. "Before my time."

Tess ignored the last comment. "Then someone

may have wrapped her up. Which is a considerate act."

"Although not nearly as much as could have been done at the time," he observed. "Why such limited assistance, given the resources available?"

"Are you suggesting that it was unauthorized?"

"I guess that's where I was headed...."

"Could be that one of the last of the cleanup crew tried to help her on his own."

"That's one way to make sense of it."

"Well, at least we still think we *can* make sense of it."

"We must be optimists," the Sheriff noted.

But Tess had moved on already. "I should keep seeing Patty."

"Why's that?" He wasn't challenging the idea. Tess usually had good reason for her assertions.

"To show this so-called insurance man that we're just friends, and that his visit didn't change anything."

"I think you might be right about that. But you can't ask any questions about Necklan's Lake or that night. No more investigation."

"I can live with that. No sense asking if I know she

can't answer, Sheriff."

"Can I trust you on this?"

"I should be offended, but I know where you're coming from. No more investigation. You have my word on it."

"Thanks, Tess. Why don't you go visit your new friend?"

Tess was satisfied. There had been no explicit prohibition against helping Patty disappear --- if the need should arise.

CHAPTER 30

Wellston, Vermont
Wednesday, April 13, 2017, 11:08 AM EDT

"Transferred? What does that mean?" Tess couldn't believe it.

"A wheelchair van showed up a little after 10:00 this morning. There was a driver and an attendant and a man in a suit with the paperwork. The head nurse made a phone call to confirm it was correct. Boy, was she angry!"

Tess' brain was still struggling to fathom it. "But she let them take her?"

"It wasn't like she had a choice. But she let them know that this facility has a 3-day advance notice policy for non-emergency transfers. I was right here. Heard every word. But when they said the insurance would pay through the end of the month, there wasn't much to argue about."

"How did Patty feel about it?"

"Oh, she got all upset. We had to sedate her."

Terrific. "Didn't she have any say in it?"

"No. She's still a minor. So her mother must have signed something. The head nurse still has the papers; so I can't check the file."

Great. Probably had to buy old mom a few drinks to get her to sign. Tess took a minute to allow her breathing to approach normal. "Well, I guess I'll have to visit her at the new place," she remarked as casually as she could. "I hope it's not too far."

The receptionist picked up a form from the counter and scanned it. "Let's see. It just says 'TBD' on the line. That's 'to be determined.'" She understood that this was not helpful information.

Tess was about to explode, but couldn't afford to lose her only source of information. "They put her in a van and took her away, but they don't know where they're taking her?"

"Oh, no. They sometimes go to a clinic for an

evaluation. The results of that determine what facility she enters next." Her face suddenly brightened. "She could be going home."

Tess really wanted to seize on that faint hope. But she couldn't manage it. "When will you know?"

The receptionist thought. "First part of next week probably. I'll give you a call as soon as I find out. O.K.?"

"Sounds like a plan. And thanks a lot."

"You're welcome. And tell Patty 'hi' when you see her."

"I'll do that." *And I'll bring her a real panda bear from China, while I'm at it. Won't that be a hoot?*

Tess retreated to her car, and drove away stunned to the core.

Her fanciful notion of spiriting Patty away from danger had been crushed by the reality of an organized resourceful enemy. One that was likely a federal agency.

Then paranoia directed her to review her conversation with the receptionist. Had Tess revealed any clue she might know that Patty was being silenced? Tess didn't think so, but she would have to follow up, as casually as she could, with the receptionist in order to preserve the illusion that she and Patty had simply been friends.

Maybe she could offer to write to Patty.

Yeah. "Dear prisoner...."

And that was the best case scenario.

CHAPTER 31

Cobbler's Knob, Vermont
Wednesday, April 13, 2017, 1:22 PM EDT

Sheriff Roy was explaining to Deputy Lucas why it was difficult to extract information from a female.

"Talking to a woman is like playing pinball. The goal of the woman is to hit as many items on her agenda as possible, regardless of their relevance to the topic. So, the matter under discussion ricochets around faster than you can follow it. When it finally emerges, it is unrecognizable. Even when the woman is really trying to convey information, each sentence she utters is subject to conversational perturbation. That's when her agenda causes the course of the conversation to deviate from its intended course."

"And why do you think that is?" Lucas asked

reasonably.

"I think that most women fail to understand that the purpose of conversation is to exchange needed information efficiently. Ask a woman if the car should be locked. She will never answer with a single word. Instead, she will tell you that she read about an unlocked automobile being stolen in some place you've never heard of. Then she will verbally assess the cultural differences between that place and where you are at the moment. Then she will reveal that her mother never locked her car, speculating as to whether the times have changed. Finally, she will ask 'What do you think?' By then you have locked the damned car anyway."

Deputy Lucas enjoyed listening to the Sheriff pontificate. Almost as much as the Sheriff himself did.

Tess took the long way back to the office. It wasn't like she had a case to work on. Sheriff Roy and Deputy Lucas were there.

"Lucas just made fresh coffee!" the Sheriff announced as she entered. "You're timing's great — as long as you're not too particular."

"That's your second cup," Lucas pointed out.

"It's really pretty good," he admitted. "Tess just looks better making it."

"Not going to argue with that."

Tess poured herself a cup and held up the pot to offer refills. No takers. She added milk from the mini fridge and hazarded a sip. "Not a thing wrong with this coffee, Lucas."

"I believe that's what they call an unsolicited endorsement," Lucas told the Sheriff, who nodded in agreement. Then innocently he asked "What's new in Wellston?"

That's when Tess finally caved. Her arms folded on her desk, followed swiftly by her head. The men thought they heard sobs. They looked at each other in surprise and mutual incomprehension.

"Ah, Tess," Sheriff Roy said tentatively. "Something wrong?"

"Patty's gone."

"What?"

"They took her away this morning."

"Who?"

"Some men in a van. They had the proper documents. So they let them take her away. Just like that!"

"Where to?"

She finally raised her head. "TBD."

Sheriff Roy wasn't processing this; so Lucas explained. "To be determined."

"To be determined?" he repeated, as if that might clarify it.

"It's my fault," Tess confessed. "For visiting her."

Now Sheriff Roy had a new concern. Had his make-work, cold case investigation caused Patty Martin to be kidnapped? It was more than possible. It was even beginning to appear likely. If so, he was to blame.

Tess had read his thoughts. "Not your fault, Sheriff."

"I'm the one who suggested you go to Wellston, Tess. In fact, I'm the one who started this whole investigation over again."

A minute passed before Lucas said. "Shouldn't we be doing something? Besides blaming yourselves? I mean actually doing something to locate Patty Martin?"

"That would be more in keeping with the job description," the Sheriff conceded. "Even if the jurisdiction is a bit shaky."

"No one else is going to lift a finger," Tess reminded them.

"There is that. Tess, you need to get a look at the patient file to see what this transfer paperwork might reveal. Maybe the name of a transport company, or something else we can use. Try to find out what clinics she might be taken too, as well."

"They don't intend to evaluate her," Tess stated flatly.

"Find out anyway. It's not like we have a world of clues to work with. Take Deputy Lucas with you."

"What for?" she asked. It was clear that Lucas wondered as well.

"Backup. He can be intimidating when he wants."

"I get to play bad cop," Lucas explained.

Tess began to see the positives that Lucas brought to the game. For one, he could distract the receptionist while Tess looked around. *O.K., he could probably charm her right out of her knickers. Whatever.*

"Let's go, Lucas. We'll discuss tactics on the way."

"Take the Jeep?"

"Yes!" The Sheriff decided for them, as they left the building.

Sheriff Roy watched them leave before he picked up his phone. After a few rings, it was answered. "Afternoon, Matt. Hope I'm not interrupting the formulation of one of your inspiring sermons." After a pause, the Sheriff chuckled. "Yes, I'm sure I have the right number. I have a situation. I think you can help. You up for a little community service?"

CHAPTER 32

Cobbler's Knob, Vermont

Wednesday, April 13, 2017, 2:59 PM EDT

"Why, this *is* an unexpected surprise, pastor," Mrs. Martin gushed as she opened the door for him to enter. It was obvious that housekeeping didn't agree with Mrs. Martin. If indeed it ever occurred to her. Then there was that unmistakable cat odor which threatened to gag him. She failed to notice his involuntary reaction to her world. Instead, she was desperately trying to recall when she'd last been to church. He was familiar with the situation.

"Just call me Matt, Mrs. Martin. I'm not ordained."

"Maybe they just haven't heard about you yet." Her conception of the workings of organized religion was refreshingly inaccurate.

"Perhaps I should speak louder," he offered, but

that seemed to confuse her. He'd come as quickly as he could, but he hadn't beat her to the bottle. He wondered if that was even possible.

"Could I get you a refreshment?"

"Just had a late lunch," he lied without guilt. "So I'm fine."

"You let me know if you change your mind." She sat down. Mrs. Martin cast a quick look at the glass on the end table beside her chair, but quickly rejected the urge to imbibe more of the wine. She had thoroughly embraced the notion that wine was the drink of queens and princesses, not to mention Jesus himself. This led to the logical fallacy that wine imparted an aristocratic bearing upon one. Therefore, that person couldn't be an alcoholic. She tried her best to appear regal, raising her chin slightly.

They both knew what was coming next.

"We've missed you at services recently. I thought I'd come by to make sure you hadn't thrown in your lot with the Devil."

"Oh, no, pastor!" She found the idea more than a bit scandalous. "I'm still on the side of the Lord."

"It comforts me to hear it." Matt nodded as if this

was indeed excellent news. "And your health?"

"I get by all right. Can't get up the stairs by myself anymore, but I have a bed and bathroom on this floor. Doesn't do any good to complain about the little aches and pains we get from time to time, does it?"

"They remind us that we are imperfect. That the love the Lord has for us is a miracle." Matt believed it, but felt he was laying it on a bit thick.

His eloquence had apparently stunned Mrs. Martin into silence; so he resumed the conversation himself.

"And how's your family?" Patty was her only child; so the general question was calculated to lead to specific information.

"Oh, the poor thing is still up at that Wellston place," she responded.

He tried a different approach. "Do they evaluate her from time to time, to see if she can come home?"

She dismissed the idea out of hand. "They told me she'll never be able to come home." She looked like she might cry.

"Oh, I'm sorry. I didn't know that." Matt sought a way to move forward. "Was this recent?"

'Yes, it was. Just the other day." Which might have been last year, Matt realized.

"How did you find this out?"

"The insurance man told me."

"The insurance man?"

"The man who brings the money." She couldn't understand his confusion. It was so clear to her. "You know, the support money."

He played along. "Oh, yes. The support money."

"Right!"

"He brings you the insurance check."

"No check. It's always cash. Says they do that to make it more convenient for me."

Matt appeared to consider this. "That's very thoughtful."

"Isn't it? And the last time he was here he told me that my Patty would never be well enough to come home." Mrs. Martin began to sob.

"There, there." Why was he saying *that?* He sounded like Cary Grant comforting a child in a motion picture. "I'm sure they'll look after her."

The sobs subsided as she latched onto this ray of

hope. "That's what they said, bless them. Said I'd never have to worry about my Patty again."

"Well then, it sounds like she's going to be well cared for."

"It's a fancy place, you know."

"Yes, I've been there to see her."

"Oh, how kind of you, pastor."

"It's nothing at all." He paused, making it up as he went. "Do you have Patty's insurance documents, in case something should happen to you? Would somebody be able to locate them?"

"They're keeping them safe for me."

"Who is?'

"The insurance company." The pastor did not seem to be following her very well. Maybe he had more pressing matters on his mind, she thought.

"Ah, of course!" He looked at his left wrist. He wore no watch, but assumed correctly that she wouldn't notice. "I need to be on my way. The Lord's work is never done."

"I certainly do appreciate your visit, pastor. And your words of comfort." She was already eyeing the glass of red liquid comfort that awaited her on the table.

"Do try to make it by on Sunday, then. Let me know if you need a ride."

"I'll be fine," she responded without addressing the matter at all.

"Then good day, Mrs. Martin."

"And to you, pastor."

The door closed. Matt counted her steps to the wine glass.

Then he returned to his car. He was meeting Sheriff Roy at *Rachel's* for a friendly glass of beer. The Sheriff was buying.

The promised draft was waiting. Matt waved, sat down and took a long sip before speaking. The first word he uttered was not promising. "Clueless."

"Can you be more specific?"

"*Utterly* clueless."

"Mrs. Martin doesn't actively participate in her daughter's care?"

"O.K. Mrs. Martin is a lush, a wino. This is what she believes to be factual. Her daughter is at a fancy place called Wellston, and will probably be there for the rest of her life. She has no idea why that might be or what is wrong with Patty. She believes that Patty is being cared for by some insurance company, that also keeps track of her health in some manner similar to a welfare agency. And, you're going to love this, this mysterious insurance company regularly makes what she calls 'support payments' to Mrs. Martin directly — in cash!"

"Incredible. Takes the breath away."

"Indeed," he confirmed as he took another sip. "I suggested to Mrs. Martin that someone would need to know about the insurance company in the event she was out of the picture. She assured me that all the paperwork was is a safe place. Want to guess where?"

"Under the mattress?"

"The insurance company is keeping it all safe for her."

"Boggles the imagination."

"What's going on, Roy? And why the cloak and dagger routine?"

The Sheriff sighed deeply. "Quite a bit, really. But if I confine my answer to Patty Martin, we can deal with it summarily. Hold up your right hand."

"What for?"

"I have to deputize you; so I can swear you to secrecy."

"Bit dramatic, don't you think?"

"I have to do it. It's a deal-breaker, Matt."

Matt raised his right hand. The Sheriff swore him in.

"Do I get paid?"

The Sheriff shook his head.

"A badge?"

"Nope. Just a benefit. You get your question answered."

"I'll take it."

"It's not the whole story, just about Patty."

"Just tell me!"

"As you've already heard, Patty's insurance coverage is too good to be true."

"So it isn't. But who's paying?"

"We don't know, but the few records in her file at Wellston disclose a Nevada shell company with a phony address and no taxpayer identification number."

Matt's eyebrows raised spontaneously at that last

bit. "So the source of funds is unknown."

"No, Deputy Matt."

The not-pastor, now-deputy frowned.

Sheriff Roy continued. "The source of funds is hidden. As in intentionally hidden by someone serious about it remaining untraceable."

"Sounds like the CIA...."

"Haven't ruled them out. But there's more."

"I'm all ears."

"My student deputy, Tess...."

"I met her. We discussed the Camp Bethany fire. She said she was working on a cold case."

"Yes, she was. Forgot she spoke with you."

"Seemed bright and eager to learn."

"Bright as a new penny," Sheriff Roy agreed. "Anyway, she visited with Patty and they became friends."

"Must have been difficult, since Patty doesn't talk." Matt was skeptical.

"I don't have the details. Not important. But she talked to Tess."

This was big news. "Did she say what happened...?"

"No. Nothing about Necklan's Lake. She apparently

doesn't remember anything about that night. Tess doesn't think she's faking."

"Still, that's great. Maybe she can come home now." Matt reflected briefly on Mrs. Martin's house and discarded that scenario. "Or at least leave Wellston."

Sheriff Roy wasn't smiling. He looked Matt directly in the eyes and said "That's the problem. She has left Wellston."

"When?"

"This morning."

"Why doesn't her mother know?"

"Nobody did until it happened."

"You make it sound like a kidnapping."

"Haven't ruled that out either," the Sheriff responded. "As I heard it, a van arrived about ten AM, unannounced. One of the men who rode in it produced some documents, a phone call was made, and he was allowed to take her away."

"What do you make of it?"

"Yesterday, an 'insurance' man showed up at Wellston. No idea if it's the same guy that pays Mrs. Martin. He saw in the file that Patty had been visited by

Tess several times. He inquired, and found out that Patty was talking."

"And now she's gone. Any idea where?"

"Down the rabbit hole. Although we're still making inquiries."

Matt whistled. "Impressive. In less than twenty-four hours? These people really are pros!"

"My greatest fear," Sheriff Roy admitted. "My other deputies are at Wellston now."

Matt still hadn't quite gotten his mind around being a deputy sheriff, but the child in him thought it was neat. "Any idea what they're afraid Patty might say?"

"Not really." The Sheriff was reluctant to reveal more, but also coming to the realization that the facts were resisting his attempts at compartmentalization. "There's this theory that a federal agency was engaged in some clandestine activity at Necklan's Lake when the Seniors turned up unexpectedly."

"And Patty might have witnessed what happened next?"

"Along those lines."

"Then said agency might have to insure her

silence."

"In an nutshell."

"Any idea what this agency might have been doing there?"

"Even if we had a firm theory, it would be need to know, Matt. And we've got no evidence at all." The Sheriff spread his hands before him in a gesture of uncertainty. "Actually the lack of evidence is the most compelling evidence we've got."

"Not enough to accuse a federal agency," Matt concurred.

"Wouldn't know which one or what to accuse them of doing. And that's not going to change, because I've closed the investigation."

"But you're still looking for Patty?"

"Quietly and discreetly."

"Glad I could help, Sheriff."

"It's appreciated, Deputy."

"Will I still be a deputy after today?"

"It'll be our secret."

"Sounds like we're one step away from you sending me the Bat-signal when you need my help."

"Just download the app on your cell phone."

Matt just shook his head slowly.

CHAPTER 33

Cobbler's Knob, Vermont
Wednesday, April 13, 2017, 5:14 PM EDT

Tess and Lucas entered the office. "We have news," Tess announced. She placed some papers on Sheriff Roy's desk. "Those are copies of the checks that paid for Patty's care." There were dozens. Sheriff Roy picked them up.

"Tess looked them over on the way back," Lucas said.

"They are all cashier's checks; so we don't have an account name or number," Tess said. "And the signature is a bank officer."

"What about the remitter — the name of the requesting party?" the Sheriff wondered.

"Professional Case Management LLC. No other identification," Tess replied.

"They all appear to come from the same bank, called BankZone. Seems to have a Spanish address," Lucas added.

"What do we know about the bank?"

"Searching it now," Tess advised from her computer. "Got it! What?"

"Find it?" Sheriff Roy asked.

"BankZone is located in Panama and chartered under its laws. I'll double check."

"How do you intend to do that?" Lucas inquired.

"Compare the routing number on the checks to the one listed for the bank."

"She's smarter than we are Sheriff."

"Just better educated. Maybe."

"Maybe not. Turns out it's something called an IBAN number," Tess said. "Read me the numbers off the bottom of the check, slowly."

That was how they confirmed that it was the same bank.

"Think the bank would tell us the name on the account number?" Lucas wondered aloud.

"I think that's one of the reasons for using a

Panamanian bank: secrecy." Sheriff Roy was pretty sure of this. "The account itself is probably in the name of the shell company anyway."

"And we're probably never going to penetrate the shell company," Tess added.

"We're never even going to try it," Sheriff Roy stated with more volume than necessary. "Not consider it for a moment."

"Got it!" Tess understood.

"Any leads on where they took her?"

"All anyone saw was a new-looking gray van with no markings."

"What make and model?"

"Not sure. But one of the male nurses said it was on a truck chassis, whatever that means."

"Means it wasn't a Chrysler product. Those are built on car frames," Lucas enlightened her. "Eliminates quite a few models."

"Was there a ramp or a lift for the wheelchair?" the Sheriff asked.

"Ramp."

"Electric or manual?"

"They said it was electric, but couldn't identify the brand."

"Did the ramp come from the side or the rear?"

"Let's see. The side."

"Vermont plates?"

"They think so, because nobody noticed anything unusual about them."

"Anything else?"

"Uh. Darkened windows."

"Figures. Which direction did they take?"

"South, but there are only two choices at that point."

"Lucas, you get onto the state police. Tell them what we're looking for — as a possible stolen vehicle. Tell them it could be in New Hampshire or Massachusetts by now."

"What about New York?"

"If we request too much, we won't get anything. Besides, I suspect they haven't gone far."

"Why?" Tess asked.

"If I had pulled something this audacious, I'd want to disappear fast instead of driving an unusual vehicle around where there aren't a lot of roads or people."

"And you accused me of having a criminal mind," Deputy Lucas reminded him.

"Maybe a state campground or cabin that hasn't been opened for the season yet. Something along those lines."

"Maybe something federal even, if we're dealing with a federal agency," Tess suggested. "Like a national forest or ranger station."

"See what's out there, open or not."

"I'm on it, Sheriff." Tess was searching the internet.

Sheriff Roy walked over to a large aerial photograph of Allen County that was pinned to the wall. He was studying the most rural areas, of which there were many. His thoughts were interrupted by her shout.

"They don't know! It just hit me! They don't know!"

"Know what, Deputy Tess?"

"What kind of vehicle is Lucas looking for?"

Lucas looked up. "Gray wheelchair van?" he ventured.

"That's it! They don't know that Patty can walk!"

"Do we know that?" the Sheriff asked.

"Patty told me she could walk."

"And now you've decided to share that possibly critical information with us. How considerate."

"You haven't gotten it yet. Her abductors don't have any idea that she could simply walk away from them. They might leave her unattended."

"Oh. That might not be good news," Sheriff Roy stated. "They aren't going to take her any place that she could escape like that. Not these people."

"So she might try it and get caught?"

"Something like that," he replied vaguely. "On the other hand, this news could make it easier to rescue her."

"Is that what we're attempting?"

"It could come to that, Lucas."

CHAPTER 34

South of Wellston, Vermont
Wednesday, April 13, 2017, 6:01 PM EDT

It had been a long day. When she awakened to learn she had been abducted, a rag had been stuffed into her mouth to keep her quiet. Then she had received a lecture from the man in the suit, warning her to cooperate or be punished. She believed him.

Just a few miles after that, they had pulled into a decrepit Irving gas station. Any thought of trying to get help vanished as the proprietor handed her captors the keys and drove off. The driver of the van pulled two large standing signs from the back. They both said "NO GAS - CLOSED." These he positioned in front of the pumps. Then the van, with her wheelchair still secured by straps, went around back. As she watched, the two men not wearing suits began to wash it. She didn't understand why until she noticed the men were getting flecks of a gray substance on their clothes.

They were washing off the gray. The van was really another color. She looked at the side mirrors. Blue.

Then the suited man reappeared. Only now he was wearing a polo shirt with khaki shorts and walking shoes. This was more in keeping with the khaki shorts and white polo shirt the aides has dressed Patty in, under explicit instructions from her abductor. He changed the license plates to a set from Massachusetts and applied tourist decals to the side windows. The two others tied luggage to the top rack. The transformation of the van was completed by a Red Sox bumper sticker.

The darkened windows remained.

Then they had wheeled Patty into the most disgusting bathroom she had ever seen and told her to "do her business" while they waited outside. One of them tied a rope around the inside door handle, so it wouldn't close all the way. This prevented her from locking them out. She could hear them talking.

"Too bad she's a cripple."

"Why's that?"

"Could have had some fun."

"Not on the agenda. Don't even think about it."

"About what?"

"That's more like it."

"Hey princess! Hurry it up!"

A half hour later, they'd continued their journey — confident that no one would be looking for them this close to their starting point. But they headed north. Patty quietly wept when they passed Wellston Care on their way. Just before the Canadian border, the van turned east towards New Hampshire.

That was when they'd given her something to drink. It had knocked her out.

So Patty wasn't aware when the van finally left the road. It passed slowly between two ruined fieldstone columns and into the woods.

CHAPTER 35

Cobbler's Knob, Vermont

Wednesday, April 13, 2017, 6:38 PM EDT

Sheriff Roy turned from the aerial photograph. He went to his desk and replaced the magnifying glass he'd been using. Then he opened the drawer that contained the files he had confiscated from Tess. He quickly located the slim file on Camp Bethany. He was looking for something in particular.

"Aha!"

The deputies gave him their attention.

"I had a feeling."

"Is that like when Gibbs has a hunch in his gut on NCIS?" Deputy Lucas wondered aloud.

"Tell us about it, Sheriff," Tess said, casting a disdainful glance at Lucas.

"I suspected that the DoD, or whoever, would have a place on site."

"At Necklan's Lake?"

"Yes indeed." He turned back toward the wall with the aerial photograph. "According to this photograph from 2014, there are still a few cabins standing at Camp Bethany. And I'll bet you the DoD is using them."

"You think they'd take Patty there?"

"I would if I were them."

Lucas pointed out that "Those cabins could be ruins inside, and the photo wouldn't show it."

"True. But then why would the chimney be smoking in the photograph?"

"Show me. Please." Tess was on her way.

The Sheriff plucked the magnifying glass from its holder and followed her. Lucas began to amble that direction, frowning. It took a couple of minutes, but soon they had identified the cabin and verified the smoke.

"I don't know what to say!" Tess exclaimed.

"Holy smoke?" Lucas suggested.

After a moment's consideration, they decided to laugh, rather than to pummel him. It had been close, though. Tension is peculiar that way.

"What now, Sheriff?"

"Yeah. Do we mount up?" Deputy Lucas was ready.

"A plan would be...." Sheriff Roy stopped in mid-sentence, a gleam in his eye. "Mount up? You may just have something there, Deputy Lucas."

"Well, I .... Really?" He hadn't caught up with the Sheriff yet.

"Do you ride, Tess?"

"I prefer wheels to hooves, but that's just because the maintenance is simpler. What do you have in mind?"

"See this trail going from the cabins to the adjoining parcel of land?"

He pointed to a thin dotted line. They nodded.

"We could use this trail to infiltrate the camp on horseback. We'd have to walk the last part, of course. Beats trying to drive right through the main gate without being detected."

"What about the owner of the adjacent land?"

"Not sure anyone lives there anymore. But we'll deal with it when we get there. Who's going to stop the sheriff and his deputies?"

There was the briefest of moments when thoughts of men wearing dark unmarked uniforms, wielding machine guns, infiltrated their minds. Then diplomacy carried the day.

"Nobody!" Tess shouted defiantly.

"That's the spirit!" Sheriff Roy chimed in. Then he looked at his other deputy. "Lucas, can you round us up some decent riding horses?"

"Now?"

"Of course not." The Sheriff replied. Tess noted that it was a textbook scoff. "Half an hour would be about right, though. And a truck to get them out there."

"See what I can do, Sheriff."

"Why does it have to be tonight?" Tess asked.

"They'll question her tonight. After that they'll have no further use for her. She'll have become a liability. I'm just hoping they don't like to dig by flashlight."

"Oh."

"Too much information?"

"The price of clarity, I guess."

CHAPTER 36

Necklan's Lake, Vermont

Wednesday, April 13, 2017, 9:33 PM EDT

"Wake up, princess. Come on. Wake up." the sounds emerged, unwanted, from a long hollow tube. There was a kind of echo. Her mind resisted them, tried to shut them off. But the sounds were relentless. They came closer. "Time to get up, sleeping beauty." Must be a mistake. She was Patty Martin, not Sleeping Beauty. She recognized the voice as male, a man. There were others too. Laughing. She resisted as long as she could.

Which was the moment she was slapped hard on the face.

Her eyes opened immediately, not really focusing. What was going on? Where was she? Who were these men? Why couldn't she think straight?

She screamed when the cold water hit her in the face. The men laughed. They were laughing at her. She got that, but had no idea why. The cold water ran down into her clothes, chilling her. Hands began to pull her from the chair. It was a wheelchair. At least *that* seemed familiar. Her knees buckled under her, as they dragged her from the chair. Then she was out the door and lying on the ground by a stone step. Cold. Wet. Freezing.

"That should bring her around."

The door shut. She could still hear voices, but couldn't make out any conversation. Just random voices in the dark night.

A little while later, a man came out and relieved himself. He stood right next to her, like she wasn't even there. She wondered if she really was.

Her brain shut down again, but she still shivered.

Patty was awakened by the sound of a truck approaching. It parked near the cabin. A man got out and walked toward the cabin. He nearly stumbled over her legs, kicking them. He was greeted inside by the others.

"You take care of it?"

"No loose ends. Fell down the stairs. Broken neck. Tragedy."

"That's exactly why I live in a single-story house," someone declared.

"You can never be too careful," another agreed. "Most accidents happen in the home." They were beginning to snicker.

It all made no sense to Patty.

As her mind cleared, she had this growing sense that matters could get worse for her. Probably before midnight.

A bear! Did she hear a bear?

She was thinking well enough to realize she shouldn't be out in the open in the woods at night. She looked around and saw that the cabin was set upon several large stone blocks. She crawled under it, then lay still. That would keep her safe from bears and moose. Not from wolves, coyotes or bobcats. Not if they found her. If she screamed, the men might take her inside. She didn't think that would necessarily improve her situation, though. The men were the predators she should fear. They were already here.

Patty willed herself to escape. Since she didn't know where they had taken her, all she could do was to run away from the cabin. And she hadn't run in years!

But she had walked. Just not where she could be seen. And she had been swimming laps in the pool, and done exercises in the privacy of her room at Wellston. She was still young and fit. She could do it. She could probably make good time on the road or a trail, but....

A revelation came to her. The men didn't know she could even walk! They would expect her to be crawling down the road. She had to take a difficult route. They wouldn't expect that. And the good news, such as it was, was that there were plenty of them to choose from.

Patty slid out from behind the cabin and sneaked in a crouch into the woods. Heading straight for the three-quarter Moon to avoid going in a circle. She was pleased to have thought of that. The drug-induced fog was lifting.

She opted for distance rather than stealth. It is difficult to track a person at night. She'd seen no dogs. They would have to track her without one. Better to break a few twigs than lose a few steps.

As adrenalin replaced narcotic, Patty raced toward

the Moon.

Something wasn't right though. There were flashes of light in her peripheral vision. She stopped and looked around. It took a minute to realize what she was seeing.

It was her. More accurately, her white polo shirt which had been bleached to the point of incandescence by the Wellston laundry. If she could see it without trying, so could her pursuers. She assumed they would be pursuing. It was the only safe way to approach the situation. After deciding it would take too long to darken her shirt by rubbing dirt all over it, she doffed it and hid it at the base of some bushes.

Patty began to run again, thankful she'd worn a tan brassiere today. She doubted that she would have been as cavalier about discarding her undergarments.

CHAPTER 37

Necklan's Lake, Vermont

Wednesday, April 13, 2017, 10:46 PM EDT

As the Moon slowly rose overhead, it became increasingly difficult to determine a direction from it. Patty scanned the skies through the branches to find a more reliable beacon. She was thus engaged when she pushed aside some growth, and stepped into air.

She dared not scream. But the involuntary sound she made upon landing would travel in the still night. "Damn it!" But the noise quickly gave way to another concern. Her back hurt. Not just from the fall into this — pit?

From what she could see, it seemed to be a pit, man-made, different from the geography around it. Large and unnaturally flat. No trees or even large shrubs.

"Probably used a bulldozer," she imagined. "But what is it doing here in the middle of the woods?"

Her arms felt for her injury. It was a wound. There was blood. It must have been a puncture wound. Made by a sharp object on the ground, like a rock. She turned over gingerly, favoring her back. Running her hand over the soil, she encountered the object protruding from the earth. She could tell by the blood that covered the object. It was smooth, but it didn't feel like a rock. The shape was wrong. More like a piece of kindling wood, one that had lost the bark. That had to be it.

She tugged on it, not really expecting to free it. But it came loose. Somewhere between the ground and her face, the moonlight shone upon it. She recognized it. Bone!

The ancient core of Patty's brain kicked in. She dropped it immediately — without thinking. It landed in front of her. She stared at it. She couldn't have accurately identified it if she had been in a medical laboratory. But she *knew* beyond any doubt that it was a human bone.

And they were seldom alone. Had she stumbled into an old family cemetery?

In the dappled light, she surveyed the pit. To her relief, she realized that she could climb out in several places. She calculated it to be about fifteen feet wide by twenty feet long. At the long end it appeared that mounds of earth had been pushed into place to provide a fourth wall. That would be where the bulldozer had entered. Patty realized she was doing this exercise to avoid thinking about the bone, the bones.

She forced herself to rise, to climb out of that horrible pit. And run.

CHAPTER 38

Necklan's Lake, Vermont

Wednesday, April 13, 2017, 10:53 PM EDT

Sheriff Roy led the way, Tess in the middle and Lucas in the rear. The horses were docile, seemingly a bit curious to be ridden in the woods late at night. The trail was barely illuminated by the scant moonlight that made it through the branches, but progress was steady. Tess was having trouble keeping her motorcycle boots in the stirrups.

They were all business. Tess had reminded the Sheriff that she had aced her marksmanship courses. After taking apart and reassembling a Glock 9 mm in less than two minutes, Sheriff Roy had issued the weapon to her. They were probably still outgunned.

The Sheriff pointed as they rode through a gap in an old wire fence. They had entered the Camp Bethany property. Less than a mile to the cabin.

No one spoke. Even the horses had become stealthy. It was contagious.

A muted cry came from their left.

"What was that?" Tess asked.

"Could be an owl," Lucas speculated. Clearly, he wasn't sure.

"Dismount. Quietly as you can." Sheriff Roy was already walking. "Tess, you stay with the horses while we investigate."

She wasn't having it. "If it's Patty, I'm her only friend, the only person she's spoken to since that night. You need me there, Sheriff."

He studied her for a moment. "Probably couldn't stop you anyway. I'm not allowed to shoot the interns. Stupid rule."

Tess smiled. "I'll take it. Thanks, Sheriff."

"Take care of the horses, Lucas."

"Right, Sheriff," he responded, then added "Do we have a signal in case something happens?"

"No, Deputy. We have cell phones set to vibrate."

"Reception's kind of spotty out here...."

Sheriff Roy sighed. But the deputy had a point. "Can you do a coyote call?"

"I can convince even the most skeptical coyote," he offered with a grin.

"That's a comfort." He turned to Tess. "I'll lead the way. Watch for branches whipping back at you."

"I'll stay back a yard or so."

"Then let's go."

"Should I be prepared to shoot?"

"Always wondered what it would be like to be shot in the back at close range," he mumbled.

Tess took that as a negative.

With no trail, the progress was slow. The Sheriff took care to maintain a course toward the source of the sound. Difficult because the sound had stopped. He used his knife to cut simple blaze marks into the bark of the larger trees as they passed. He'd obviously done this before. Tess took note. It would never have occurred to her.

He was on the lookout for Patty, but he was also prepared to find someone else, someone hostile.

They found neither. They found the edge of the pit.

"You stay up here and keep looking," he whispered. Sheriff Roy scrambled down into it. He put his flashlight close to the ground and began to move the dirt around with his ballpoint pen. Several minutes later, he unearthed the first bone. The second and third followed quickly. All of them clean. The expression "picked clean" came to mind. He placed the flashlight against the bone, at an angle. There were regular grooves. "Teeth marks?" he asked himself. He pocketed the bone.

Then he rose and strode several paces, where he repeated the process. He thought he'd prepared himself for it, but the human skull he uncovered shook him nonetheless.

He rocked back on his haunches and landed on his behind, dropping the light.

"You O.K., Sheriff?"

"Been better," he grumbled, as he made his way out of the pit. "Seen or heard anything?"

"Nothing."

"Let's head back then."

"What did you find?"

"Trouble," he answered in a tone that suggested the

end of that conversation.

CHAPTER 39

Necklan's Lake, Vermont

Wednesday, April 13, 2017, 11:14 PM EDT

A trail! Patty found a trail to follow. It looked unused, but it was wide enough to have been a horse trail. And it seemed to lead to the cabin; so she ran down the trail in the opposite direction as fast as she could.

Until she saw horses. Tied to a tree. Before she could change course, she heard "Well, look who's here."

Her heart stopped. She'd run right into the hands of her pursuers. Patty dropped to her knees, her dream of escape crushed. Hope gone.

A man approached her from behind. She made no effort to turn around. She was ready to die if that's what was in store for her. She thought she was prepared for anything. But she was wrong.

Her heart nearly stopped when the man howled —
like a coyote.

"Patricia Martin, you are a *sight* for sore eyes," the
man exclaimed. Not what she'd expected. Not at all. And
his voice, that smooth baritone....

Lucas swooped down and lifted her into his arms.
He felt the blood. "Are you injured?"

"Yes." Then she kissed him on the cheek and
passed out.

He was still holding her, wondering what to do
next, when Sheriff Roy whispered from nearby. "Need
help?"

Deputy Lucas swung around to the face the
speaker, wondering if he should drop Patty and pull his
Glock .45. By mid-swing, he'd recognized Sheriff Roy's
voice.

"She needs medical attention."

But the Sheriff was cautious. He'd sent Tess
around the other side of the trail. "They're alone, Sheriff."

"Stay concealed," he instructed her. Then he
stepped onto the trail with his Colt .45 Close Quarters
Battle Pistol drawn. "Put her down and mount your horse.

Now!"

Deputy Lucas was confused. "But...." He lowered Patty to the ground.

"Draw your weapon and ride down the trail the way we came in. Stop after the trail has turned enough that you can't see us, and wait. Just do it!"

Deputy Lucas started back down the trail as instructed.

"Tess! Come on out and give me a hand with Patty."

They quickly confirmed that she was bleeding from a wound to her lower back. They had to get her help. But first things first.

With Tess pulling from horseback and the Sheriff lifting from the ground, together they managed to get Patty in the saddle, just forward of Tess. Sheriff Roy was winded by the effort. "Remind me not to be so quick to send off Deputy Lucas in the future."

Holding onto Patty rendered Tess defenseless. But Sheriff Roy brought up the rear, ready to exchange fire the moment it became necessary. He silently chided himself for not bringing a second magazine for the pistol. Each one held only seven rounds. He wasn't prepared for a serious firefight. He hoped Lucas' coyote call hadn't alerted the men in the cabin. Probably not. It actually had sounded like a coyote. The Sheriff made a mental note to stop underestimating his deputy.

And the more he thought about it, the more he figured a Department of Defense team would probably take him out before he could empty the first magazine anyway. Not that it made him feel any better.

As they caught up with Lucas, the Sheriff motioned for him to take the lead. "See if you can get the emergency squad to meet us at the trail head." He couldn't be bothered to remember that they were called EMTs now. Emergency Medical Transport? Team?

"On it, Sheriff." He pulled out his cell phone.

Her mind in a fog, Patty awoke briefly. There was something familiar about the man they called Lucas. She turned to face him, but found that she was in the embrace of Tess instead. She thought this curious, and even a bit funny.

Patty smiled tentatively at Tess. Then she patted the horse's neck before losing consciousness again.

CHAPTER 40

Necklan's Lake, Vermont
Thursday, April 14, 2017, 12:38 AM EDT

"She's crawled off somewhere!" Thus were the inhabitants of the cabin informed of Patty's escape by one who had stepped outside to relieve his bladder. "Drop everything and help me look for her."

"Afraid she can crawl faster than you can run, Captain?"

The man he'd called Captain pulled his gun. "Only reason you're here is to help me."

A major attitude shift occurred. "Can't argue with that. What's it like out?"

"Not raining, but soggy and cold. Good moonlight. Bring your flashlights anyway."

The men donned their coats and stepped outside.

They began to search under and around the cabin. Two ventured up the road a bit, only to return. "No sign of her."

"When's the last time anyone saw her?" Captain asked.

"Has to be almost an hour ago," one of them ventured. "She was unconscious or asleep right here by the step."

"Check your vehicles to make sure she's not hiding in or around them. She'd be a fool to take the road, but we don't know that she isn't; so two of you take the road — one in each direction. Call out if you find anything."

"I think the road away from the camp entrance peters out after a while...."

"Then peter out with it! And keep going in that direction. Remember, she won't stay on the road once she sees or hears you coming."

Two men began to jog down the road in opposite directions, flashlights scanning the sides of the road. The vehicle searches had been completed.

"Any trails leading away from here?"

"One goes to the other cabin over there. The one

with no roof."

"Two of you, check it out. Cabin could be a good place to hide; so be thorough. After that, fan out from that cabin. She might have headed there first, then decided to keep going."

There were three of them left. "Each of you start at one side of this cabin and work your way out. I'll take the back of the cabin. She's wearing a white shirt. It should be easy to spot in the moonlight."

And it was, even though she had attempted to hide it. One of them found it within fifteen minutes. "Over here!"

He was searching the area when the rest began to assemble around him. "What?" Captain barked.

"Found her shirt. Intact. She must have taken it off. Maybe realized it would be easy to spot."

"What are you looking for now?"

"The kind of recent disturbance of the ground and foliage that you'd see if someone was dragging her legs behind her."

"Uh oh." Others began to examine the earth as well.

"I'm no tracker, but I think this is a footprint. A small one. Could be her."

Captain was stymied. "The rehab center told us she couldn't walk." He shook his head to clear it. "She was in a damn wheelchair!" he said with a volume that had nothing to do with stealth. "Did any of you see her walk?"

"No, Captain. She made no attempt to move her legs when we took her from the wheelchair."

Captain struggled to regain control. "Then she suckered us in, gentlemen. Outsmarted government agents. An amateur! Do you have any idea how bad this is going to look on our records?"

"We'll find her, Captain. We're still faster and stronger than she is."

"O.K., then. Let's assume she is still moving away from the cabin. Spread out and all move in her presumed direction. On the double, but be sharp!"

Off they went at a trot, in the direction of the pit.

By the time they'd reached the pit, Patty Martin was miles away.

CHAPTER 41

Cobblers' Knob, Vermont

Thursday, April 14, 2017, 1:21 AM EDT

"Ah, Sheriff. This is a veterinary clinic," Tess pointed out.

"Won't be looking for her here. Help me get her inside. Doc's already here."

When they opened the back door, Deputy Lucas just scooped Patty up like she was a pillow, and headed for the front door. So the Sheriff closed up the car instead, after retrieving something. Tess went to open the door to the clinic, but it opened from the inside to reveal Dr. McAdams, dressed in what appeared to be a jogging outfit. "This way," he indicated to Lucas.

"She's lost some blood," Tess advised.

"I've brought several pouches. Let's get an IV

started."

Lucas set Patty down on an operating table. "There's the wound."

Doc McAdams took a moment to study it, then resumed setting up the IV line. "Has she been awake? Talking?"

"Not for the last half hour."

"Skin's like ice!" he exclaimed.

"She was like that when we found her. Tried to warm her up in the car on the way," Sheriff Roy explained.

"Hypothermia again. Not as bad as last time. Seems to be in shock too."

"Wouldn't be surprised," the Sheriff said. "She's been through a lot today."

"Is she on the run?" the doctor inquired casually, as he completed the assembly of the apparatus to transfuse Patty. "Do I want to know?"

"Let's just say her photo isn't in the post office."

"Fine by me then. Let's see if we can turn her over without disengaging the IV." Within a minute, Patty was face down on the table and Doc McAdams was examining her back. "Good thing puncture wounds don't bleed too much." He picked up a syringe and administered a local anesthetic in several places around the cut. "Any idea what caused this?"

Sheriff Roy produced a plastic evidence bag containing the bloody bone.

The doctor examined it closely. "Appears to be human...."

"That's what we thought," Sheriff Roy admitted.

"And not recent. Exposed to the elements. Can't imagine where this could have happened. Cemetery?"

"Any idea just how old that bone is?" Sheriff Roy inquired as offhandedly as he could manage.

"Not now. But after I tend to my patient, I'll take another look." Doc McAdams began to gently cut away the skin that had been pushed into the wound. "Just missed her kidney. Lucky, that." Then he washed and disinfected it. Twelve minutes later, he was suturing it closed. He bandaged it and wrapped gauze around her waist. "This should prevent her from moving in such a way as to open the wound," he explained. "Now will you tell me what's going on?"

The Sheriff pondered this for a moment before responding. "Tell us about the bone first. It might help with the explanation."

Doc McAdams gave him a skeptical look, but picked up the evidence bag. "Is this actually evidence?"

"I'm pretty sure it is. Can you keep it in the bag for now?"

"Won't be able to tell as much that way, but I'll try."

"What bone is it?"

"It appears to be the ulna of female, fully grown or nearly so."

"Teenager?"

"That would fit," he agreed. "Any idea who it belonged to?"

"Not really, but we're investigating. How long has it been?"

"Since she died?"

"Yes. Since she died."

"If exposed the whole time, it would be several years. A proper forensic exam would narrow that down."

"What about DNA?"

"Possible, although a bone with more marrow would be more promising on that score." The doctor looked up. "Are there other bones?"

"This is all we brought, but we intend to look for more at the site. We just needed to help Patty first."

"Sounds like a crime scene. Has it been secured?"

"It's open and remote. I'm still trying to figure out how to secure it," the Sheriff explained. "We'll need daylight." *Not to mention a small army,* he added silently to himself.

"Well, you'll want to get this bone to the state lab, along with any others you dig up. It's going to take some serious testing to reveal anything."

Patty stirred, but didn't awaken.

"She's ready to go. I don't want to know where you're taking her, but I should check on her within 48 hours." Doc McAdams began to wash up. "Preferably not in the middle of the night."

"No argument there," Sheriff Roy said.

"But call me right away if the wound opens or bleeds."

"We'll take good care of her, doctor. I'm Deputy

Tess, by the way. Good to meet you." She offered her hand, which he shook.

"Likewise, Deputy." To the Sheriff he asked "Is she old enough to be a deputy?"

"She's a student at Dartmouth, majoring in Forensic Science," the Sheriff replied.

"What you do is a science now?"

Sheriff Roy considered the question. "Not the way I do it," he admitted cheerfully.

Lucas carried Patty to the car, while the others chuckled at the Sheriff's answer.

"Keep her warm!" Doc McAdams called out.

CHAPTER 42

Necklan's Lake, Vermont
Thursday, April 14, 2017, 1:23 AM EDT

"Help!" The searchers had arrived at the burial pit. "Could use a little help over here!"

Captain arrived at the edge and put the beam of his flashlight on the agent lying on his back in the dirt. Others gathered round, then some descended to assist.

"Those of you who aren't helping him scour this area for signs she was here." barked Captain. "How is he?"

"Ankle's twisted bad. He's done for the night."

"Take him back to the cabin. Will that take more than one of you?"

"It'll take two of us to get him out of this hole. If we cut over to the road, I should be able to take him in from there. The other man can come back."

"Do it!" He turned to the others. "Any sign of her?"

"Someone's been here recently, maybe tonight. But I'm seeing a large man's footprints. There's some blood on the ground. He might have been looking at it. I'm no expert, but it looks like she was here and he was too. His prints seem to cover hers in places; so he might have come by later."

"She couldn't have arranged to meet someone. She's been out of contact, and she didn't even know where she was." Captain was as confused as he was unhappy. "Anything else?" He'd thought the question had been rhetorical. He'd been wrong.

"Up here, Captain," called a man from the far edge of the pit. "There are some boot prints. Child or woman. Not the type of shoes the girl was wearing."

"Fresh?"

"Could be from earlier this evening."

Who'd have thought these woods would be so busy tonight?

"Let's try to follow them. All of them."

"Captain, I found something that looks like a bone...."

"Don't touch it!"

"What *is* this place, Captain?"

"Knowing that won't help us find her. Move out now."

"Captain! There are blazes on the trees. Definitely recent. Found them following the footprints."

"Which footprints?"

"The man's shoes and the boots."

"As long as the prints and blazes don't divert, follow the blazes. It'll be faster. What about the girl?"

"Looks like only she and the man came into the hole. She didn't exit where the man did. Probably, they weren't here at the same time."

"You two keep following her trail as best you can then."

Captain scrambled up the side of the pit, then turned for one last look at it. After all this time, he'd almost managed to put it out of his mind. Now it was back. A reminder of the impossibility of accounting for all potential variables in an experiment. Especially when the experiment was being conducted in the north woods at night. But the review committee had concluded that the experiment had not contributed in any way to the incredible carnage. What haunted Captain was the fact that his team had been unable to prevent it. If they had moved when they first heard the music. Had they not been stunned by the arrival of the students. Had they not tried to cover up the experiment before assisting the students.... That had been his decision. It had been more of a reaction than a decision. That was why Captain couldn't sleep.

And now they'd lost the girl — the only survivor of the slaughter. It looked like someone else might have found her. But who? Who else was tromping around these woods in the middle of the night? Hunters? What did people hunt in the middle of the night? Bats?

The team following the trail blazes was moving quickly. The men following the girl were on a parallel track, moving slowly. So the blaze followers reached the trail first. "We found a trail, Captain! Think it's the same one that becomes the road that goes to the cabin."

"Anything else?"

"Fresh horse droppings, sir!"

"How many?" Then he realized they might be

counting the droppings. "How many horses?"

"At least two, for sure. Maybe three."

"Where'd they go?"

"Away from the cabin. Came from that way too."

By then Captain had arrived at the trail. Coming from the direction of the cabin were more men who had been tracking Patty.

"She came this way," one of them announced. "She met someone over here. A man's boot print. Don't see any more of her footprints. No horseshoe prints here either. He might have carried her over to the horses."

"So we have at least three other persons and at least two horses, probably three."

"And she went with them."

"We'll never catch them. Not on foot."

"Don't think we can get a car through here, Captain."

He surveyed the trail. He had to do something, even if it was futile. "You two go on up this trail. See where it leads. If you find a highway, find the route number; so we can pick you up. Then report by phone."

He watched the two men wander down the trail.

"Anybody find anything here besides footprints and horse apples?"

Nobody had.

"Back to the cabin then." Captain led the way back down the trail, still talking. "If she's injured, she may be in a hospital or a clinic. Not much in the way of medical facilities in this neck of the woods. Let's find her!"

CHAPTER 43

Cobblers' Knob, Vermont
Thursday, April 14, 2017, 2:40 AM EDT

When they had settled in the car, Sheriff Roy called Lucy Thornton on his cell phone. The Bluetooth was activated; so the others could hear. That wasn't what the Sheriff had planned. It was another trap set by modern technology.

"Good morning, Lucy." That was his opener.

"It's not morning! It's the middle of the night! You lose your watch — or your brains?"

The Sheriff had expected no less. The deputies' eyes grew wide and they stifled laughter. Yet Sheriff Roy had convinced himself that he held a rare conversational advantage over her this time because he was wide awake. He quickly moved to press that advantage. The secret would be to stay ahead of her. He hoped he could.

"Fear not, fair damsel! I beseech thee at this accursed hour to pursue only the noblest of purposes!"

"You old coot! How many times have I told you not to switch to whiskey after drinking beer?"

Tess snorted involuntarily. Lucas bit his finger in a vain attempt not to. But the Sheriff rose to the challenge.

"Ignoratio elenchi!" he shouted. "False cause. A logical fallacy, m'lady. I am among the soberest of mankind at this wretched hour. And verily upon a quest so noble as to make Sir Lancelot envious of my endeavors."

There was silence.

"M'lady, I beseech thee to hear me out."

"O.K., Roy. Let's hear it."

But the Sheriff was too deep into his role to abandon it now. "A most grievous wrong hath been perpetrated upon one of our fair citizens...."

"Is Tess available?"

"Hi, Lucy! It's me. We're all in the car together," Tess advised.

"That's a relief. I thought I'd awakened in the wrong century."

Sheriff Roy beamed with pride. Even in the darkened automobile interior, one could see it. It kind of glowed.

"Do you have an electric blanket?"

"Did I hear you right? Are you planning an orgy?"

"No. That's next week," the Sheriff interrupted.

"What would you be doing there? Keeping order?"

"Electronic orgies?" Lucas mumbled.

Tess intervened. "It's a long story, but Patty Martin is with us. She's suffering from hypothermia. So, do you have an electric blanket?"

"Oh! Yes. My cousin who moved to Orlando sends me one every Christmas. Bitch that she is. I've got dozens!"

"Have you got a spare bedroom?"

"That too. Bring her right over."

"Can you make coffee?" Sheriff Roy asked.

"For you, I'll throw in a doughnut. Call it the law enforcement special." Lucy was fully awake now. "Just give me five minutes to get dressed."

"What's the fun in that?" the Sheriff inquired.

"Randy old coot!" Lucy hung up.

After a minute, Tess commented. "You two are meant for each other, you know."

Sheriff Roy already knew this. "Neither of us is sure our relationship could survive marriage. Might ruin everything."

"Might make it better...."

"Not sure that's possible, young Tess. Life does not always fit into the neat parameters dictated by conventional lifestyles."

"Who are you? And what have you done with Sheriff Roy?"

"I have me moments, Tess."

"It's best to stop talking to him when he's like this," Deputy Lucas advised.

"The young swain is quite correct, of course," added the Sheriff.

Tess could think of nothing to say. That was a comfort. A perplexing comfort, but a comfort nonetheless.

It was 3:16 AM when they arrived at Lucy's house. True to her word, she had hot coffee and warm doughnuts set out for them on the antique harvest table in the dining room. Even Patty ate some of the doughnuts. And Lucy had fixed her a cup of hot chocolate, as well. She had a second.

How could Sheriff Roy not be in love with Lucy? Tess was completely enamored of her, in a platonic way, of course. She would have been a terrific aunt or something. So wise, and so irreverent and open.

Lucy, having had at least a few hours sleep, took Patty away from the tables and put her to bed, while the others pretended to be awake, aspired to being alert.

"She's asleep already. I took her temperature. It's 96.2° already. She's going to be fine. So, why don't you finish your doughnuts and go home? I'll call you, Sheriff, if there's any problem. I'll nap by her side until daylight. Just in case. O.K.?"

"Ah! To sleep. Perchance to dream. Aye, there's the rub," Sheriff Roy philosophized with exaggerated movements of his limbs, as if performing to a rapt audience.

"That it is. Even worse, I'm out of doughnuts. So, vamoose!"

Tess rose first. "Thank you, Lucy."

"Yes, Ms. Thornton, thank you for your hospitality in the middle of the night," Deputy Lucas added.

"Couldn't have said it better myself — give or take a 'forsooth' mind you."

Lucy turned to the deputies. "Believe it or not, the Sheriff played Hamlet in the Senior class play. Quite well, all considered. Never quite recovered, it appears."

The Lucy kissed Sheriff Roy on the forehead and said "Forsooth yourself, yon varlet!"

That was their cue to leave.

CHAPTER 44

Necklan's Lake, Vermont
Thursday, April 14, 2017, 3:02 AM EDT

The search team was back at the cabin. "Before we begin the next phase of this search," Captain began, "you should know why this girl is so important. Several years ago, we attempted an experiment right here at Necklan's Lake. I can't reveal the classified portions, but I can say that just as it was beginning, a group of teenagers, most of whom appeared to be intoxicated, arrived in cars to party by the lake. This activity included drinking, blasting a radio and swimming in the lake without benefit of bathing attire."

"Skinny-dipping," someone said.

"I know what it's called."

"Yes, sir."

"Unknowingly, these kids had placed themselves in harm's way. The experiment was already underway. It was too late to stop it. Our team was more than a half mile away from the teenagers, although we quickly became aware of their presence. The result was that every teenager but one died that night. Before we could reach them or do anything for them. That one survivor was Patty Martin, the girl who has escaped tonight. She was highly traumatized and unable to speak. We have monitored her recovery since that night. We just found out that she has regained her ability to speak. We don't know what, if anything, she remembers about that night. But she may have top secret information. That is what we brought her here to determine once the tranquilizers wore off." He paused. "Gentlemen, we need to find that girl!"

"Officially?"

"No. No I.D. No hint of who we are. If anyone makes you as being from the government, deny it and casually leave. Use misdirection. Pretend you're looking for more than one person. A couple that is overdue somewhere. You think they might have been in an accident. Teams of two. Hit the local clinics and hospitals that are open. Can't be that many."

"What about law enforcement?"

"No. Not now. Only if we strike out with the medical angle. And only when I make that call. Not before."

Someone said "Understood."

"Each team will have a list of the facilities you are to check. So get going. Report in when each time you finish at a facility."

"What if we find her?"

"Assess the situation. How can we get her back? Call me right away."

Thus the search for Patty Martin continued.

Captain and a man called Sparks remained. It was a nickname from his time as a Navy radioman. He was still the communications specialist. He turned to Captain and asked "Why were the kids there?"

Captain went to the coffee brewer and poured himself a cup before answering, gathering his thoughts. "We found out later that it was prom night. There was this stupid tradition of going down to Necklan's Lake after the Senior Prom to party." But he wasn't done. "Part of that tradition included getting sufficiently fortified with alcohol to jump into the icy waters of the lake."

"Brrr!"

"I second that reaction. Probably close to freezing this time of year. Stupid kids!"

"Not sure that would stop them from skinny-dipping. Not teenagers. Especially drunk ones."

"Yeah. I can see the macho guys going right in, then taunting the others until they all went in."

"Why'd the girls go in?"

"Damned if I know."

Sparks became thoughtful, then inquired "Won't happen again, will it?"

"Not if I can help it. We know what night the Senior Prom is being held. We're barricading the entrance to Camp Bethany and posting guards just out of sight, in case someone tries to get through."

"That ought to do it."

"And the experiment is scheduled for a full week *before* the prom," Captain added, looking pleased with the preparations.

"You've thought this out." Sparks purposely

avoided jinxing the preparations by saying anything more, like they'd covered all the bases. That would have been like saying *What could go wrong?*

CHAPTER 45

Cobblers' Knob, Vermont

Thursday, April 14, 2017, 8:58 AM EDT

Tess was surprised to see that Sheriff Roy was already at the office. He was standing in front of her espresso machine with his hands in his pockets. Just staring at it.

"I'll make the coffee," she volunteered cheerfully.

"Make it strong." He plopped back into his chair with a sigh. "You're just too darn chipper for being up half the night."

"Didn't sleep well?"

"Didn't sleep much. Hardly at all," he replied. "Trying to make sense of all this."

"The big picture?"

"Exactly. How does now fit with then?"

"Why don't you start by telling me what that pit in the woods is about?" she asked. The espresso machine was making encouraging sounds. Maybe life would be restored.

"I've been considering that for much of the morning, Deputy Tess. We need to confirm my theory by visiting in daylight, but I don't want to stumble onto the feds and whatever they're up to."

"No argument there. I can wait till they're gone." She brought him a mug of coffee. The writing on the mug said LIVE FREE OR DIE!

"I put two sugars in it. You need the energy."

"Don't forget yourself"

"I'm putting three in mine. Got to keep ahead of you somehow."

"That shouldn't be too difficult this morning." The Sheriff inhaled the steam rising from his mug. "Say, I think this might work!"

"Try drinking it." Tess fussed with her own mug. "And you haven't told me about the pit yet."

He became somber. The Sheriff began slowly, as if the words he uttered were incredibly heavy on his tongue.

"I believe that pit was hastily dug using earth-moving equipment. Its purpose was to bury the remains of the Seniors who died that night. To conceal them."

She did not notice that she had dropped her mug until it crashed into the floor.

"That's why you have to supply your own crockery," Deputy Lucas informed her as he closed the door behind him. Then he stopped cold. Despite the stream of coffee running across the hardwood floor, Tess wasn't reacting. Something was wrong. Really wrong.

He moved to her, putting his hands on her upper arms, steadying her. "You O.K.?"

Her response was to slowly sit down on the edge of the nearest desk. "I'll be fine. Just not sure when."

Lucas moved away slowly, to make sure she did not need his support. Then he went to the espresso machine and took the roll of paper towels from beside it. Without a word, he began to mop up the coffee and collect the pieces of the broken mug. Only when the floor was dry and the pieces had been deposited in the trash did he attempt conversation.

"Ah, Sheriff...."

"Thank you, Lucas," Tess said softly.

Sheriff Roy put his eyes upon Lucas. "I was just telling her that I thought that the pit we found was dug to bury to Seniors."

"The Seniors?"

"From the prom."

"Oh." Lucas walked slowly toward the espresso machine, trying to figure it out. Finally he turned and asked. "What pit?"

"Last night, before you found Patty Martin, Tess and I discovered a manmade pit in the woods. It had human bones in it."

"The bone you showed Doc McAdams?" Lucas asked.

"Yes." Sheriff Roy paused, then announced "I found a skull too. Left it in place."

Tess recovered. "You didn't tell me that!"

Sheriff Roy put his forehead in his hand. "You didn't need to know at that time. It had nothing to do with finding Patty," he explained. "That's the only reason we were there."

She looked like she was going to say something

more, but Tess just said "Right."

"I wanted to think about it before I told you. I wanted to figure it out first."

"I understand, Sheriff. It would have been a distraction at the time."

"Not to mention outright speculation." The Sheriff turned again to Lucas. "I tried all night to find other explanations for what we'd found, but nothing else fit."

"My God, Sheriff. We have to find out for sure."

"And we will, but we don't want to run into the federal people. Not while we've got Patty Martin."

By now, Lucas had his own mug of coffee. He had just realized that Tess needed a new one. He held up a mug for her to approve. "BRAKE FOR MOOSE O.K. for you?"

Tess nodded and got up to help Lucas make her coffee. "Thanks, Lucas."

"You all right now?"

"Good enough. What do we do now?"

"I think we need to move Patty — far away. Before they find her. Let's face it, they could search every inch of Cobblers' Knob in two days or less. Probably already started."

"We don't want Lucy involved in that," Tess observed.

"It has to be some place that has no connection to any of us," Sheriff Roy said. "They'll be looking at us pretty soon."

"If they're feds, we shouldn't be talking about any of this on telephones," Lucas added. It was this comment that made them all realize for the first time the extent of the danger they were in. Nobody spoke for awhile, as they considered whether it was even safe to speak.

"Can't have bugged this office. Not yet, anyway," the Sheriff said. "But we need to move now. Deputy Tess, why don't you ride over to Lucy's house now on your bike. To pay her a friendly visit."

"On my way, Sheriff."

"And, if Patty is feeling all right, you and Lucy could maybe give her a make-over. Might pick up some hair color to take with you."

Tess sparked to the idea. "We'll give her a boy's haircut!"

"That's the kind of thinking we need!"

"Poor Patty," Lucas said to no one.

CHAPTER 46

Cobblers' Knob, Vermont

Thursday, April 14, 2017, 10:26 AM EDT

"Now," said Lucy, "we'll disguise you; so those creeps who took you from Wellston won't find you."

Patty shivered, just once. "Why did they do that?"

Tess answered. "They wanted to find out what you knew about prom night. Your prom night."

"You mean at Necklan's Lake?"

"Yes, Patty. They think you might have seen something you shouldn't have. Maybe a secret."

"But I don't remember anything about that night. At least not after the prom."

Lucy interrupted. "I can believe that. I had some of the punch. Wonder it didn't eat through the punch bowl."

"Pyrex," Patty said with a glint in her eye. "So

what's the disguise? I went out as Wonder Woman one Hallowe'en. But the cotton kept falling out of the top."

"Maybe that's why she was called Wonder Woman," Lucy posited. "You wondered how much filling there was in her top."

"We're going the other direction, I'm afraid," Tess declared.

"Flat-chested?" Patty sounded a bit disappointed.

"Among other things...."

Now she was worried. "What?"

Tess began to explain. "They are looking for a young lady. So we will disguise you as a teenage boy. No surgery required."

"And you won't have to wear make-up or earrings for a while," Lucy added.

She appeared to be envisioning it. Then she frowned. "But my hair...."

"Will grow back before you know it." Lucy completed the sentence for her with the authority only a high school principal can employ.

Patty gulped.

"Need a baggy sweatshirt to hide that voluptuous figure," Lucy declared.

Patty blushed. She was sitting amidst the remnants of her previously shoulder-length hair. She wasn't bald, but most high school boys had more hair. So did Miley Cyrus.

Tess agreed. "Just the thing. Do you have one?" This last part was yelled after Lucy, who had left the room.

"If I can find it...." There were the sounds of drawers opening and closing, then "Eureka!"

"Redwoods!" Tess called back.

Lucy re-entered the room with something behind her back. "I wasn't playing word-association, wise-ass!"

"Oh. Then I didn't win anything?" Tess responded in mock disappointment.

"No, but Patty did." Lucy pulled the sweatshirt out for display. It had been dark blue, but was unevenly faded. The bold white lettering across the front proclaimed 64TH NANTUCKET REGATTA. It was several sizes too big. In other words, *perfect*.

"That's actually pretty cool." Patty admitted as she

took possession of the garment.

"Darn right it is! I had to sail in driving rain two days and fight off drunken sailors at night. I *earned* that sweatshirt. Try it on," Lucy suggested. And she did. It hung down to almost mid-thigh.

"I may not need pants," Patty teased.

"Let's not go that route," Lucy admonished. "For one thing, your legs are shaved."

"True."

"What about pants? And shoes?" Tess wondered.

"Can't help there. Not without her looking like a vagrant."

"I'm sure I've still got stuff at home. Mom never goes upstairs, where my room is — or what used to be my room."

Lucy looked to Tess. It was her call.

"Too risky for you, but maybe I can go there. I'll tell your mother I'm going to visit you and that you asked me to bring some clothes to you. Show her my badge if she doubts me."

"Bring me some jeans and athletic shoes — not the pink ones."

"Kinda figured that out myself," Tess said.

"Sorry. I've got some socks like boys wear, too."

"You're quite the cross-dresser," Lucy teased.

Patty blushed again, but defended herself. "You can't climb Mount Washington in a ball gown and high heels."

"I'll take your word for it," Lucy conceded, smiling. "But it leaves me wondering if you've ever tried to."

"I took the cog railway," Tess intervened to end the discussion.

"Tenderfoot!" Lucy snorted, in good humor.

"Do you need any undergarments, while I'm at it?"

"All you can carry."

"Got a couple shopping bags I can use, Lucy?"

"Better yet, how about some rolling suitcases? She's going to have to pack anyway."

"Brilliant. Bring 'em on!"

"And one more thing, please."

The both looked at her sternly.

"At least one outfit that will let me be a girl again."

"What do you think?" Lucy asked.

"If I can fit it in, sure." Tess was not sympathetic.

After all, she was the one who might be risking her life for the clothes.

CHAPTER 47

Cobblers' Knob, Vermont

Thursday, April 14, 2017, 11:19 AM EDT

Tess parked Lucy's practical sedan in the back of the Martin house. She saw a car in the garage through the horizontal row of windows. It appeared to be an older American model. She left the suitcases at the back door, hoping she could retrieve them out of sight of the street. It was just beginning to rain, as she knocked on the front door. While she waited, she looked through the narrow window beside the door. Just opposite the door was a solid old staircase leading to the second floor. There were rooms to the right and to the left of the door. A hallway that went to the rear of the house flanked the staircase. So there would be a faux Oriental inside the door or one of those braided rugs, she predicted. Standing on tiptoes, she could see the floor.

No rug. Instead there was a body. A woman she assumed to be Mrs. Martin was sprawled at the bottom of the stairs.

Tess began to knock loudly on the door, but stopped when she realized the noise might summon a neighbor.

The body had not moved.

Tess was having trouble breathing. She noticed that her legs were gently lowering her to the porch floor. She reached for her cell phone.

This was way above her pay grade. It was time to call Sheriff Roy.

Although the Sheriff approached the Martin house at a reasonable speed, with nary a siren or flashing light, the plan to quietly liberate some of Patty's clothes was blown. The word "smithereens" came to mind as Tess watched Doc McAdams pull in behind the Sheriff. Then Deputy Lucas, seeing no space left in the driveway, pulled over the curb, leaving his right wheels on the lawn. He emerged from the Jeep, quickly scanning in all directions, as if there might be snipers in this otherwise serene neighborhood. Tess figured Lucas had been waiting for an excuse to do that.

Sheriff Roy already had his lock picks working. Once the troops had entered the house, she introduced them to the body and retreated to the front porch. Sheriff Roy was standing inside on the third stair, looking down at Doc McAdams as he examined the body. Deputy Lucas was searching the house for who knew what. He had discovered the suitcases at the back door and rescued them from the rain. Upon seeing Tess, he silently stepped behind her and asked "Looking for these?"

Startled the Hell out of me!

Tess was too occupied stifling her gag reflex to speak just then, but she managed to point upstairs. She stepped around the doctor and the corpse to ascend the staircase. Once clear of the stairs, the place was musty. Seriously musty. She found Patty's room and opened a window. Lucas brought the suitcases in.

"Planning on collecting a lot of evidence?" he asked.

"No. I'm after wardrobe."

"Oh. I guess Patty didn't bring her clothes from Wellston."

Tess was tearing through the closet, throwing items in the bags. "That's part of it." She emptied a drawer into the second suitcase, then picked up another. Indicating the suitcase she was closing, Tess asked "Would you help me get these downstairs?"

He didn't bother with the wheels. Lucas simply picked one up with each hand and carried them out of the room and down the stairs with no discernable effort --- like they were pillows with handles. Maybe there was some truth to the weaker sex tradition. She followed, feeling like she should be carrying something too.

Deputy Lucas awaited her on the front porch, still carrying the suitcases. She had paused at the door, looking at the Sheriff.

"What's the verdict, Doc?" Sheriff Roy asked.

"As you can see, it looks like she fell going downstairs."

"Not going up?"

Tess realized that she wouldn't have thought to ask.

"No. She would have landed on her back or side if she'd been going up. She wouldn't have twisted around to face the one direction that offered no way of arresting her fall. It's instinctive."

"Makes sense."

Tess suddenly understood that the Sheriff already knew this. This was his way of having it explained to her. She was grateful. But there was something she needed to tell them, if she could only figure out what it was.

"She has the smell of alcohol. Wine, I think. Can't tell how much until we test for it, but she definitely ingested alcohol prior to this. Could have caused her to lose her balance. Of course, I may discover that she had a stroke. Or a heart attack. Either of those could have caused her to fall. From the position of the body, I can't really tell if she tried to break the fall. She was frail; so any such preventive action wouldn't have accomplished much, I'm afraid."

"Ready?" Lucas asked. He was still holding the heavy suitcases.

"Put those down for a minute." He complied.

"What is it?" Sheriff Roy wanted to know.

But she turned to Lucas again. "What rooms are on this floor?"

"Well, there's this foyer, the living room, the kitchen, a bathroom and another room which looks like it was the dining room. Then you're back here."

"Full bathroom?"

"No tub. Just a small shower — kind of jury-rigged, like it's not an original part of the house."

"What was that about the dining room?"

"It's the closest big room to the kitchen, has crown molding and a chair rail; so it should be the dining room."

"But what?"

"It has a bed in it, with a night stand and an armoire and a chest with drawers and a mirror. I think there's a chair too."

"That's it!" Tess blurted out.

"That's what?" Sheriff Roy asked.

"Patty told me that her mother couldn't climb the stairs anymore without assistance. She must have lived down here."

"Yes...." Either the Sheriff had grasped the implications, or he was letting her work it out by herself.

"So how did she manage to fall down the stairs if she couldn't climb them in the first place?"

After a moment of intense silence, the Sheriff turned to Doc McAdams. "Keep that in mind when you perform the official examination."

"I couldn't forget it if I tried, Sheriff."

CHAPTER 48

Cobblers' Knob, Vermont

Thursday, April 14, 2017, 1:14 PM EDT

They were still on the front porch. Tess had an idea. "Do we have any tape that says EVIDENCE to put on these suitcases?"

"Should be some in the Jeep," Sheriff Roy answered. "You been gathering evidence here?"

"No. These are clothes to take to Patty, but with all the neighbors watching, I thought...."

"Say no more. I've managed to grasp the intricacies of your plan of deception." The Sheriff turned to Lucas. "See if you can find some of that tape and plaster these suitcases with it while they're up here on the porch. So everyone can see what a bang-up job we're doing."

"Just like the big city," Tess offered.

"Good thinking, Deputy Tess. When they're properly marked as evidence, I'll have Lucas put them in the Jeep and take them to the office. We'll leave them in the back until the courthouse has shut down. Then we'll put them in the trunk of.... Is that Lucy's car in the driveway?"

"Yes, it is. I rode my Harley over to her house."

"Well, you just go on back there for now. I'll call you when you can pick up the suitcases. Make sure there's a space next to the Jeep; so the transfer can be quick — and, hopefully, unobserved."

"Should I go now?"

"Yes. But, just in case, drive out to *Rachel's* and pick up a couple sandwiches to take back to Lucy and Patty. Get one for yourself, as well."

"But that...."

"Will give you ample opportunity to see if anyone is tailing you. It may also convince any such person that you are not harboring Patty."

"Oh. I hadn't thought of that."

Sheriff Roy was thorough. "If someone appears to be tailing you, just get the sandwiches. If the tail is still there after you leave *Rachel's*, come straight to the station and we'll figure what to do. Call me right away if you think you have a tail; so we can check it out as you pull in."

"You've done this before, Sheriff."

"Not my first rodeo, Deputy."

"I'm learning a lot here."

"The kind of stuff they don't put in books," he supposed aloud.

"None I've read so far."

"On your way, then. Keep your eyes peeled for someone following you. I don't really think that's going to happen, but I'd hate for you to lead the bad guys to Patty."

"What happens if I think I'm being followed and have to come back to the office?"

"I guess the Sheriff's department will have a decent lunch for a change."

"Sheriff, you might just be devious yourself."

"Thank you."

Deputy Lucas returned with a roll of evidence tape. "You just figuring that out?"

"Let him do it," the Sheriff advised. "I don't want

you to be associated with those suitcases."

Tess swung her head around, taking the suitcases out of her view. Ignoring Deputy Lucas, she went to Lucy's car. And she left the property as unobtrusively as she could, considering that the Sheriff and Doc McAdams both had to move their vehicles to let her out of the driveway.

"Cloak and dagger," she said to herself. "Cloak. And. *Dagger!*"

CHAPTER 49

Cobblers' Knob, Vermont

Thursday, April 14, 2017, 1:38 PM EDT

Tess took an indirect route in order expose anyone who might be tailing her. But after seeing no vehicles at all behind her through several turns, she decided to cut the melodrama. This was still Cobblers' Knob, after all.

Tess reminded herself to put on a cheerful face as she pulled into Lucy's driveway. She did not intend to divulge anything about Mrs. Martin. There were still too many questions. But the real reason was that she needed Patty to be focused on the plan to hide her.

Lucy met Tess at the back door. "Hasn't said more than six words. None of them particularly informative. Ate like a lumberjack, though. You didn't happen to bring any pancakes with you?"

Tess smiled and entered the kitchen. "Fresh out, I'm afraid." Patty sat at the kitchen table, drinking tea or coffee --- maybe hot chocolate. Something hot, at any rate. Tess called out to her. *"Bonjour, Patricia! Comment allez vous?"*

"Je suis tres bien, merci. Et vous?" Patty replied, indicating she was well.

"Aussi."

"Tell me she speaks English," Lucy implored Tess.

"Se claire. Of course. French is just the key that unlocks the door," Tess sort-of explained.

"Hadn't thought of it that way," Patty announced. She found it to be curiously accurate. "What now?"

"We have to wait a bit on the clothes. There were other people at the house." It wasn't a lie, but it sure wasn't an accurate representation of the situation. Tess felt badly, but a bit excited. She was unaccustomed to intrigue.

"Funny," Patty commented. "She never had much company."

"Peculiar it may be," Lucy corrected, "but she may have changed her routine after you moved away."

"I suppose so." Patty conceded without conviction.

CHAPTER 50

Cobblers' Knob, Vermont
Thursday, April 14, 2017, 5:07 PM EDT

Sheriff Roy had been tied up with administrative duties all afternoon. He'd pick up a form, groan, and then go to work on it. Lucas was out on patrol. According to the Sheriff, driving around Cobblers' Knob aimlessly was the only aspect of police work that the townspeople understood. That may have been an exaggeration, but at least the citizens could see for themselves that something was being done. And if it discouraged a single crime per year, it was worth the effort.

So he was a million mental miles away when the phone rang. Tess answered, but it was for him.

"Who?" he asked while she was still talking.

"Doctor McAdams."

"The Sheriff picked up. Tess hung up. But then the Sheriff gestured for her to get back on the line. This was new.

"I had to send the body to the state medical examiner in Burlington, Sheriff. They picked it up this morning. The immediate cause of death was a broken neck. That's not surprising. But I couldn't find any evidence to account for the fall. No stroke. No heart attack. Of course, she could have just tripped."

"But...."

"Her face. You saw it. It's smashed in. Her front teeth are broken off. The nose, her septum, was driven back into her brain. She didn't get her arms in front of her before she hit the floor."

"I thought that was instinctive."

"Exactly. It's a reflex, meaning it doesn't need to be thought out."

"Was she drunk?"

"I just got the preliminary lab results back. She was not drunk by the Vermont legal standard for a DUI. I also had them check for medications that could have caused her to lose consciousness or even become unstable. They even checked for combinations of alcohol, medications and other substances. Nothing."

"Being old and out of shape, she might have just been clumsy," Sheriff Roy ventured.

"No doubt about it. But that doesn't explain the lack of a defensive reflex when she landed at the bottom of the stairs."

"Well, then what would explain it?"

"If she was fully conscious when she began to fall — and we're not sure she was — then I've only come up with two possibilities. I'm sure there are more, but these are the most probable. They are not mutually exclusive."

"Enough preamble, Doc. I know you don't have a sophisticated laboratory with experts tripping all over each other to get you results. Let me hear what you think. I won't even write it down." He gestured to Tess to take notes.

"The main reason for her not to have taken effective defensive measures would be that she was traveling too fast. She didn't have the time."

"Maybe her reactions were slow."

"Probably the case," the doctor admitted, "But

reaction times don't vary that much. Wouldn't explain it."

"Don't all objects fall at the same rate?" the Sheriff wondered.

"Galileo proved that two objects of similar size and shape, but of different mass, when dropped from the same height, struck the earth at the same time."

"So how would Mrs. Martin have achieved a higher velocity than normal?" Sheriff Roy could hold his own in the scientific language arena. Deputy Tess was impressed.

"If she was pushed hard."

"I see. And was she?"

"Let me tell you the other possibility first. As I said, they could work in concert."

"It's your story, Doc. Tell it the way you see fit," the Sheriff conceded.

"The other reason for lack of defensive action would be surprise. Even when you trip, you know you're probably going to fall before you actually begin to fall. It's only a moment, but it's enough to rearrange your thinking and priorities."

"I can see that."

Doc McAdams paused to deliver the clincher. "So

what if both reasons happened to Mrs. Martin?"

There was a thoughtful pause.

"I'd say it might not be an accident." Sheriff Roy had made the leap.

"Remember that your alert deputy, whom I can hear breathing into the phone, told me that Mrs. Martin couldn't use the stairs without assistance."

"Good afternoon, Doctor McAdams," Tess said. "The Sheriff asked me to get back on the phone."

"Good afternoon to you as well, Deputy."

Sheriff Roy interrupted the greetings. "So it appears that someone assisted Mrs. Martin *up* the staircase, maybe the whole way. It doesn't matter. In any event, that same someone was assisting her *down* the staircase when he suddenly pushed her forward with great force."

"And her reaction time was slowed by the elements of surprise and shock. But she also was approaching the bottom of the stairs much faster than she would have if she had simply fallen. That scenario would explain why her hands and arms were not deployed to protect her face."

"Any evidence to support that theory, Doc?"

"Yes. After I figured out what had probably happened, I went back to my examination notes. I was looking for bruising from a hard shove to the back or a kick, either of which would propel her forward. But I didn't find any."

"That's too bad."

"Not so bad, after all. While looking for bruising on her back, I took another look at a horizontal mark I'd found on the back of her neck. I no longer had the body, of course, but I'd photographed it and sketched it in my journal, with the dimensions. Sometimes when a forehead hits a surface hard, it can cause a compression bruise where a cervical vertebra has fractured. This is what I had initially thought had occurred. But now I realized the mark was more consistent with a blow to the back of her neck. Like a karate chop."

"So that's what broke her neck?"

"It's likely. And it would make effective defensive measures highly unlikely."

"Excuse me," Tess said, "but did this karate chop kill her?"

"I believe that it did, although she could have still been alive when she hit the floor a moment later. We may never establish whether her collision with the floor killed her, or just complicated our analysis by providing a second likely cause of death within an extremely short time frame. But in the ultimate analysis, she would not have died if she hadn't been struck violently from behind while descending the staircase."

Sheriff Roy was ahead of them. "Wonder what they wanted upstairs...."

CHAPTER 51

Cobblers' Knob, Vermont
Thursday, April 14, 2017, 5:54 PM EDT

The suitcases had been transferred into Lucy's car once the courthouse parking lot had emptied out. When the circuit judge was sitting in another county, not much happened after 4:30 when the recorder's office closed.

Patty had approved of the clothing selection. Everything she had tried on so far still fit. She was happily reunited with her garb. Even if she did look like a boy.

"Where am I going to wear these outfits?"

"Not around here," was the best Tess had at the moment.

"I didn't ask where I *wasn't* going to wear them."

"Still working on that one, I'm afraid."

"I've been thinking," Lucy said. They both looked

at her expectantly. "And I haven't come up with an answer, *per se*. But she can stay here until we figure it out."

"It's nice, but I can't stay indoors for the whole summer."

"Wasn't suggesting that. We'll have to see. At least until we determine you're safe."

"What if I'm *never* safe?"

"We'll have to revise the plan. But let's not get ahead of ourselves. At least you won't be in Wellston...."

"Or in that pit," Tess added.

"What pit?" Lucy asked.

"When we went looking for Patty over in the old Camp Bethany, Sheriff Roy and I stumbled on some kind of pit. It was obviously artificial. At least several years old. The Sheriff found some bone fragments. He's going back to investigate sometime...."

"You mean you haven't figured it out?" Patty was incredulous.

"Figured out what?" Lucy asked.

"Those bones are my friends! The missing Seniors! Or what's left of them."

"I...." Tess couldn't put her thoughts into words. Finally she asked "How could you know that?"

"How could you not?"

Lucy intervened. "Calm down, both of you." She turned to Tess. "Does that make sense?"

"Sheriff Roy thinks so, but he can't prove it until the forensic team can process the site. Which is problematic right now." Tess paused to allow Lucy to digest this. "That would explain why the Sheriff couldn't find any remains at the lake. They'd already been transported and buried."

"In a mass grave," Patty added. "I was going to tell the other deputy, the man who found me. But I was too exhausted to remember."

"Deputy Lucas?"

"Lucas?"

"He went to high school with you. He was a class or two ahead of you."

"It was two," the principal advised.

"Do you remember him?" Tess was trying to sound casual, but she was desperate to establish the connection.

Patty was trying to remember, but coming up

short.

"Rode a motorcycle," Lucy offered.

An internal light went on. It lit up Patty's face, making it even prettier.

"Oh, *him!*"

Lucy nodded to Tess. "Deputy Stud made an impression."

"How well did you know him?"

Patty blushed. "Hardly at all. It's just that all the girls thought he was...."

"Including you?"

"Oh, yeah."

"Was he in the Drama Club with you?"

Patty frowned. "I don't think so."

Lucy cleared that up for them. "He played football, basketball and ran the 440. He didn't have time for Drama Club. But I do think he had a part in one of their plays, a major role."

Now Tess was interested in Lucas. "Was he any good?"

"Not so much at acting, as I recall. But made all-state as a halfback, Single A Division. Not too shabby in the other sports either. The coaches were sorry to see him graduate. Of course, they were the ones who gave him the good grades in their classes."

"Good grades?" That didn't reconcile with Tess' assessment of her fellow deputy.

"Not Honor Roll, mind you, but respectable. He didn't plan on going to college; so he didn't apply himself."

"If I had played three sports, I wouldn't have had the strength to study," Tess admitted.

"There was that too. But I always had the feeling that he could have been a top student if he had been motivated."

"But he wasn't?"

"Life was working out just fine for him without the grades. Probably still is. There are people like that, you know."

"Just amazing." Patty had finally found the words to describe Lucas.

They all laughed.

But Lucy continued. "Watch him carefully, young Tess. He's smarter than he pretends to be. He has a sort of native cunning. Instinctively understands situations and people."

"He has surprised me already. I'm wary."

"But intrigued?"

She hadn't thought in those terms, but she admitted "Possibly."

"He's so cool." Patty said, as she continued, unabated.

Tess had an inspiration. "Did he ever take you for a ride on his motorcycle?"

Patty had a recollection. "Before that last football game of the season in his last year, he walked over to the cheerleaders in his uniform...."

"Looking like a gladiator," Lucy threw into the conversation.

"And told us to cheer our pretty little tails off, and if we won, he would give each of us a ride on his Harley."

"Did you win?"

"Yes, we did. It was close, but we knocked off the only undefeated team in the league."

"Tore down both goal posts," Lucy contributed. "At $463 apiece. Shot the athletic budget all to Hell. Had to return the spiffy new track suits for credit."

"And did you cheer your pretty little tails off?"

"You bet. We were totally exhausted by the end of the game."

"Did Lucas make good on his offer?"

"What?"

"Did he give you each a ride on his motorcycle?"

"No. Not that night. Except the senior cheerleader. She rode off with him right after the game, and they didn't come back."

"Sounds right," Lucy commented.

"So you took a rain check?"

"Yeah. I guess the rest of us did."

"When did you cash it in?"

"I guess I didn't." Tess thought she was finished, but she wasn't. "See, I didn't just want a quick ride, with another cheerleader waiting for us to get back. So I told him I'd let him know when. Then I kept it there for when I wanted it. Kind of like a dream."

Tess could taste what was coming. She was going to *love* law enforcement. "So you were going to call him when the time was just right?"

"That was my plan."

"When would that have been?"

Patty had misinterpreted the question. "Oh. When I needed something really special, I guess."

"Like a hot date for the Senior Prom?" There. It was out there, to be caught or fumbled.

But Lucy interrupted. "Only Seniors are allowed at the prom."

Determined to keep the thought in motion, Tess asked, "But *after* the prom?"

Patty had nothing to say, but she sure had plenty to think about. "After?"

"Good-bye, Fred. Time to cash in your rain check for a prom night you'll never forget."

"What?" Patty was confused, but not denying it.

"You climb onto the back of his Harley, the whole bike is pulsating with the power of the engine. He asks you where you want to go, and you say Necklan's Lake...."

"Oh." Patty could picture it. Perhaps too well. She began to whimper.

"Stop it!" Lucy shouted. "Just stop it now, Tess."

Tess reacted like she had been slapped in the face.

"Oh my God! I'm so sorry, Patty."

"Go make some coffee, Tess."

But Patty stopped sobbing long enough to say "No."

Both of them looked at her, astonished for different reasons.

"I'm so confused. I really don't remember, but it sounds ... possible."

"Let's let her gather her thoughts," Lucy suggested. "And I'll make the coffee."

There would be no further discussion of Deputy Lucas that night.

CHAPTER 52

Cobblers' Knob, Vermont
Friday, April 15, 2017, 8:07 AM EDT

Tess walked out to his car as Lucas pulled in. She opened the passenger door, and got into the official Jeep. "Good morning," he said with surprised amusement.

"Drive."

"Where to?"

"Rachel's."

"Not open yet."

"Perfect."

Lucas backed out again. After he was on the road, he asked "What's this about?"

"Deputies' meeting."

"Are we going to join the union?"

"There's a union?"

"Not up here in the woods."

"Good, 'cause that's not what this is about."

"Should I get a lawyer?"

'Only if I read you your Miranda rights."

"Works for me. So what do you want to know, Deputy Tess?"

She went straight to the heart of the matter. "Why did you abandon Patty at Necklan's Lake the night of the Senior Prom massacre?"

"Patty Martin?" They both knew he was stalling. It was painfully obvious.

"The same."

After an awkward minute of silence, Lucas said "The Sheriff closed that investigation."

"It's not an investigation. Just one simple question."

"No, Tess. It's a complex question. In a court room, it's called a leading question. To answer the question as framed requires admissions that go beyond the question itself."

Lucy was right. He was smarter than he let on. "You still aren't answering my question.

"Well, it doesn't have a simple answer."

"Then I'll try really hard to follow it."

"It began with a promise to give her a ride on my motorcycle."

"That she twisted into a promise to take her whenever she asked. Already know that."

"Oh." Lucas quickly reassessed the new deputy. "Then you know she managed to get me to take her to Necklan's Lake after the prom."

"And get naked in the lake. Yeah. Got all that."

"It was *her* idea."

"Maybe. Not relevant."

Lucas wasn't letting it go at that. "Look, she was a bit drunk, presumably from the spiked punch, but I didn't take advantage of her."

"How did you know the punch was spiked?"

"It's *always* spiked at the Senior Prom."

"You certainly didn't take her to an AA meeting."

"I didn't realize she was high until we were in the water."

"Naked."

"Yes, naked. Like everybody else. We didn't get a

chance to talk on the Harley, and once we arrived, she was stripped and wet before I reached the shore."

"And you joined her."

"Of course. That's what happens on prom night."

"Sure."

He ignored her sarcasm. "Anyway, she swam over to the rocks and beckoned for me to come over."

"Beckoned?"

"It's just a word, Tess. Actually, she jumped up and down, so I could see her breasts, and waved to me."

"And what did that tell you?"

"Several things...."

"How about in order?"

"O.K. Nice body. Too eager. Moonlight."

"I think I get the first two, but moonlight?"

"There was enough moonlight to see really well. It was sort of reddish that night. She glowed in it."

"How convenient for you." Tess realized that her sarcasm was guiding her. She checked herself and switched back to interrogation mode. "O.K. So you went to her?"

"Yes. And when I got there, she began to kiss me.

Deep, passionate kisses. But I hardly knew her. And she jammed her body up against mine."

"How terrible that must have been for you."

"But I had no feelings for her," he explained.

"So you forced yourself to have sex with her, just so she could have a good prom night? That what you're telling me?"

"No. I sensed danger."

"What?"

"No matter what you think, Tess. I saved Patty's life that night."

He sounded sincere. That stopped her cold. "But you left her!"

"I had to. I had to leave."

"Right then. In the lake. In the middle of the night."

"Right then. Couldn't wait. And I couldn't bring her along."

"So what was this urgent business?"

"Can't tell you. The investigation is closed. Remember?"

Tess nodded. She was angry, but he was right. And

Lucas hadn't closed the investigation. The Sheriff had.

"I answered your question, and a couple more."

He had kept his end of the bargain. Neither had any idea what her end might have been. She forced herself to calm down, as he pulled into *Rachel's* parking lot. "Can I head back to the office now?"

"Might as well."

Tess remained deep in thought for the return trip. But when the car stopped, she turned to face him. They made eye contact. "You saved her life. Not an exaggeration?"

"The literal truth. A fact." His green eyes didn't flinch.

"I believe you are telling the truth, as you perceive it," Tess admitted.

"My perception is accurate. I saved her life."

"O.K. Thanks for answering my question."

"Does that mean I get an espresso?"

The tension was broken. "With hazelnut creamer. Just the way you like it, Deputy."

"Thank God. I could sure use one now."

CHAPTER 53

Cobblers' Knob, Vermont

Friday, April 15, 2017, 9:19 AM EDT

The promised espresso had been made and consumed. Deputy Tess was making notes, trying to figure out what was the danger Lucas said he had sensed. And why he had to leave Patty in the lake. And where he'd gone and what he'd done. And the big enchilada: why he thought he'd saved Patty's life. Of course, she was alive and everyone else was dead; so....

Deputy Lucas was filling out some reports about patrol routes taken and gasoline consumption. He looked bored. Every now and then he would glance over at Tess, as if she were a volcano that might suddenly erupt. Or blow, like Mount St. Helen's had.

But it was Sheriff Roy who blew. "What in the devil

are they doing out there!"

Thus was the investigation reopened, at least a crack.

"Was that rhetorical, or can we speak?" Tess inquired.

The Sheriff didn't respond. Looked like he might *never* answer.

"Maybe we could toss a few ideas around," Lucas offered, to Tess' surprise.

"Already did that," Sheriff Roy said. "Don't remember coming up with any solution to the case."

"Maybe we've learned something since then," Tess suggested. "At least, we've had more time to think about it."

"Ah. Guess that's true enough. But I'm looking at this from the perspective of when are they going to leave; so I can get on with investigating that pit. The cold case stays that way."

"If it's the same outfit, they won't be around much longer." Lucas seemed confident.

Sheriff Roy wondered "Why do you think they'll be leaving soon?"

"Based on what we think we know, they're here for a specific event — or experiment. Right?"

"Keep talking."

"They seem to be working in a rundown old cabin...."

Tess interrupted. "That's right. Patty told me the cabin was primitive. Just bunks and few old wooden chairs."

Lucas continued. "So it's temporary. They will leave after this event occurs."

"Makes sense," the Sheriff admitted. "Anything else?"

"Yes. They left the last time."

"We can't be sure of that."

"Actually, we can."

"And why is that?"

"Because I personally combed every square foot of Camp Bethany searching for them. There wasn't a soul around, Sheriff."

"Well, I know we did a pretty thorough search, but...."

"No. After that. I searched it myself."

Sheriff Roy was astonished. "Why would you do that?"

Tess couldn't wait to hear the answer herself.

"Because I couldn't believe it happened. Not the way it did. People don't just vanish in the night without a trace. O.K., maybe one or two, but fourteen?"

"Did you find the pit?"

"Yes. But it was pretty well covered. I didn't have the tools or the time to excavate. Never occurred to me that it might be a grave. Found the cabin. They'd been using that. Cleaned up real well, but didn't bother to remove the ashes from the fireplace."

"Find anything else?"

"Tire marks, including farm or earth-moving equipment tires. I figured it could have been a backhoe. And huge tread marks from the trailer that brought it in. And took it back out."

"They brought a backhoe in to dig the pit?"

"I don't think so. The backhoe was probably brought in to construct what may have been a trap of some kind."

"A trap," the Sheriff repeated dully. "Just keeps

getting better."

"Like those you see in the movies. Where the ground looks solid, but collapses when a man or animal steps on it. But without the bamboo spikes at the bottom. I guess it wasn't designed to kill."

"You're describing a camouflaged hole?" Sheriff Roy was incredulous.

"Actually, it was a deep trench, about thirty-five feet long. I paced it off."

"Wait! How did you pace it off?"

"It was easy. After I fell in."

"You fell in?" Tess gasped.

"That's when I noticed there weren't any sharpened spikes."

"How deep?" the Sheriff asked.

"Close to twelve feet. Higher than I could reach by several feet."

"How'd you get out?"

"I dug my way out. I always carry my Bowie knife with me in the woods or I'd still be there. Took me almost two hours to get out."

"No cell phone reception?"

"Not a single bar."

The Sheriff plodded on. "This trap was well disguised, then?"

"I didn't see it in broad daylight. Not that I was particularly cautious. But no one would have noticed it at night."

"It had been dug by a machine?"

"No doubt about it. I could see the marks."

"Where is this trap?"

"About half a mile from the lake. But it's not there anymore."

"What?"

"I went back with my camera a couple days later.

Tess broke in again. "Why didn't you take a photo with your cell phone?"

They could see it dawn on his face. "I guess I still think of it as a phone --- period. Anyway, it was gone."

"Completely?"

"Yes. That's why I didn't report it. But then I noticed something else, about fifteen feet beyond the trap itself. There were six round holes in a row. Like post holes. Several feet deep. Hadn't noticed them before."

"Any idea what they might have been for?"

"Not at first. But when I pictured them with posts in place, it could have been a fence — or a firing squad."

"That's it!" Tess shouted.

They both looked at her.

"No. That's not it, but you pictured it right."

They just stared harder.

"A firing squad. A man is tied to a post prior to being killed. Picture it!"

"A sacrifice?" Lucas guessed.

Sheriff Roy shouted. "The intended victims of the experiment."

"If they were the intended victims, then why was the trap there?" Tess asked.

"The trap would have prevented a predator from reaching them," the Sheriff agreed. "Which changes the function of the men at the posts to bait!"

"Whoa," Lucas admonished them. "You think that these feds were trying to lure some predator into a trap?"

"A predator that would prey upon men. That should narrow it down quite a bit."

"And multiple baits suggests multiple predators,"

Tess concluded. "I don't mean different types of predators, just a group of the same kind."

"Hunting together, in a pack," said the Sheriff.

"But there aren't any wolves in the area," Lucas added.

'Maybe these wolves, or whatever, have a larger hunting area than we're used to seeing."

"Any species will go beyond its usual geographic limits if food becomes scarce," Tess contributed,

"Don't know how a city girl knows that, but it's true."

"Anthropology 101," Tess admitted.

"So what now?" Lucas asked.

Sheriff Roy went into deep ponder mode. Tess got up to make more coffee. Not espresso this time. Her mind was already bouncing off the walls of her skull.

Lucas shuffled the papers on his desk. He could do this indefinitely.

Finally, the Sheriff spoke. "Because of the paucity of reasons for the federal government to send a weapons team to this neck of the woods, I think we need to assume that these two events are part of the same project." He looked them in the eyes before continuing. "And the information so belatedly revealed by Deputy Lucas confirms that they were here to trap animals, possibly for use in weapons research of some type. The size of the trap which Deputy Lucas *so cunningly* discovered indicates they expected a hunting pack. Which pretty much means wolves. At least to us. But these government men — let's call them the DoD --- have been involved with this for quite a while. So it's a given that they know a lot more about this than we do. But let's just say wolves for now. Anything else?"

"Just a clarification, Sheriff. It's now clear that the DoD men came here because the wolves were here. That's the *only* reason," Tess said.

"Agreed."

"And it follows that the Seniors got in between the wolves and the trap. They unwittingly became the new bait. And the DoD was caught by surprise, unprepared for what happened and unable to stop it."

"That makes sense. Doesn't make me feel any better about having the Department of Defense conduct secret weapons projects on my turf, mind you. And to avoid calling attention to the project, they just cleaned it up and left town. Left me holding the bag."

"Just one thing, Sheriff," Lucas said. "Are you saying that the DoD *lured* the wolves to the lake that night?"

"All I'm saying is that the DoD put out bait, then the wolves showed up. Why?"

"So the wolves wouldn't have been hunting there, but for the DoD?"

Sheriff Roy considered this. "Seemed perfectly obvious a minute ago."

Tess chimed in. "But what if the opposite is true?"

"Any idea what she means by that, Lucas?"

"What if the DoD people were there because they *knew* the wolves would be coming to the lake that night?" she hypothesized.

"Well, that does put the shoe on the other foot."

"It means the bait was just to lead them into the trap," Lucas concluded. "Not to get them to the Necklan's Lake in the first place. They were already coming."

"Got to admit that fits better. Even wolves wouldn't have picked the scents of the men from a mile away."

"What if they were bleeding?" Tess asked.

"Good question, my morbid young Deputy." Tess blushed. "Let's just leave it at the wolves weren't attracted to Necklan's Lake by the bait. It's *your* hypothesis."

"Aye-aye, Sheriff. So how did the DoD know when the wolves would be arriving?" Tess wondered aloud.

"It's just possible that the DoD has access to resources even greater than those available to the Allen County Sheriff's Department. I know it's a difficult concept, but try to imagine such a thing. As a favor to me."

"Satellites, drones, airplane reconnaissance," Tess ventured.

"They may even have spotters and trackers on the ground. Could have mapped their migration patterns," Lucas said.

"So let's assume for the moment that the DoD has employed at least some of these techniques to study this pack of wolves for years. If so, the DoD could have accurately predicted they would be hunting at Necklan's Lake that night."

"And been prepared to capture some of them," Tess

added.

Sheriff Roy nodded.

"What's so special about these wolves?" Lucas asked.

"No idea, but if the DoD went to all that trouble, you can bet there is something — and it's pretty amazing."

Sheriff Roy turned to Tess. "I think you're on the way to solving your first cold case, Deputy Tess. Shame you won't be able to write it up. But congratulations anyway."

"Thanks, Sheriff. But you and Lucas share the credit."

"Um. Aren't we forgetting something?" Lucas asked.

"What would that be?"

"They're back. The DoD is back."

"Not officially."

"What difference does that make?" Tess wanted to know.

"Makes them trespassers. Lawbreakers."

"You plan to arrest them?" Lucas was shocked.

Sheriff Roy chuckled at that. "No. Not me. I plan to

be an amused spectator, along with both of you."

"But you're going to do something?"

"I'm going to start the ball rolling, that's all."

CHAPTER 54

Cobblers' Knob, Vermont

Friday, April 15, 2017, 12:58 PM EDT

"Thanks for meeting me here, Doc."

Sheriff Roy slid into a booth a *Rachel's*.

"Pleasure's all mine, Sheriff. Been wanting to talk to you about that bone you found. You say there were more?"

"Lots more, Doc. It's a mass grave."

"What?"

"Figure it's the Seniors from the massacre. Did you and the state lab find anything that would contradict that?"

"No. That would fit with what little we know. Have you been back to investigate?"

"Not yet."

"What's keeping you? This is an amazing discovery."

"Have I sworn you in lately, Doc?"

"What?"

"You know, have I deputized you?"

"I don't think so. Why?"

"Because I should have done it when we brought the girl to you. But we were all tired that night; so I probably forgot."

"Is that necessary?"

"I hope not, but I really can't tell you any more unless you're officially on the team. Consider it an honor."

"Do I get paid?"

"No. That's why it's an honor. Why does everyone ask that?"

"O.K. Get on with it then."

The brief ceremony was concluding when Matt arrived. "Congratulations, Deputy Doc," he said. "I take it this is an official meeting."

"Deputies," the Sheriff began, "I need your help. Some strange events have been happening in *our* jurisdiction." He watched them react to their inclusion.

Each of you knows part of the story; so bear with me while I bring you both up to date. Everything I'm about to tell you, even if you already knew or suspected it, is secret. You've each sworn an oath. As deputies, you will not reveal any of this unless, and to whom, I tell you."

"I may have to hand in my badge," Matt replied. Doc McAdams nodded.

"You don't have one," the Sheriff reminded them. "Just hear me out."

"You buying lunch?" Doc inquired. "Could make a difference...."

"Why not? You guys are already acting like seasoned deputies."

"Let's hear it, Sheriff." Matt was listening.

"The short version, if there is one."

The waitress came then and took their orders. He waited for the drinks to arrive before starting.

"Short version. My rules. Questions after. Patty Martin, the only survivor of the Necklan's Lake Massacre. You know who she is." Both men nodded to indicate the affirmative. "She was traumatized, couldn't walk or talk. She's been at Wellston doing rehab for the past few years.

Well, she was kidnapped and drugged this past Wednesday by unknown persons who presented the staff with what appeared to be the appropriate documentation. Acting on little more than a hunch, we went looking for her in a remote part of Camp Bethany late that same night. Sometime after midnight, we found her. Actually, she found us. She had escaped her captors by pretending she was still drugged. She'd also left secret the fact that she had regained the ability to walk. Clever girl."

"Indeed," Matt commented. Off a look from the Sheriff, he pointed out "That wasn't a question."

With a look back, the Sheriff conceded the truth of that, and continued. "Patty was injured and exhausted; so we immediately extracted her for medical treatment." He nodded to Doc. "It was not the time to confront her abductors. Deputy McAdams here stitched up her wound, gave her some antibiotics and checked her over in the middle of the night, at a secret location that was not a medical facility. We didn't want her captors to find her in the Emergency Room of the local clinic. And, thanks again, Doc. She's doing well."

Doc McAdams nodded.

"Then we took her to an undisclosed location. That means neither of you needs to know where. On Thursday, the next morning, slightly before Noon, Deputy Tess arrived at the Martin house to retrieve some of Patty's clothes. She found Mrs. Martin dead at the foot of the staircase. She'd been dead long enough for *rigor mortis* to have set in. Doc here examined her. When did you see her, Matt?"

"She was alive and well when I left her house at about a quarter past three on Wednesday afternoon. How did she die?"

"Doc?"

"Broken neck. Looks like someone pushed her down the staircase. There was bruising on the back of her neck consistent with a karate chop. The state lab has confirmed this. It's being treated as a probable homicide."

"But why?" Matt asked.

"We don't have a motive for her death. Or for the kidnapping either. But I don't believe the two events are unrelated. And we do know where the kidnappers are — for now. And Matt, while searching for Patty Martin, we found what appears to be a mass grave located on the grounds of Camp Bethany, near where the kidnappers have been staying."

"Mass grave?"

"Might be the missing Seniors."

"Oh, no."

"We need to investigate as soon as we can. But there's a problem."

"If you are trying to recruit an assault force, you've got the wrong man," Matt let him know. "I'm in the turn-the-other-cheek business."

"No. Not you two anyway. According to Patty, these guys are armed to the teeth, and there are at least a half dozen of them. This is way too big for my department. That's why I need your help."

"We'll do what we can, Sheriff." Doc McAdams was ready.

"Doc, I want you to tell the state medical examiner about the bones and the mass grave, and how we can't get to it because the area is occupied by a gang suspected of murder and kidnapping."

"I know the ME well enough to do that. Went to med school with his father. Come to think of it, I'm his

Godfather. But what is he supposed to do about it?"

"Tell him to call the governor, let him know about the mass grave. And you Matt...."

"Call the governor now."

"Exactly. You know him."

"He's my cousin. We used visit each other as kids for weeks at a time. I can get through to him."

"Good. Tell him that there's an armed gang which has set up in an old summer camp in Allen County. That they definitely kidnapped a local girl and are suspected of murdering her mother. That there are more than six of them, and they're heavily armed. Then tell him you're afraid the local sheriff might attempt to arrest them himself, with only one deputy to assist him."

"My apparent goal is to keep you from being slaughtered, then."

"Such a graphic term. I just don't want to be cut down in my prime."

"Too late for that, Sheriff," Doc McAdams observed.

"No respect. You guys really picked up on deputy conduct fast."

The tension broke, but Matt still had to ask "Any chance you might try to take them on yourself?"

"That's Plan Z."

CHAPTER 55

Cobblers' Knob, Vermont
Friday, April 15, 2017, 3:26 PM EDT

At his desk, Sheriff Roy finished the call on his cell phone. It was the second one this afternoon. He looked immensely pleased with himself. "Deputies, let's take a walk." That was unexpected. "Leave your cell phones in the office." That was *really* unexpected.

But that's what they did. After putting the answering machine on. They walked over to the courthouse and slipped right through the unattended scanner at the entrance. It was only used when the circuit judge was sitting. Then they hit the vending machines just off the lobby for snacks. The Sheriff was buying.

"You know we have food at the office." Tess reminded him.

"We're here for the privacy." He looked around. No one else was in sight. Friday afternoons were not exactly rush hour at the Allen County Courthouse. He began to crunch NECCO wafers. "Should have known they'd get stale in the machine."

"Why do you always buy them then?" Lucas inquired.

"Loyalty to local business. NECCO stands for New England Candy Company."

"At last, the name makes sense," Lucas volunteered.

"I believe you said something about privacy," Tess prompted.

"From now on, we assume that the office is bugged and the telephone is tapped. We're up against an enemy with formidable resources. Even outdoor conversations could be snatched right out of the air."

His deputies took a moment to digest that, along with their candy bars.

"Mounds," the Sheriff observed Tess eating. "Coconut is the asbestos of the fruit world. Catches in your throat."

"Thanks for that, Sheriff.," Tess responded. But she kept eating.

"What about our cell phones?" Lucas inquired.

"We're getting new ones from George's Hardware. The Robinson boy, Earl, is fixing us up with some untraceable burn phones. Won't be smart phones, like you both favor. I guess they'll be dumb phones. But you will use them for all matters concerning Camp Bethany, the pit there, Necklan's Lake and Patty Martin. If in doubt, use the burn phone. And remember that your half of the conversation can be picked up in the office or outside by eavesdropping equipment."

"Is this necessary?" Tess couldn't believe what she was hearing.

"We'll only find out if we don't do it. And then we'll wish we had." Sheriff Roy paused. "There's more. You can still use your regular cell phones for other matters. In fact, you should. That way no one will know you've got a second phone. But, the NSA can turn your cell phone on without you knowing it and hear whatever you say. So keep your regular cell phones where they won't hear anything we don't want them to. Tess, you can keep yours in your purse at all times when not it use. Lucas, it's closed desk drawers and glove boxes for us, I guess. Don't think the good citizens of Cobblers' Knob are ready for law enforcement men carrying purses."

"Wasn't planning to start anytime soon," Lucas commented drily.

"And they can track them too. So don't take it any place you don't want to be followed."

"When do we get these burn phones?" Tess asked.

"They'll be ready by five o'clock today. Tess, you can drive over to the hardware store to pick them up in a little while. Be discreet. Don't let anyone see what you're getting. Earl's been told to keep it quiet."

"I suppose you deputized him," Lucas wondered.

"That I did," Sheriff Roy admitted. "Tess, call him Deputy Earl, as long as no one can hear you."

"Poor geek must be thrilled out of his mind," Lucas noted.

"That's no way to talk about a fellow deputy," Sheriff Roy admonished.

"You've deputized half the county, Sheriff, and the other half's waiting."

"As long as we don't have to pay them all." Sheriff Roy turned to address his other real deputy. "Tess, the first call you make on your new phone should be to Lucy. Before you return to the office. Tell her the people after Patty should be moving on in a few days. Ask her if she can keep Patty at her house until then. And I mean inside her house, dressed like a boy. Give her your new phone number and tell her to forget the old one. And no further contact with either of them till I say so."

"O.K., Sheriff. What have you done?" Tess asked point blank.

He glanced around. They were still alone amidst the vending machines. Folks would be getting their snacks elsewhere on a Friday afternoon. "I'm taking the DoD public."

"Uh, how's that work?" Lucas asked.

"The state medical examiner has told the governor about the mass grave. And the armed trespassers at Camp Bethany, whose presence is preventing investigation of the site. It has also been brought to the governor's attention that some of these same trespassers probably kidnapped a young girl and are suspects in a murder investigation." He crossed his arms and leaned back against the wall, a satisfied look on his face.

Tess recovered first, possibly because she couldn't be fired. "Why didn't you just nuke 'em?"

"Saving those for Independence Day."

Lucas had recovered. "What is our role in this --- exercise?" He'd almost said "charade."

"Undetermined, so far. But it's just getting started. I'm going to suggest that we advise whoever is sent about how to approach the DoD agents. Then we step back."

"Do we tell them that they're dealing with federal agents?" Tess wondered.

"We don't really know that, do we? If they are federal agents, I'm sure it will come up during the introductions."

Her frown gradually morphed into a smile.

Lucas was actually chuckling. "You sure know how to throw a party, Sheriff."

"But won't the DoD pull rank?"

"Won't matter. I figure they'll skulk off once their operation has been uncovered. And the state medical examiner's team will be moving right onto the site to investigate the pit. Can't see them hanging around for that, seeing how they put the bodies in it in the first place."

"Wow, Sheriff." Lucas liked the plan.

"Think it'll go down like that?" Tess asked.

"Seldom does, but I believe we will rid ourselves of the DoD — at least for the time being."

"If this works, I might just kiss you on the cheek."

"I'll just buy you a beer," Lucas volunteered.

"That's a relief."

"But only during Happy Hour," Lucas cautioned.

"Bless your stingy heart."

Tess laughed, and it spread. It was relief. They headed back to the office.

CHAPTER 56

Cobblers' Knob, Vermont

Saturday, April 16, 2017, 10:07 AM EDT

Even though it was Saturday morning, none of them had any place else they wanted to be. Tess was showing the Sheriff how to set up the speed dial on his new cell phone. For simplicity, they were all going to be set the same.

1 - Sheriff Roy

2 - Deputy Lucas, and

3 - Deputy Tess.

So if Tess were to pick up Lucas' phone, she'd know the speed dial settings without having to think about it. It was Sheriff Roy's idea, even though he had needed help to implement it. Tess had, once again, been impressed by his ability to foresee potential problems and eliminate them before they could occur.

She doubted that any metropolitan police department would have come up with it. Too many people, too many opinions. She briefly thought of Einstein sailing his boat when it was calm, and smiled to herself.

They sat around the office, fiddling with their new phones and drinking coffee until the Sheriff's new cell phone emitted several shrill beeps. "Can I help you?" No mention of his name or of the Sheriff's department. "Why yes, I'd love to attend." He listened some more, then offered "Can I bring anything?" The conversation ended with "I'll be there."

The Sheriff pointed toward the door and quietly put his old cell phone down on his desk, watching to see that his deputies did the same. The courthouse was closed for the weekend. So he led them to the rear exit door, and opened it with his key. "We need to be eating snacks from the vending machines when we leave," he advised them. "I hope one of you has some change."

When they reached the vending machines, he simply said "Seven AM tomorrow. They'll be driving through the entrance to Camp Bethany in force. They'll stop for anyone they see, but some will proceed straight to the cabin no matter what. We're to wait at the entrance in case someone shows up. In other words, they don't want us along."

"Fine by me," Lucas said. "I'd rather not have the DoD mad at me."

"Me too." Sheriff Roy agreed. "Both sides outrank us. Let them work it out."

"What about the kidnapping charge?" Tess wanted to know.

"We don't know which of them did it. Could be someone who's moved on. Couldn't make a case without testimony from Patty. That's kind of the opposite of hiding her."

"Murder?"

"All we've got so far is a body with a suspicious bruise. And the victim was an alcoholic old woman who might just have fallen down the stairs. And the only suspects are federal agents. Not exactly a prosecutor's dream."

"Put that way, I guess not."

"Any idea when the state will release the body?"

Lucas asked.

"Not until next week."

"When can we tell Patty?" Tess asked.

"Tell her what?"

"Oh. That her mother fell down the stairs and broke her neck, I guess."

"You're getting the idea, but I don't think it should be you. You know too much."

"How about Lucy?"

"So does she. Besides, why would she know about it?" the Sheriff asked. "No. I was thinking Matt, our minister. At least he wasn't at the scene. And giving comfort to the bereaved is part of his job description anyway."

"Perfect choice, Sheriff."

Lucas bought a package of six powdered mini-doughnuts from the machine. "To complement the coffee," he explained.

Sheriff Roy led his deputies back to the office. As they entered, he explained to Tess "Law enforcement is just part of the job in a small town."

"So I'm learning."

"And there are some functions that combine the two, like providing security for the Senior Prom."

"I'd like to do that," Tess volunteered. "When is it?"

"Next Saturday."

"So soon?"

"Lucy realized that the final exam scores were impacted by the prom. The scores improved once the Senior Prom was moved ahead a month."

"Smart lady."

"And then some," the Sheriff agreed.

"So can I work it?"

"Assignments have already been made," Sheriff Roy decreed.

"Damn it, Sheriff, you sound like this was New York City! It's only the three of us!"

Lucas laughed. The Sheriff smiled sheepishly, but stuck to his bureaucratic guns. "Don't see any reason to change the assignments. I suspect you still want to investigate the massacre."

That was part of it, Tess admitted to herself.

Lucas surprised them by pointing out that the prom had originally been scheduled for Saturday, April

30th when the assignments had been made. It had been changed to Saturday, April 23rd after the baseball team unexpectedly made the state finals game to be played in the capital on the 30th. "Really got better things to do on the 23rd. I've made plans."

"Done, then. But you will be able to work on Sunday, right?" Sheriff Roy asked rhetorically.

"No problem, sheriff."

"Well Tess, looks like it's going to be the two of us."

"Think we can squeeze in a dance?"

"Don't see why not," he admitted.

"Can you Charleston?" Lucas asked.

"Not without bruising my knees," she admitted.

"He's kidding," said the Sheriff.

"True. But our Sheriff and the fetching principal always show the kids a step or two," Lucas explained. "Best let her have at him first. Give him a chance to practice. Might save you from a stomped foot."

"Sounds like good advice," Tess agreed.

"All part of the protect and serve thing."

"I'm going out on patrol. Lucas, you'll be relieving me at five o'clock. Tess, you're not on duty today; so I'll see you tomorrow morning at Camp Bethany. Last one to leave the office closes up."

"We'll finish the doughnuts first," Lucas said.

"Only to prevent them from getting stale, of course," Tess added.

"Your dedication is overwhelming," the Sheriff observed as he left.

As Sheriff Roy's car pulled out of the lot, the telephone rang. Deputy Lucas, whose mouth was currently occupied by the bulk of a doughnut, nodded to Tess.

"Allen County Sheriff," she answered briskly, as she noted the unfamiliar number of the incoming call.

"Could I speak with the Sheriff?" She recognized Lucy Thornton's voice, but remained professional.

"He just left. I'm Deputy Chandler. Can I assist you?"

"Oh. This is Principal Thornton. I was just calling to remind him about the Senior Prom. I'm at my office, catching up, and had a note to remind him that it's this Saturday at 8:00 PM."

"Then you'll be pleased to know that the Sheriff has already made the assignments. He and I will be attending."

"Glad to hear it. That's one more thing off the endless list."

"Should we be in uniform?"

"No need for that. Everybody knows the Sheriff. And since you've been in town more than a week, they probably know who you are, as well."

"Well, then?"

"Sheriff Roy always wears a sport coat. Hmm."

"What?"

"I just pictured him in it, and he always looks the same. He's either got several similar jackets or he trots the same one out every year."

Tess held back a laugh. "Maybe you can put a mark on it; so you can check next year."

"I may just do that, Deputy," Lucy said. "You should just dress up a bit, as long as it's something easy to dance in."

"Sounds like soft duty, principal."

"From your lips to God's ears, Deputy."

"Any other advice?"

"Stay away from the punch."

"No drinking on duty. Got it."

"That about covers it then. I guess I'll see you at the prom."

"I'm looking forward to it, Principal."

"Sounded innocuous," Sparks commented, after hearing the conversation that was heard throughout the cabin.

"But, it's Saturday," declared the Captain. "And she could have called next week."

Sparks was surprised, but said nothing.

Captain made his case. "Not just that, but the whole tone of the conversation indicated a friendship, not just business."

"Point taken, Captain. Should we follow up?"

"I think so. Shouldn't be hard to track down the school principal. Especially if she's still at the school. It's not like we have any other leads."

"I'll get someone over there now. Then I'll get a photo of her driver's license."

"Get her automobile registration too. Easier to identify her car in the lot than her face. Have them follow her, but loosely, since we'll have her address."

"Aye, aye."

"How long has it been since you left the Navy?"

"Going on four nautical years, Captain."

"Stow it, sailor." But he was grinning.

It was great to have a lead.

CHAPTER 57

Cobblers' Knob, Vermont

Sunday, April 17, 2017, 1:22 AM EDT

The sound from the kitchen told Lucy that Patty was raiding the larder again. She wondered at her metabolism that allowed her to eat pretty much constantly and not gain an ounce. Lucy began to drift off again.

Was that the back door?

Lucy was out of bed and into her slippers in a heartbeat, a mature adult heartbeat — not exactly a flash. She moved quickly through the open bedroom door and turned toward the stairs. And into the vicious blow to her solar plexus that doubled her over, unable to breathe. A huge hand on the back of her neck pushed her hard against the wood floor. Unable to move, she felt her ankles being taped together.

Her arms were roughly pulled behind her back and secured together with a plastic zip tie. Then a dark fabric sack was put over her head, the drawstrings tightened uncomfortably. *Trussed.*

Then came the hypodermic needle, jammed into her arm without pity. The last thing she remembered was being lifted like a feather and thrown over a large shoulder for the trip down the stairs.

Lucy awoke in a bed. Not so much a bed as a bunk. That must have been it, because she was staring at the underside of a top bunk. The wall next to her was logs. A bare light bulb hung from the ceiling. *A cabin.*

The sack had been removed from her head. But she was lying on her back, unable to look around. Once she had taken in the view available to her, she closed her eyes to concentrate on her other senses. Taste told her she had been drugged, hardly a revelation. Strange how you could taste something that had never been in your mouth. The musty smell more or less confirmed the rustic cabin. Touch wasn't a factor. Her hands appeared to be tied to the supports for the upper bunk. A half-hearted attempt to move her legs indicated a similar arrangement binding her feet. *At least I'm still in my nightgown.*

Hearing was the only useful sense left to her. There was the low throbbing hum of a generator, a large one. There were hushed voices, some shuffling of feet. Someone was typing intermittently on a computer keyboard. Someone was approaching.

"The old one's awake."

The old one! Must be me.

"Check the girl."

"Stirring."

"Wake her up."

"What?" Patty said. She wasn't yet able to form a sentence. "Hey."

"Good morning, Patty."

"Who?"

"You Patty. Me Tarzan."

Other men chuckled. *At least three of them.*

"Hand me an ice cube."

"Just one?"

"Should be enough."

Lucy heard an ice chest being opened and closed.

"Hey!" Patty shouted. "What are you doing?"

"Waking you up."

"Stop it, you freak!"

"But it's working so well," the voice taunted.

"No! Stop!"

"Are you awake?"

"Yes, damn it! Stop!" she shouted.

"But it hasn't melted yet...."

"I'm awake! Wasn't that the idea?"

"Then say something intelligent."

"How did you find me?"

"That's good," the man decided. "If you'd bothered to close your robe when you raided the fridge, we'd have thought you were a boy. But you didn't."

"I didn't know you were out there."

"That was the point. Nice boobs, by the way. Seems a shame...."

"I'm not afraid to die," she announced defiantly.

"Of course, you're not. Death is just an abstract concept to you now. I'm going to give you a sample. Who knows? A few hours from now, you may be begging to die."

"What do you want?"

"The truth, Patty."

"O.K...." Tentative.

"About the night of your Senior Prom. Specifically what happened at Necklan's Lake."

"I don't remember anything about that night. Doctors told me that if I didn't remember after a year, I probably never would."

"Medicine is called the healing art. That's art, not science. Doctors are wrong. Often."

"That means they're right often too."

"I suppose it does. My job is to find out what you know about that night anyway."

"Are you going to torture me?" she asked with false bravado.

"If necessary, yes," he replied calmly. "It is one of my special talents. However, we can start slowly to give you a chance to fully recall that night before we arrive at the point where your recovery is no longer an option. You see, you are in the unfortunate position of being expendable. Not a healthy place to be."

"You're not the first to ask me. I've tried to remember, really. I just can't," she sobbed.

"Did anyone ever try hypnosis?"

"Yes," she answered. "It didn't work."

"Well, we're going to try again tonight. It's a technique known as enhanced hypnosis."

"Enhanced?"

"As in drug-induced. It starts with a syringe. But the real enhanced part has nothing to do with the drugs. It employs fear. And if that doesn't work, we move on to terror. And then there's the pain that comes with bodily harm. It's progressive, you see. If your memory hasn't been sufficiently revived by then, we can move on to removal of eyeballs, amputation, disembowelment — just a whole bunch of nasty things you don't want to happen. I say this to encourage you to be forthcoming."

"Because you really don't want to do them?"

"No," he chuckled. "Because they're messy as Hell."

"Oh." *Didn't like that answer.*

"So, let's get started, shall we?"

"Do I have a choice?"

"Don't waste my time," he growled. "Gentlemen,

move the victim to the table and secure her by her hands and feet."

"Remove the robe?"

"Yes."

"Using sodium pentothal?" Captain asked.

"No. That just makes people want to talk, but they can be led to say whatever you want. Handy for a confession. Tonight we're going straight to the hard stuff."

Lucy heard Patty being positioned on the table.

"But I can't remember...."

CHAPTER 58

Necklan's Lake, Vermont
Sunday, April 17, 2017, 6:54 AM EDT

Everyone was there, but the Vermont State Police weren't going to move in before the appointed hour of 7:00 AM. They were sticklers for adherence to the plan. So, three SUV-loads of SWAT forces in their Darth Vader outfits, backed by a medical van with a trauma team, seemingly had nothing to do but to intimidate the Sheriff in his old Jeep. After making it clear for the tenth time that local law enforcement was to remain behind at the entrance to Camp Bethany, they finally moved in.

Sheriff Roy swung into action. He and his two deputies drove down the road to the first bend; so they couldn't be seen from the entrance. He pulled the Jeep sideways across the road to block it and turned on the rack of modern flashing gumballs. "Lucas, I want you and your rifle concealed over there. So you can cover me, the vehicle and a good twenty-five feet up the road toward the entrance."

"Tree?"

"If suitable. But not too high. I want you to have mobility in case we need it. The usual hand signals. Warning shot first, if there's time." Lucas headed into the woods. "Tess, I want you over there, well concealed, but near the drive. Make sure to get a position far enough back up the road to avoid being in Lucas' line of fire. Somewhere that you can clearly see what's going on here at the Jeep. You take the second rifle from the Jeep and your Glock."

"What do I do after that?"

"You are our last line of defense. If either Lucas or I get into it with anyone, you remain in place and watch carefully."

"Aw, Sheriff...."

"Now listen. This is important," he admonished. "If Lucas and I get taken, you remain still. Be patient. I'll want them to think there's nobody else. Then they'll drop their guards. And you can come to our rescue. But only if they're all together and we're not in the line of fire. That last part's real important, by the way."

"What if I'm challenged?"

"If there's any indication that lethal force is about to be directed at any of us, fire at the chest. If the barrel of your weapon tends to rise when fired, adjust downward accordingly. Don't hesitate. Don't analyze. Just react. Your only edge will be the element of surprise. Use it. It won't last a second."

"O.K.," she said. Her eyes were a bit wider than normal.

"If you have to fire, keep firing. Don't assume the others will surrender. That's not likely. Be prepared to take them all out. That's the default setting for these guys."

"Got it."

"On the other hand, if we're all just chatting, just keep yourself hidden and observe."

"I've never shot anyone before."

"Let's hope you can say that this afternoon. But don't plan on it. That would slow you down."

"O.K.," Tess said without conviction. "Good luck, Sheriff." She ambled down the road, scouting places for concealment.

"Same to you, Deputy." *That girl's got guts.*

Suddenly she broke into a run, hiding quickly.

The Sheriff heard a car approaching. He positioned himself behind the open driver's door of the Jeep, shotgun in hand. The best way to avoid a confrontation is to appear ready for it.

A gray Explorer rounded the curve and applied the brakes. Two men in front exchanged words, then the passenger emerged to approach the Sheriff.

"What's going on?"

"Crime scene down the road. Trying to preserve it till the forensics team arrives."

"Really? Some kind of accident?" All innocent curiosity. The guy was good.

"That's what they'll try to find out. Not for me to say." The party line. Then, "What's your business here?"

Sheriff Roy could see the fellow's mind working, deciding whether to pull out the badge. "Our business can probably wait. Any idea when they'll be done?"

"Sorry, I'm not in that loop. Why don't you come back tomorrow?"

"Might be best. Let me just check with my partner."

"Sure. Invite him over."

That had clearly not been his plan, but he waved casually to the driver to join them. Then he explained what the Sheriff had disclosed. It was clear that the passenger was in charge; so the discussion had been a ruse, a delaying tactic.

"We really need to get in today, Sheriff. The sooner the better."

"I have my orders, gentlemen." The Sheriff wasn't budging. "You're welcome to wait, but I'd recommend grabbing some breakfast and then checking in later. Maybe some lunch too."

"What if we just drove around your car and promised not to disturb your crime scene?"

Sheriff Roy raised his left arm. A bullet hit the ground a foot in front of the two agents. Both reacted nicely.

"You gentlemen just got lucky," Sheriff Roy confided. "My deputy is an inconsistent shot. Next one might hurt."

"We'll be back," the passenger growled as they retreated to their vehicle.

"See you then," the Sheriff responded jovially. Then he hollered "Hold your positions until I say to come out." Just in case the men in the Explorer decided to come right back.

That went well.

CHAPTER 59

Necklan's Lake, Vermont

Sunday, April 17, 2017, 7:08 AM EDT

"Vermont State Police! Open the door now!"

Captain shouted "Be right there. Have some ID ready." He looked over at Patty Martin, tied to a table, and hooked up to an IV line. There was no way in Hell he could explain that. Then there was the principal, tied to a bunk bed in her nighty, duct tape over her mouth. He made a command decision as he strode toward the door. "Coming."

Captain had intended to blast through the door and confront them with his Department of Defense credentials. That's not how it went down. He was a step from the door, badge in hand, when Patty screamed.

The cabin door imploded, ripped from its hinges, and carried him with it. It landed on top of him. His credentials flew under a corner bunk. The SWAT team charged into the cabin, guns drawn.

"Vermont State Police! On your knees now! Hands behind your heads. No talking!" Glancing around at the two women, the leader continued, "You are under arrest! You have the right to remain silent...."

Some men are so arrogant that they think they're invulnerable. "Hold it!" one of them shouted, as he reached for his credentials. "We're on the same...."

A hailstorm of bullets tore through his chest.

"Cease fire!" came the order, as the remaining DoD men dropped to their knees in compliance. "Cuff 'em!"

"You're going to regret this."

"Shut up while I read you your rights. You are under arrest. You have the right to remain silent...."

The other members of the SWAT team secured their DoD captives' hands behind their backs with zip ties. Then one called in the medics to treat the women. There was nothing to be done medically for the man who had been shot in the chest. The man under the door was still unconcious.

"This girl has been interrogated and tortured. But I don't see any life-threatening wounds."

One of the SWAT team casually spat on a DoD agent. "Oops. Didn't notice you there."

"The other lady doesn't appear to have been tortured. Drugged maybe."

That was when Lucille Thornton suddenly arched her back from the pain.

"Code Blue! Bring the paddles! Stat!"

During the medical pandemonium that followed, Lucy's heart was restarted and she was stabilized.

"Nearest hospital! Now! The Sheriff can direct you. Pick him up on the way out."

"The girl?"

"Take her too! What's keeping you?"

By the time the ambulance reached the St. Johnsbury Regional Hospital, Patty was awake and worrying over Lucy. Sheriff Roy was busy barking the directions to the Emergency Room entrance. Lucy was mildly sedated. The acute pain was gone. The anticoagulants were working.

The DoD agents were taken to the Vermont State Police barracks for individual interrogations. Their mouths had been taped shut until then. The FBI had not been notified because the kidnapping appeared to have been confined to a single state.

The Chief State Prosecutor had forgone his usual church services to attend. He was dictating a list of potential charges to his hungover paralegal. "Two counts of kidnapping with all the lesser included charges. One count of first degree murder. Trespassing. Conspiracy all around. Maybe RICO if they were looking to profit, but we would have to have ironclad proof of that. Otherwise, forget it. Resisting arrest?"

"The man who did that didn't survive, sir."

"Oh." He hadn't heard that. "Then forget resisting arrest — as a charge. We can still use it to justify the need for a SWAT team at trial though."

"Why would that be necessary?"

"The defense always alleges use of excessive force, even when it's irrelevant. It creates sympathy for the defendants."

"I see," the paralegal replied. "What about witnesses?"

"We have the two women who were kidnapped. One is a school principal. Should be credible as Hell."

"If she makes it...."

"What?"

"She had a heart attack during the rescue, sir. We don't know her status."

"Well, find out."

"Yes, sir." The paralegal pulled out his smart phone.

CHAPTER 60

Necklan's Lake, Vermont
Sunday, April 17, 2017, 9:42 AM EDT

The Sheriff had ordered Deputies Lucas and Tess to remain at the gate to Camp Bethany to discourage anyone from attempting to enter.

Tess had asked if she should offer to show the state police the pit. The Sheriff had told her to let them find it themselves. "It will make it more exciting for them," he'd explained. When she hadn't responded, he'd added "That translates into more vigorous prosecution. Human nature."

The Vermont Bureau of Criminal Investigation was scouring the cabin and surrounding area. It wasn't long before they found the pit.

"It's a mass grave!"

"Get out of there. Don't touch anything else. Get the Medical Examiner here. Tell him what we've found and to bring a team. But first, contact the interrogation team and tell them. They're probably still at it. They need to know about this."

"Found something in the cabin, sir. It was in a corner, under a bunk. Didn't catch it on the initial sweep. It may have been in the hand of the man who got in the way of the cabin door. Thought you should see it."

The search leader looked at the proffered leather wallet with foreboding. He opened it as if the contents might bite him. Which they did --- figuratively.

"Department of Defense? Holy crap! Make sure the interrogators...." He stopped. "No. Nobody says anything about this to anyone for now. We don't know its significance. Could have been there for months. Might have nothing to do with the suspects in custody." He'd always reverted to proper law enforcement language when making questionable decisions.

"But, if these guys are feds...."

"Then they'll probably tell us, sooner or later. But maybe not. Maybe they're hiding something."

"Like what?"

"Could have had nothing to do with their employment."

"You think it's a black op?" he asked, clearly excited by the prospect.

"That's the CIA. So, no. But it could be a sideline. Or an legitimate operation gone wrong. Be interesting to see how they play it. That is, if they are DoD."

"Yes, sir."

CHAPTER 61

St. Johnsbury, Vermont

Sunday, April 17, 2017, 11:53 AM EDT

Doc McAdams had joined Sheriff Roy at the hospital. As Lucy's primary care physician, he'd brought along her case file. This had allowed him to contribute to the discussion of what procedures might be appropriate. It also allowed him to tell the Sheriff that there would be no open-heart surgery for Lucy. "So stop worrying, and find us something to eat."

It wasn't long before Matt arrived. He encountered Sheriff Roy just as he'd embarked on his journey of culinary discovery. Together they drove the official Jeep toward an interchange with Interstate 91. There was always fast food at these places. If the Sheriff didn't crash the car before they found one.

"Calm the Hell down!" advised the Lord's representative to Cobblers' Knob, as he scanned the dashboard in front of him for confirmation of the existence of a passenger side air bag. He really didn't believe Hell was a location, even a celestial one. He thought it was more of a situation. "If Doc McAdams told you she's going to be all right, then she will be."

The Sheriff slowed to 55 mph. "Right. Got to trust Doc." He said it like he really wanted to believe it. "It's just that I can't imagine Cobblers' Knob without Lucy."

"And *vice versa*."

"What?"

"It's Latin for she cares about you too. You hadn't noticed?"

Sheriff Roy thought a moment. "She did buy me a beer at *Rachel's*...."

Matt smiled. "See? Just like Romeo and Juliet."

The Sheriff grinned back at him. "Cobblers' Knob version."

"Exactly. So what are you going to do about it?"

"Well, Rita Hayworth hasn't returned my calls...."

"She's dead, Roy. Sorry to be the bearer of sad

tidings."

"That's just an excuse. Everyone lies in Hollywood."

"Either way, Sheriff, you need to move on — while you still can."

"I don't know if it would work. We're both pretty set in our ways."

"Well then, why don't you just go to a movie? And try not ask for her hand in marriage, at least until they roll the credits at the end."

"She likes Paul Newman. I'm more of a John Wayne guy."

"I don't think that will be an obstacle."

"Maybe I could take her to that *Rocky* movie that they show at the multiplex on Saturday nights. That's Stallone, right?"

"I think I see a Burger King ahead on the left."

By the time they returned to the hospital, Patty was in a private room. She was a bundle of bandages, but she smiled when they came in. The smile grew when she saw the burger bag.

"How are you feeling?" asked Sheriff Roy.

"Hungry."

"You look like a mummy." He tossed her a cheeseburger, which she unwrapped greedily.

"Thanks."

"You remember our preacher, Pastor Matt?"

"Just Matt. I'm not ordained."

"Yes. He visited me at Wellston."

"That I did, but you were...uncommunicative. Nice to hear your voice, Patty." He stepped closer to observe her many bandages. "What happened to the other guy?" It was an old joke. So Patty didn't recognize it.

"They shot him dead. He deserved it." She was serious.

"Well, such decisions are supposed to be.... Did he do all this to you?"

"He cut me. He burned me. He shocked me. He gave me drugs that made me convulse. He waterboarded me. He...."

"Probably deserved to die," Matt agreed.

"What did he want to know?" asked the Sheriff.

"He wanted me to tell him what I saw at Necklan's

Lake on prom night."

"What did you tell him?"

"That I didn't remember what happened." Her smile had been banished.

"You know what, Patty? That might be a good thing. If you'd remembered, he might have killed you and Lucy Thornton."

"I think he might have anyway."

"But you kept him busy until the state police arrived. He never had the opportunity."

That was a new concept. It took a moment to get her head around it. "In that case, I kept him occupied long enough to get him killed."

"It wasn't your fault."

"Fault? I'd like to claim *credit* for it." She turned to Matt. "Is that bad, Pastor Matt?"

"No, it's not," he proclaimed. "But it's certainly Old Testament."

The Sheriff smiled at this, but Patty challenged Matt. "The Book of Leviticus sets forth the proposition that the punishment should fit the crime. He should have been tortured to death."

"Point taken," he conceded. "On the other hand, you aren't dead. But vengeance is mine, thus sayeth the Lord."

"I never said *I* wanted to kill him."

Sheriff Roy stepped in. "You read the Book of Leviticus?"

"I read the entire Bible. I had lots of time to read at Wellston."

"What version?" Matt asked.

"Not King James. This one was in English."

"Then I congratulate you," Matt said. "That takes determination."

"Thank you. And it sure does," she confirmed.

"Would you consider leading a Bible study group at the church?" Matt inquired.

"Me? I'm not qualified."

"Neither am I, in terms of credentials. But here I am."

"I don't know. I mean I just resumed talking a few months ago. Public speaking is another thing altogether."

"Why don't you just join a study group then, and we'll see who becomes the leader?"

She thought for about fifteen seconds before replying. "That could work, but don't introduce me as an expert."

"You'll be God's ringer."

"God has ringers?" the Sheriff wondered aloud.

"I like the sound of that. Like Esther."

"Oh, she's good," Matt said to Sheriff Roy.

Patty smiled at that. "Got any fries?"

"Real good," Matt said as he handed her a small box of French fries and two ketchup packets.

"Enjoy your fries, Patty. I've got to leave," Sheriff Roy said. "Tess will be around later."

"What about Lucy?"

"She's going to be in intensive care overnight. Maybe you can see her tomorrow."

"I'm leaving now too, but I'll try to get back later. Should I bring you a Bible?"

"There's one in the bedside stand already. A Carolyn McCray novel would be better."

"You crave even more action, then?"

"Not as a participant. Thank you."

"I'll see what I can do."

They met up with Doc McAdams outside the main operating room. "The surgeon inserted a stent into her aorta to prevent another embolism from causing cardiac arrest."

They really tried to look like they understood, but must have failed. Doc sighed, and tried again.

"They put a small slinky in her artery to keep it from closing."

"Oh. How long will it be there?"

"Eternity, I suppose. That's more up Matt's alley than mine."

"Eternity works for me," Matt concurred. "Barring cremation, of course."

"Recovery time is minimal, but she'll be under observation here for a few days. The main complication would be infection. If none occurs, I want her out before the weekend."

"So she can attend the Senior Prom?" Sheriff Roy asked hopefully.

"So the weekend staff doesn't kill her."

"Oh. Good to know," the Sheriff said.

"We appreciate you being here to run interference for the ladies and to keep us informed in a way we can understand," Matt added.

"Glad to help you, not to mention my patients." Then he added "Was this what you were worried about when you brought Patty to the veterinary clinic that night?"

"Pretty much. Thought we had it covered though. Guess the bad guys got lucky," Sheriff Roy explained. "They found her at Lucy's, looking like a boy. Guess they weren't fooled."

"That explains the haircut," Doc deduced.

Matt spoke. "I don't expect, even as a duly sworn deputy, to be completely in the loop on this. It's O.K. with me. But, with all this going on, how did Patty react to the news about her mother?"

Doc McAdams looked at the Sheriff.

"Ah. It's good that you brought that up."

"You haven't told her?"

"Not yet. We just found her, you know. But now might be the time to do so," the Sheriff suggested. "But since we don't have the results of the state autopsy, I don't see any point suggesting it might have been a homicide. We don't have proof, and she's been through a lot already."

After a few moments, both men nodded their agreement.

"If the autopsy states the probable cause of death to be intentional homicide, we have to tell her then. I don't want to lie to her. Matt, why don't you tell Patty? You weren't at the scene; so you don't have any first-hand knowledge of the grim circumstances."

"It's also part of my job description."

"Yes. There's that."

"We'll wait here," Doc McAdams said. "In case you need us."

They weren't completely abandoning him. Not officially.

CHAPTER 62

Burlington, Vermont

Sunday, April 17, 2017, 12:41 PM EDT

"Lawyered up. Every one of them," the voice on the phone said.

"Thanks." Chief State Prosecutor Leigh disconnected the call. "That was the non-surprise of the day."

"Are we done here then?" his paralegal wondered. He was sure that a few more hours in the rack would dramatically improve his outlook on life.

"Not yet. Given the suspects' Department of Defense credentials, I expect it to be an interesting afternoon. I don't believe that the DoD has the right to kidnap and torture United States citizens on U.S. soil for *any* reason. But I have a feeling some Pentagon attorney is going to try to convince me otherwise --- soon. So scramble your associates and get me a summary of law on this issue."

"Not a brief?"

"Might need one tomorrow, but concentrate on a summary today. Is there any federal law that would override the right of the State of Vermont to prosecute kidnappers who abducted and assaulted two residents of Vermont completely within the geographical boundaries of the State of Vermont? Even if said kidnappers were engaged in an authorized project that was in some way tangential to the kidnapping? That's how to frame the issue."

"Put that way, they don't have a chance." Hungover or not, the paralegal was becoming interested in this case.

"It's called advocacy," his boss explained. "They've probably heard of it in Washington too. So start making those calls."

"Yes, sir!"

"Did you call that number they found at the cabin?"

"Yes. 321-433-1561. I called it twice. A stern

woman's voice advises the caller to provide an authorization code before you can proceed. If you haven't punched it in within a few seconds, it disconnects. She's real serious about it."

"Sounds right," he figured. "I want a draft by 2:00 PM sharp."

"Computer or hard copy?"

"Both."

"Dumb question, I guess...."

"To be an effective advocate, you're going to have to anticipate what other people want from an event. What they plan to take away from it."

"Thank you, sir. Excuse me, while I rally the research team."

"Everything comes through you. You're to coordinate the effort, review the work in progress and put the draft together."

The call came before the prosecutor had completely read the draft summary of law. He hadn't even looked at the cases cited yet. He would have to trust his researchers regarding their applicability. He smiled, not because of the legal precedents in his favor. He'd been taught to smile in the face of adversity.

"Prosecutor Q. Franklin Leigh." He pronounced his last name as Lee. "To whom am I speaking?"

"This is the Attorney General."

"Jeff? Doesn't sound like you."

"Of the United States," the man said. "I apologize for any lack of clarity. I'm usually dealing with people who recognize my voice."

This guy is good. Made me feel like an idiot, then reminded me I wasn't part of the big picture. And I don't even know how to address him.

"What's on your mind today, sir?" *As if I shouldn't be bothered with his trifles.*

"I had hoped you might have an inkling, but since you obviously don't, I'll try to bring you up to speed on events.

"Please proceed then."

"Your state police have abducted and restrained ranking employees of a federal agency without cause or proper jurisdiction." The Attorney General had paused for effect, but Chief Prosecutor Leigh moved into the silence.

"That's not quite accurate. They shot and killed one of your agents while he was resisting arrest."

"What?" the Attorney General asked, furious that he hadn't known.

Who's the one without an inkling now, big shot?

"He ignored the order to put his hands behind his head. Instead, he reached for his pocket. There were three automatic weapons pointed at him. He was either brave or delusional."

"He was unarmed," the Attorney General assumed.

"He did not even claim to be unarmed. And he was standing at a table full of knives and other instruments of torture that he obviously knew how to use. You see, they caught him in the act of torturing a half-naked young girl." It was irrelevant to why the man had been killed, but Leigh wanted to get it on the record. He felt good that he'd been able to.

"So your men killed the torturer?"

"They aren't my men, sir. They are members of the Vermont State Police, including the Bureau of Criminal Investigation."

"Where are the survivors of this reckless raid being

held?"

"The suspects are presently at the state police barracks at Burlington, awaiting their respective attorneys for interrogation to commence. The local judges require that attorneys who appear of record be members of the Vermont Bar Association. It's an integrated bar."

"Is there an airport there?"

"Burlington *International* Airport, airline code BTV, offers daily commercial flights on several major airlines to New York, Boston, Toronto and other important destinations. There may even be one to Washington." *Take that!*

"Good. I'm sending a team to pick up the survivors."

"I hope they enjoy their stays. We try to be hospitable to visitors. And, give them time to pack. The suspects can't be released until the arraignment hearing tomorrow. And the subsequent bail hearing, which is usually several days after that. That's if bail is set, which is doubtful because you've just informed me that you intend to have them removed from our jurisdiction. Never telegraph your punches."

"Then I'll let you guess what is going to happen next. Here's a hint. You won't like it."

"Then thank you for the warning and the stimulating conversation."

The line had gone dead before he'd finished.

Oh, boy! If a man is known by his enemies, I'm about to become famous.

He motioned for his paralegal to come in. "Time to move on to the brief. We're going to need cases denying bail. He made it clear that the suspects will be removed from Vermont as soon as possible. That makes them flight risks."

"He told you that?"

"Word for word."

"Who is this bozo?"

"The Attorney General of the United States. Himself. Unlike here, it's a political appointment."

"What's he going to do?"

"Send a team to extract the suspects. But don't take that to mean he's going to break them out of jail."

"What then?"

"I think he'll try to by-pass our state judicial system

entirely. Go into federal court. Emergency hearing. He'll select a friendly judge and show up with an intimidating retinue, maybe a letter from the Secretary of Defense as well. And I'll just be a voice on the speaker phone. *Habeas corpus.*"

"But Vermont has jurisdiction," he protested.

"You've been reading the Constitution. Read *Wickard vs. Filburn* before you prepare the brief. The federal government will assume jurisdiction on one pretext or another. Then Vermont will have to appeal. That's a losing situation. An *expensive* losing situation."

"Are you telling me the wrong side won the Civil War?"

That was a surprising comment, but he got it. "It's called the War Between the States in the South. They didn't believe there was a federal government as we think of it. As they saw it, the *national* government was more of a customs union and defense alliance."

"So the war wasn't about slavery?"

"Is that what they taught you in school?"

"Pretty much, sir."

"Then ask yourself how Lincoln got elected before

the country divided. He was not an Abolitionist. Not that he was a fan of slavery, but he knew that the economy of the South depended on the plantation system --- which rested squarely upon the institution of slavery. His goal was to reunite the nation in a viable condition. But after the war had thoroughly decimated the South, he knew that could never happen. The damage was done. So he issued the Emancipation Proclamation, freeing the slaves."

"It makes sense."

"Check it out. After you finish the brief."

Alone in his office, Chief Prosecutor Leigh made a call to the state police to let them know that the FBI or another agency might show up to liberate the suspects. It was a longshot, but he was passing along a warning from a credible source. And every police chief in America knew that the FBI had acted in a similar manner in the case of Barry Seal. He suggested that they be moved to a secret facility which was part of the state police properties. The knowledge of where they had been moved should be known to as few as possible. The officers who participated in the move should not return to Burlington, but remain unavailable. Prosecutor Leigh did not want to know any details. Nor did he want anyone in his office to know where or even *whether* they had been moved. Complete deniability, in case a federal judge questioned him under oath.

Then he requested state police protection at his home. Like most Americans, he feared the excesses of the federal executive branch.

Look what they'd done to that girl. *Res ipsa loquitur.* It speaks for itself.

CHAPTER 63

Burlington, Vermont

Sunday, April 17, 2017, 3:46 PM EDT

Damn, he'd moved fast!

"Good afternoon, Prosecutor Leigh. This is Judge Randolph of the United States District Court in Burlington."

"Good afternoon, Your Honor. What can I do for you?"

"I have before me a petition for *Habeas Corpus* which has been prepared by the staff of the Attorney General for my immediate consideration. It bears his electronic signature and was presented in person by the Assistant Attorney General, who made the trip to Burlington to present it to me. He brought several staff attorneys with him."

"So I'm outnumbered."

"That could be an understatement," Judge Randolph commented. "Are you anywhere near the Federal Building over on Elmwood?"

"I could be there in half an hour if I don't need a suit and tie."

"We're not too formal here on Sundays," he remarked drily. "I'll tell them to let you in. Come to my chambers. Bring your research. I'm going to decide this one today, if I can."

"I understand, sir. I'm on my way."

"Thank you."

Of course, Judge Randolph was no stranger to Prosecutor Leigh, even though they worked in different legal systems. Burlington was too small for them not to have been acquainted. But they didn't belong to the same club or play golf together. Nor did the Judge know his nickname: "Quite," as in Quite Frank Leigh. There would be no hometown advantage for the Prosecutor.

This was underscored by the very formal reception he received at the federal courthouse a short time later.

But the judge was obviously intent upon conveying the message that there would be no favoritism in his court. Introductions were made around the polished walnut conference table. But before the Assistant AG could begin, Judge Randolph turned to the court reporter. "Madame Court Reporter, kindly leave the room while we briefly discuss this matter off the record."

She complied, leaving her equipment in place.

"Now gentlemen, I have acquainted myself with the federal government's case and understand this to be a matter of great importance to the Attorney General. I have also read the persuasive summary of law submitted electronically by the Prosecutor's office. And I can't bring myself to believe that the kidnapping and torture of a young woman was an integral part of a legitimate Department of Defense operation."

The Assistant AG stirred, but held his tongue.

"But, it's not my first day on the job. I don't believe for a minute that the issue will be resolved by a denial of the petition for *Habeas Corpus*. To the contrary, I would expect an immediate appeal and further escalation. And quite frankly, gentlemen, I hate to subject the American public to the spectacle of the Department of Defense engaged in a tug-of-war with the State of Vermont over several government employees who are alleged to have committed heinous acts. So we're going to have a chat to determine if that outcome can be avoided."

"Now, Prosecutor, I understand that the person alleged to have been the torturer is dead."

"They killed him, Your Honor." The Assistant AG had lost his grip upon his tongue.

"Resisting arrest, Your Honor," Prosecutor Leigh rejoined.

"Gentlemen, you have failed to grasp the concept. This is not the time for argument. All that is relevant is that the accused torturer is dead. Is that the case, Prosecutor?"

"That appears to be the case, Your Honor."

"Then I request that you consider dropping all charges related to the alleged torture as part of a package of concessions to be elicited from *both* sides. I don't want an answer now. Just consider it."

Prosecutor Leigh nodded, as non-committally as he could.

"I am going to proceed on the assumption that the State will agree if we reach some other common ground today. I am not looking to settle this matter, but to streamline it and make it efficient. And return it to the state courts of Vermont, where it belongs. So, I am requesting that the Department of Defense advise me which of the men being held actively participated in the alleged kidnapping."

"The men who removed Ms. Martin from the facility at Wellston were not kidnapping her. They had the legal right to take her, You Honor."

"Assuming for the purposes of this discussion that to be the case, then the persons to whom I refer would be the men who abducted her from the home of the local school principal, taking her along as well. That would include the men who planned and oversaw the alleged kidnapping."

The Assistant AG looked to his companions. One of them handed him a note. "We believe that these are the three persons involved in the alleged kidnapping, You Honor. We would need to be able to confirm this when we can talk to the men being held. He handed the list over to the judge."

"That is understandable. You will be able to confer with them prior to the arraignment tomorrow. You can accompany their local counsel. I assume you've arranged for local counsel. We'll call this a tentative list until then. Please remain mindful of the fact that both ladies have seen the faces of their abductors and can probably identify them. I will abide no chicanery."

"Quite so. And we have arranged for local counsel, Your Honor."

His Honor turned to face Prosecutor Leigh.

"I can't tell you how many times I've seen the prosecution attempt to ensnare everyone associated with a crime, only to have the jury acquit them all because the case against the peripheral suspects was so weak. So I am going to suggest that you drop the kidnapping charges against the men who did not actively participate in the actual abduction."

"But they're accessories after the fact, You Honor."

"Acting under orders, as well. But this isn't Nuremberg. So think about it," His Honor admonished. "Also forget any ideas about the felony murder rule."

The Assistant AG provided the information. "If the State of Vermont drops all charges against those who did not participate in the planning and execution of the kidnappings, that would leave just three suspects in custody, to be arraigned."

The Judge Randolph said "I'm asking you to agree to have them submit to arraignment and a bail hearing for each. Perhaps you will be able to agree upon a recommended bail amount to present to the judge. In any event, the Prosecutor would not oppose bail."

"What if either of the women who were kidnapped has been permanently injured or dies?" Prosecutor Leigh asked.

"Any deal we make here today is based upon the restoration of both women to full health. It's a basic material premise. If either of them dies before the trial commences, we will endeavor to amend our stipulation accordingly. Should we fail to do so, it will no longer be valid."

The Assistant AG had been thinking. "I've been told that the project these men were working on is highly sensitive, top secret. It can't be made public, Your

Honor."

"Keeping them quiet about this project is the job of the Department of Defense and the trial attorneys. But I think both sides should agree in advance that the project itself is irrelevant to the kidnapping charges, and therefore off limits as to discovery and testimony."

"If the defendants take the stand, they will be asked about their employment," Prosecutor Leigh pointed out.

"You're going to have to stipulate that they work for the federal government and that the nature of their employment is irrelevant. You don't need me for these details," the judge said. Then he added "Besides that, they may jump bail...."

"I've considered that possibility," Prosecutor Leigh offered. "In that case, the bondsmen would send out bounty hunters, but the State wouldn't pursue it."

"I guess the Department of Defense will have to post cash bonds, then," the judge concluded.

The Assistant AG nodded glumly. He had no doubt they would jump bail. That was the plan.

"I'm going to recall the court reporter to take down

the stipulation we have just made. If I leave out anything, let me know. But please wait until I've finished."

Prosecutor Leigh was amazed. He'd conceded away the torture charges and agreed to free all but three of the alleged kidnappers. Yet, he'd won! He'd still bring kidnapping charges, do his job. Of course they might jump bail and disappear before trial. So he had to push for a high number on the bail. To punish the Department of Defense, if nothing else.

He might not get a conviction, but he'd teach the feds that they couldn't run roughshod over Vermont. That was enough.

CHAPTER 64

St. Johnsbury, Vermont
Sunday, April 17, 2017, 6:22 PM EDT

Tess had brought candy. Lots of it. Different brands. She hadn't known what Patty liked. But everyone liked some kind of candy. Zero bars, 3 Musketeers, Baby Ruths, Tootsie Rolls, Snickers, Mounds, Hershey's dark and milk chocolate, with and without almonds, Crunch, Dove with raspberry and with orange. She'd also brought York Peppermint Patties, Dots, Scotties, Jelly Bellies, Gummi Bears, Allsorts, Jolly Ranchers, chocolate covered cherries, Maple and Vanilla Buns, toffee and three flavors of fudge. She had been salivating in her car on the way to the hospital. "Don't let Patty be a diabetic," she'd pleaded to no one in particular.

It turned out that Patty liked all of them, although

she had never tried some of them before. Generous contributions were made to the hospital staff when it had become clear that there would be plenty left over.

They spoke limited French and laughed a lot while they sampled the different varieties. Occasionally, one of them would act like she was sampling a fine wine at a wine tasting, sniffing the candy first, rolling it around in the mouth — but never spitting it out. Perish the thought!

Somewhere during the evening, they invented the chocolate-covered jelly bean. Then they decided to un-invent it, because mankind wasn't ready for it. Couldn't handle it. In the midst of this frivolity....

"Did you know my mother died?"

"What?" Tess had heard the question. It was just so completely out of context that she couldn't believe she'd heard correctly.

"Pastor Matt told me my mother died last week. Did you know?"

"Yes, Patty. I did." Honesty is always easier than prevarication.

"Why didn't you say anything?"

Tess paused to gather her words. "In spite of our

friendship, I still feel like a stranger here. I never met your mother." *Technically correct.* "I was told that Pastor Matt would break the news to you. That seemed right. You know, appropriate. Then, of course, you were kidnapped. And I couldn't have told you anyway. And when we found you, there was so much going on...."

Patty wanted to be convinced, but still had doubts. "But you went to the house and got my clothes...."

That was the implied question Tess had been dreading. *What had Patty been told about the time of death?*

"Yes, I did," Tess stalled. Then she went for it. "Your mother had already passed."

"I wish you'd have let me know."

"I guess I should have," Tess conceded. "I'm sorry."

"Wait! How did you get in?"

"The Sheriff let me in. I'm a cop, remember?" *Also technically true.*

"Oh yeah." Patty thought for a minute, then asked "She fell down the stairs?"

"That's what I heard." Tess knew that wasn't enough. "Did Pastor Matt mention the autopsy?"

"State law that persons who die alone must be autopsied to confirm it was a natural death."

"It's probably a good policy, in general," Tess opined.

"You know, she lived on the first floor. Never went upstairs."

"I heard she'd set up a bedroom in the dining room. Why did she do that?"

"She had problems keeping her balance. Some inner ear thing that couldn't be fixed medically. At least not in Cobblers' Knob. The alcohol had to be a problem too. Messed up her coordination. So, she was afraid to take the stairs."

"But there are stairs to the front and back doors," Tess commented.

"Not so many in the back, where she parked her car. And she'd had railings installed on both sides."

"Well, she must have needed something that had been left upstairs."

"I guess so." But Patty had more to say. "She drank too much. Pretty much all the time. And I couldn't make her stop. Hell! I didn't even want to go home any more."

"Don't do that to yourself. You'd been through a lot. You were still fragile. You didn't need to contend with those problems at home until you were better."

"I was selfish. I used Wellston like a spa."

"It must've worked. You recovered. That was the idea, wasn't it?"

"Yeah. I guess it was," she admitted. "But I feel like I should have tried to help my mother, even though it probably wouldn't have worked out."

"You needed to heal yourself before you could help anybody else, Patty."

"That's about what Pastor Matt said." Then she added "More eloquently, of course."

Tess smiled. *"Se claire.* But, of course."

"I wonder what chocolate-covered peanut butter fudge tastes like."

"Sounds delicious!"

They resumed their concocting.

Chocolate-covered peanut butter fudge turned out to be incredible.

"This stuff can't be legal!"

CHAPTER 65

Burlington, Vermont

Monday, April 18, 2017, 8:58 AM EDT

Tess decided she had a sugar hangover. Plus, the overdose of chocolate had made sleeping difficult. Attempts at conversation with Sheriff Roy in the car on the way over had pretty much ended with "Did you ever have a chocolate-covered jelly bean?"

The Sheriff had responded by quoting someone called Ogden Nash. A poem about a purple cow, of all things. That had been the last nail in the conversational coffin.

Now they sat in a courtroom, waiting for the arraignments to begin. Their presence was unofficial. They sat with the public, which appeared to comprise the relatives and friends of the various accused. Amid the tears, there were whispers about the alleged crimes and how bail might be arranged. It was substantially less than cheerful, but it was new to Tess. And it was an essential step in the criminal justice system she longed to be part of. So she paid close attention.

By the fourth arraignment, she'd decided she'd learned all there was to know. After another forty-eight minutes, the judge instructed the bailiff to clear the courtroom. Sheriff Roy stood up, but made no move to leave. He indicated that Tess should stand, as well.

"Your Honor," he said. "I'm Allen County Sheriff Leroy Hughes. This is my deputy. We investigated the kidnapping case and participated in the capture of the defendants. If you would let us remain, it would avoid us having to catch up later outside in the hallway."

"It's a privilege to have you both in my courtroom. You may remain." After he had made this ruling, he'd asked the attorneys "Any objections?" This was obviously a formality. No one had objected.

Once the spectators had left, the judge asked counsel to step forward with their clients, who were wearing business suits, but were shackled --- which diminished the sartorial impact considerably.

"Criminal Case No. 2017-793, Defendant Ross Mansfield, Charge of Kidnapping and lesser included offenses. How does the defendant plead?"

"The defendant pleads Not Guilty, Your Honor, and requests that bail be set at the earliest time convenient to the Court."

"Noted for the record."

Tess figured out the "the Court" meant "the Judge." There was a lot of ritual involved. And "Ritual" might mean "Bull," she thought, but reserved judgment on the issue.

Two other kidnapping defendants were similarly arraigned. Then the judge called the session to a close.

"All rise," shouted the bailiff, as the judge exited stage right.

"What about the others?" Tess asked the Sheriff.

"Must have made some kind of deal." He waved to Prosecutor Leigh, who indicated he would meet them outside.

"I'm Sheriff Roy Hughes and this is Deputy Tess

Chandler, who's interning with us from Dartmouth. She's majoring in Forensic Science. She's been involved with this case from the beginning. Been a big help."

"Pleased to meet you both. I'm State Prosecutor Frank Leigh. I suppose you're wondering why there are only three defendants...."

"It did come as a surprise."

He looked around to make sure no one was within hearing distance.

"The man accused of torturing Ms. Martin died at the scene. The federal government threatened to make a case of excessive force over that. The Attorney General of the United States told me that himself yesterday. Then he filed a *Habeas Corpus* petition in federal court. Sent up an attorney from Washington immediately. There's a lot of interest in this case."

"The participation of the other men was determined to be peripheral to the kidnapping and the other charges. We could have charged them as being accessories after the fact, but frankly, we just wanted the perpetrators. Makes for a cleaner case, easier to present to a jury. So we struck a deal at the Federal Building yesterday which allowed the State of Vermont to go forward with its kidnapping case against the three men who were arraigned today, in return for dropping all charges against the others. And the threat of excessive force went away."

"Wow," Tess said softly.

"It's legal realism in action. Don't see enough of it any more." The Prosecutor turned his full attention to Tess. "Bet they didn't cover that at Dartmouth."

"Actually, it was mentioned. But it was an abstract concept until now."

"When do you graduate?"

"At the end of the summer session. There was a course I wanted that wasn't offered until then."

"How would you like to work for the State of Vermont?"

"What would I do?" she wondered.

"Investigate cases that are sent to us by law enforcement. Determine whether the cases are solid enough for us to proceed. Whether there is a likelihood of conviction. I know there's a rumor that prosecutors won't take cases they might lose, but there's more to it than that. The State has limited funds and prosecutions cost money. The Governor doesn't like to waste it."

"I appreciate the offer, sir...."

"Think about it. You'd learn how the prosecution works before you had to find out the hard way."

"The man has a valid point, Tess," Sheriff Roy interjected. "And it would look great on your résumé."

"I don't think I'd want to do it permanently," Tess explained.

"The person you'd be replacing will probably come back from maternity leave by next Spring," Prosecutor Leigh said. "She's come back before. Then you can stay or leave. With your new experience."

"It's sounding like an opportunity I shouldn't pass up. Can I call you in a few days?"

"Call my office manager, Sybil Green. Here's my card. I'll tell her to expect a call from Deputy Tess Chandler. You'll have to be approved by Human Resources. It's part of the bureaucracy we contend with these days. But, don't worry. It's just a formality. Contingent upon you graduating, of course."

"Sounds like the fix is in," the Sheriff ventured.

Tess was appalled.

But Prosecutor Leigh chuckled. "Except it's not a race. She's the only entry."

"My kind of odds, Prosecutor," Sheriff Roy replied.

"Thank you so much, Prosecutor Leigh. I was wondering what to do next after graduating. This sounds ideal."

"Then I look forward to working with you next fall, Deputy Chandler."

"So, are you going to convict those DoD agents?" the Sheriff wanted to know.

"I'm sure going to try, Sheriff. The next step is to get bail set as high as I can. It appears that the Department of Defense is going to provide the funds needed in cash; so they'll probably make bail no matter what. After that, well — it's going to be interesting."

"You mean they might jump bail?" Tess asked.

"They might be *ordered* to. Even though they did stray pretty far off the reservation."

"What would happen then?" Sheriff Roy asked.

"With no bondsman, there'd be no bounty hunter tracking them down...."

"What about the Vermont State Police?"

"If they're stupid enough to come back to Vermont and get caught, they'll be arrested and held for trial without bail. Otherwise, that's it I'm afraid."

"Doesn't seem fair," Tess commented.

"It's not about fairness. It's about justice. We don't have a fairness system, Deputy."

"Understood, sir. Another abstract concept just became real."

CHAPTER 66

St. Johnsbury, Vermont

Monday, April 18, 2017, 11:54 AM EDT

"You up for a little detour to the hospital, Deputy?"

"Absolutely, Sheriff. We may be able to visit Lucy by now."

"That's what I thought. She might need some cheering up."

But Lucy was her feisty self already.

After Tess had left them to go visit Patty, Sheriff Roy suggested "When you get out, I'd like to see more of you."

"You're not likely to see any more of me than you can while I'm wearing this hospital gown. Drafty little thing!"

Feisty, all right.

The Sheriff rebooted his approach. "What I meant was that we might spend a bit more time together."

She just stared at him.

"Go out for dinner. Maybe a movie. That sort of thing."

She appeared to be considering it. "No hanky-panky?"

Sheriff Roy actually blushed. "Ah, just dinner. Maybe a movie."

Lucy sighed. "A girl can dream, I guess."

He had no idea how to respond. So he evaded. "Just give it some thought. No rush."

"Easy for you to say. You're not the one who just had the heart attack."

"Lucy, the doctors fixed the problem. You're good to go, as they say."

"And what about you?"

"Well, I guess the warranty has expired by now. But Doc McAdams thinks I'm good for lot more miles."

"That's a terrible metaphor, Leroy," Lucy said.

"Maybe you could help me with that."

"Aha! You have an ulterior motive for asking me out."

"I guess I do," he admitted. "I thought about you not being around any more. I didn't like it."

"I reached a similar conclusion," she said. "And decided I needed to liven things up a bit."

"Does the humble Sheriff of Allen County have a part in that?"

"I might get a motorcycle."

O.K. Way past feisty.

This was so far beyond dinner and a movie that the Sheriff went blank. "Oh," was the only response he could muster.

"You could get one too, Roy. Then you wouldn't have to ride behind me, hanging onto my breasts to keep from falling off."

"Doesn't sound so bad...."

"Which doesn't sound bad?"

"They both sound pretty good." *Wait! Not the right response.* "I think I'd prefer my own bike, though."

Meanwhile, in another part of the hospital, Patty

was discussing her new life with Tess. "So the first thing I have to do is get back to the house and put it in shape. No idea how long that will take."

"Will you move in right away?"

"No sense delaying it. I'll work outward from my bedroom, doing what needs immediate attention." Patty continued "Then I have to find my place in society --- as they say when they mean get a job."

"What about college? Had you applied before graduation?"

"No. I'd planned to stay around town, at least for a while."

"Doing what?"

"Whatever I could find. Maybe secretary or receptionist. I know my way around a computer, thanks to my neighbor Fred. Or at least I did. Probably need to catch up a bit now."

"Maybe Earl can help," Tess suggested.

"George's Hardware?"

"You paid attention."

"You never know when useful information might enter the conversation."

"I don't mean to pry...."

"You're a cop. Go for it."

"Do you stand to inherit anything besides the house and the car?"

"No idea, but I'm not planning to buy a yacht any time soon."

"If you change your mind, can I have a ride on it?"

"Tess, you can have a stateroom."

Tess remembered that Patty had been institutionalized for a long time. "You do know how to drive, don't you?"

"I took Drivers' Ed. Passed it. I've got a license somewhere. But I'm out of practice."

"As in potential menace to the highways?"

"Probably," Patty admitted. "But I'll stay off the freeways at first."

"Not much of a challenge around here."

"Do cars still have that round thingy in the front seat?"

"Your mother's car has just such a device — a steering wheel, I believe it's called."

"That's it! You know your automotive vehicles,

Deputy."

"Would you like for me to drive you home from the hospital when they release you?"

"I'd appreciate that. Perhaps you could show me how to start the car, too."

"I'd be honored to."

"Which?'

"Both."

"I don't have the car key; so it might not be easy." Patty frowned. "Come to think of it, I don't have a key to the house either."

"Relax. Your local sheriff's deputy has that covered."

"You do come in handy at times."

"That she does," Sheriff Roy agreed as he entered the room. "Good to see you on the mend, Patty. You're going to have to excuse us. We've got to get back to the office before Deputy Lucas decides he's in charge."

In the Jeep, Tess was silent.

"What's on your mind, Deputy?"

"What will happen to Patty?"

"She'll be safe enough. After all the light that's been put on her abduction, she might be the person least likely to be kidnapped in all of Vermont."

"You really think so?"

"Yes, I do. And Lucy will keep tabs on her. Feel better?"

"There are still so many unanswered questions."

"That investigation is over. At least for us. The state Medical Examiner has it now. I assume they'll use DNA testing to identify the remains."

"But what happened to the Seniors?"

"There are more questions than answers, Tess. We may never know the answer to that one."

"I think Lucas knows." *What did I just blurt out?*

"Our Lucas?"

"I shouldn't have said that."

"But you did. You can't un-say it," he pointed out. "So, what gave you that idea?"

"It's kind of a long story, but Lucas was the one with Patty at Necklan's Lake that night."

"I thought I told you to stop investigating."

"You did," she confirmed. "And *I* did. But the

information just kept coming, and I couldn't ignore it."

"Did you ask Lucas? Just Yes or No," the Sheriff added hastily. "I want a one-word answer."

"Yes."

"Did he deny it. Same rules."

"No."

"You couldn't have just finished your internship and gone back to college without telling me?"

"I tried, Sheriff. Sorry. I didn't mean to complicate your life. I like you. I like Lucas too."

"So why didn't you leave well enough alone?"

"Didn't seem to fit the job description, Sheriff. Especially since you'd assigned me the cold case."

"And now you've solved it?"

"Not by a longshot, Sheriff," Tess admitted. "I still have no idea what happened to the rest of the Seniors that night."

"Lucas didn't tell you?"

"All he would say was that it happened fast, while he and Patty were hidden in the rocks in the lake. Like there was nothing he could have done to stop it."

"So he might not have been able to see what was

going on?"

"That's the impression he gave," she said. "As you suggested, I went swimming there at night --- with Deputy Lucas. If he and Patty stayed behind the rocks, hidden, they wouldn't have seen what was happening on shore. They'd have heard the shouts, of course."

"You think that's what might have happened? He didn't see?"

"He didn't *look*. Didn't want to be seen. But, you tell me. He's your deputy. What would he do in those circumstances? What should he have done?"

"That might be a good way to approach it. Was he armed at the time?"

"No. He was naked, too."

"Oh, my. Didn't need to know that." Sheriff Roy thought a moment. "He was with Patty Martin at the time?"

"Yes. Also naked."

Sheriff Roy cringed at the image. "I see. Under those circumstances his training would have dictated that he do what he could to save her and himself from a threat that appeared to be overwhelming. Any other action on his part would have been reckless."

"I hadn't thought of it that way. But you're right, of course. He did say that he'd saved Patty's life that night. He believes that."

"Lucas couldn't accurately identify the nature of the threat. Especially since it came from some secret DoD project --- although he didn't know that at the time."

"So you think Lucas did the right thing?"

"In the situation as you've described it. There didn't seem to be any other viable options, Tess."

"So why didn't he tell you this himself?"

"There's more to Lucas than meets the eye. I think you've seen this yourself," Sheriff Roy began. "I think it has to do with Patty Martin. He couldn't tell his story without incriminating her. And he knew that telling it wouldn't solve the case, because he hadn't seen enough. And he wasn't even my deputy then. So why do it?"

"So you condone his silence?"

He took a minute to reply. "I guess I do."

"Then so do I." *But I still suspect Lucas knew what was going on.*

They had fallen silent after that.

"So what did Lucy have to say after I left?"

"She's thinking about getting a motorcycle. I suspect you had a hand in that."

"What?"

"Thinks I should get one too."

"Sheriff, that would be great. I was worried that she'd become one of those people who become ultra-cautious after a heart attack."

"No worries there, Deputy."

"I guess not. Well, I can teach you how to ride one."

"That might be a good idea. I've ridden a bicycle, of course."

"Lesson One: Don't pedal."

"Starting with the basics, are we?"

"Yes, indeed, Sheriff. Don't want to put local law enforcement at undue risk."

"I appreciate that."

"Just doing my civic duty."

CHAPTER 67

Burlington, Vermont

Tuesday, April 19, 2017, 8:59 AM EDT

The court session had yet to begin.

"I hope this is the end of it," Sheriff Roy whispered to Tess. "Getting up an hour earlier than usual is a lot harder than it used to be."

"At least there wasn't a foot of snow on the road. Or black ice."

"I hate black ice," he said. "One minute you're sailing along without a care in the world, and the next you're fully engaged in trying to make a ton of machinery defy the laws of inertia."

"Hear ye, hear ye! The Superior Court of the County of Chittenden is now in session, Judge Wilson presiding. All rise." His Honor gathered his robes and ascended his throne. He glanced around the court room. It appeared everyone was assembled and ready. He gave the gavel a sharp rap to begin the bail hearing.

There had been no stipulation as to the amount.

Prosecutor Leigh began by introducing himself for the record. "Your Honor, what I say now applies equally to all three of the defendants in this case of alleged kidnapping. All three of them are presently employed by a federal government agency. The nature of this work is not relevant to this case. Furthermore, it is subject to stipulated gag order issued by the federal court. Normally, such employment would argue against the defendants being flight risks. However, I have been advised personally that they will leave the State of Vermont. I have no reason to doubt my source."

Judge Wilson interrupted. "Can you reveal your source?"

"If defense counsel has no objection...."

"Objection, Your Honor!"

"Sidebar, gentlemen."

The attorneys approached the bench.

"What are your grounds for objecting?"

"I'm sure Your Honor is aware of the federal court stipulation limiting the evidence to be presented in this trial."

"That's not an answer, but I confirm that I am familiar with it. Proceed."

"The identity of the prosecution's source is protected by that stipulation."

"I disagree, Your Honor. That person has no direct relationship with the employer of the defendants or with the work they were engaged in."

"Is that true?"

"They are both employees of the federal government, in the executive branch."

"That's the connection?"

"Yes, Your Honor."

"Then why don't *you* tell me who it is? So I don't have to overrule your objection."

"The defense withdraws the objection Your Honor, but requests that the identity not be disclosed in open court."

"It will still be on the record."

"Understood."

"Well, Prosecutor?"

"The source is the Attorney General of the United States, Your Honor."

Judge Wilson expressed surprise, then amusement. "I believe that you have a credible source. Please proceed."

The parties resumed their pre-sidebar positions. "The stipulation states that the prosecution can not oppose bail, but does not restrict its efforts to set it high enough to discourage flight."

The defense attorney nodded his agreement. He was less than cheerful.

"Given the resources available to the defendants' employer, the State proposes that bail be set at One Hundred Million Dollars each."

Judge Wilson had expected a large number. But this was beyond large. "That is an unprecedented amount, Prosecutor."

"These are unprecedented circumstances, Your Honor."

"Please resume your seat, Prosecutor. I imagine counsel for the defense feels the need to contribute to the discussion."

"Yes, Your Honor, we do. It is not the intent of the defense to call into question the veracity of the Prosecutor. The defense has confirmed that the conversation did take place and that it could not have been characterized as friendly. The Attorney General did indicate that he might send a team to pick up the surviving members of the raid by the Vermont State Police. Those survivors included the defendants before the Court today. But the Attorney General had just been informed that one of the government employees had been killed in that raid. His comment was a reaction to that shocking news. But it was just a conversation. And it occurred *before* the hearing in federal court, at which time a number of issues were settled amicably."

"But bail was not one of those issues, I take it ," Judge Wilson ventured.

"Actually, bail was discussed. And it was stipulated that the prosecution would not contest the granting of bail."

"Let me stop you for a moment, counselor." The Judge turned to the Prosecutor. "Do you agree with the defense so far?"

"The facts, yes. The spin, no."

"Proceed then."

"After having stipulated to allow bail, the prosecution is attempting to deny it *de facto* by requesting an impossible amount. That violates the spirit of the stipulation, Your Honor."

"Prosecutor?"

"That is not the prosecution's intent, Your Honor. The only goal here is to set bail in an amount that will reduce the likelihood that the defendants will leave the jurisdiction and fail to appear for trial. A great deal of thought went into this request. Given the resources of the defendants' mutual employer, One Hundred Million Dollars each might just be enough. But there is only one way to find out."

"Does the defense have an amount in mind? An amount that will take into consideration the resources of the defendants?"

"We do, Your Honor. We have researched Vermont case law and determined that the highest bail ever to be set that was upheld on appeal was Five Million Dollars.

And that gentleman owned a jet aircraft and maintained a home in Brazil."

"Any response to that, Prosecutor?"

"The defendants' employer has single-use weapons that cost that much, Your Honor."

"Thank you, gentlemen, for your stimulating arguments. I intend to set bail in the same amount for each defendant, since neither of you has raised any argument against that approach. Bail is hereby set in the amount of Seven Million Dollars each. You are dismissed."

"Hear ye, hear ye. All rise."

"Wow," Tess said. "Who won?"

"The judge," replied Sheriff Roy. "As usual."

"Prosecutor Leigh doesn't look too unhappy."

"He came in a close second."

They'd congratulated Prosecutor Leigh before they left, and Tess had confirmed her intent to accept employment in his office after graduation.

Then they had stopped off at the hospital again. Lucy had become somewhat mobile overnight. She greeted them from a chair, instead of a bed. She wore real pajamas and a robe. Her hair was brushed. She glowed. Sheriff Roy was smitten by her.

"Looks like I'll need a ride home Friday afternoon," she announced. "Not on a motorcycle — yet." Somehow she managed to stare at both of them at the same time.

"I'll bring the Beetle then," Tess replied after it became clear that she should be the one to volunteer.

"Oh, dear. I had one a long time ago."

"They've come a long way, Lucy. It even has air conditioning."

"Then I insist on being conveyed in your VW, Tess. I need to keep up with the times."

Patty joined them at that point and advised that *she* would need a ride home tomorrow afternoon.

"The Allen County Sheriff & Jitney Service is at your disposal ladies," the Sheriff assured them. "Express service to Metropolitan Cobblers' Knob and points north."

"He's trying to keep me away from the office," Tess explained.

"Nay, fair Deputy. "Tis noble duty that calls thee from thy throne and venerable desk."

"Cut it out, Hamlet," Lucy said. But she was smiling.

"Your wish is my command, m'lady." And he closed his mouth as though he might never open it again.

Lucy rolled her eyes dramatically.

Patty giggled. "I'll call you when they give me a time," she said to Tess.

"Then add an hour," Lucy advised. "They don't just open the door and wave good-bye."

CHAPTER 68

Cobblers' Knob, Vermont
Wednesday, April 20, 2017, 2:27 PM EDT

"On my own. With a house and a car. It's a bit overwhelming!" Patty said.

Tess was driving. "You didn't mention money."

"That's because I don't have any. The hospital was curious about that too."

"I'll bet they were."

"A long time ago, my mother and I set up a joint account at the local bank branch. I doubt that she ever changed that."

"Maybe we should check that out on the way home. Money's kind of handy."

"You know, I've been living without it for so long, I sort of forgot about it. At least as it applied to me. I guess it's time for me to practice capitalism again."

"Socialism has become *passé* here in New England."

"*Ouí.*"

"I didn't mean to start speaking French. I don't know if I can even do it while driving," Tess admitted.

"O.K. Concentrate on driving then." Patty then went on to say "You know, it's kind of fun to ride in a car without being tied up or injured."

"You have an interesting perspective on the subject," Tess commented. "Which bank is it?"

"There's more than one now?"

"Boom times in Cobblers' Knob, I guess."

"Sure," Patty replied, drily. "It's Merrimac Savings."

"Right downtown," Tess said. "Next stop."

A bank officer confirmed the existence of the joint money market account and requested to see Patty's identification. Of course, everyone in town had heard about the lone survivor of the Necklan's Lake Massacre. Patty had a certain celebrity status in the region. So her lack of photo ID was easily surmounted by Tess displaying her badge and vouching for her.

"What's the balance?" Patty asked.

The officer tapped on the computer keyboard, then smiled. "It's $48,853.21," she announced. Scrolling down the page, she continued "It appears that there have been no withdrawals for several years. So the direct deposit social security payments and interest just kept adding up. Of course, social security will stop now that your mother has passed away. In fact, they may even reclaim part of the final payment. They're quite precise in their bookkeeping," she added with a hint of approval.

Patty walked out with Three Hundred Dollars and a smile. Once she presented her driver's license, she would be issued a debit card. The bank's records indicated that checks had been issued. Patty was encouraged to look for them.

"And I was about to offer to lend you money," Tess commented.

"That was a nice surprise. I'm going to try to conserve it."

They entered the house through the front door. To Tess' immense relief, there was nothing unusual to be seen. No crime tape. No body outline on the floor. No blood.

Patty went right upstairs to her room. "It's creepy here without her. She's always been here."

"You'll get used to it."

"I don't know. After living in one room, it seems so big. Maybe I'll sell it and get an apartment."

"Think about it awhile. You've got time. There's no mortgage, right?"

"Never was. At least not in my lifetime. She inherited this place from her parents."

"That's good. So where are you going to start?"

"I need to get my bedroom in order first if I'm going to stay here. After that, I don't know."

"I suggest you check out the refrigerator first. Could be green milk or festering vegetables."

"You've done this before."

"College roommate had a mini fridge. She unplugged it when she left, but forgot to remove her yogurt. It had turned all fuzzy by the time I found it."

"To the refrigerator, then."

Once the refrigerator contents had been vetted, they sought out Mrs. Martin's records, many of which were still upstairs in a battered old metal file cabinet. The more recent records were in a bureau drawer in the bedroom that had been established in the former dining room.

Apparently she had been a *functioning* alcoholic, tending to her affairs in the morning before imbibing away the rest of the day. Matters seemed to be in order. Her income taxes had been reported and paid for the previous year. That was a good sign. It also appeared that she had visited her records on the second floor recently, which supported the theory that she might be returning down the stairs when she fell to her death.

But no records could be found related to Patty's injuries or rehab. No newspaper clippings. No medical bills. Nothing about insurance payments, or any other kind. It was as if Patty had ceased to exist on the night of the Senior Prom. In fact, the section of the file drawer after a cardboard divider marked "P" was completely empty. Tess knew the Sheriff would find this interesting.

With a promise to come back later and take Patty to dinner at *Rachel's,* Tess left. She went straight to the Sheriff's office to report. What had become a small act of kindness had become part of the investigation. Tess was beginning to understand how law enforcement could become a 24-hour a day job.

CHAPTER 69

Cobblers' Knob, Vermont

Wednesday, April 20, 2017, 5:47 PM EDT

"This is what's known as a restaurant," Tess advised Patty as she pulled the Beetle into *Rachel's* parking lot.

"Roadhouse is more like it," Patty corrected. "But the burgers are great. At least they used to be."

"They still are. The mushroom and Swiss cheeseburger is amazing."

"Where do I sign up?"

They were seated at a rustic wooden booth when the waitress approached. "What can I get you two to drink?"

"Draft lager for me," Patty replied, handing her

driver's license to the waitress as she ordered. After a look from Tess, she said "It's been years."

"Same here," Tess ordered. The waitress went on her way.

"You disapprove?"

"No. I just have trouble remembering that you're an adult. That's all."

"It's O.K. So do I. It's like I've been dropped into adulthood with no preparation."

"Join the club. College is about as artificial an environment as Wellston."

"At least you get a degree at the end."

"There's definitely that."

"I got kidnapped."

"Well, that's more interesting than a graduation ceremony. Certainly more colorful. Makes a better story."

"Actually, I was kidnapped twice," she reflected.

"That's like a Master's Degree in kidnapping," Tess figured.

"Must be worth something...."

"Know what?" Tess became excited. "It could be. Victims Reparations."

"What's that?"

"It's when the guilty party is ordered to pay compensation to the victim of his crime. I can't believe I just thought of it."

"Do these guys have money?"

"Oh, yeah. Bail was set at Seven Million Dollars --- each. And they'll probably raise it."

"Do I know how to pick 'em, or what?"

"Don't get sassy, now. But I'll mention it to Prosecutor Leigh."

"You can just call him?"

"I'm going to work for him after I graduate."

"Now who's sassy?" Patty said. "Is he handsome?"

"Yes," she answered too quickly. "In an mature sort of way."

"That didn't figure in your decision?"

"Only in the sense that he wasn't repulsive."

"I tend to believe you, but I haven't seen him yet."

"O.K., then. He reminds me of Johnny Depp."

"So he's weird too?"

"Forget it, Patty."

"Sorry I inquired."

The drinks arrived. They toasted to Victim Reparations.

They passed up dessert in favor of a second beer. "You're not going to go crazy and rip off your clothes now?" Tess inquired.

"I need the proper stimulation for that. It's not just alcohol."

"The night just got lovelier," Lucas said. "Good evening, ladies." Neither had seen him approach.

How does he do that?

While Tess was wondering whether to ask him to join them, Patty scooted over to make room for him. He accepted the invitation and, with the slightest gesture of one hand, managed to order another round for them and a large draft for himself. Maybe it was like Lucy had said. Some people are naturally better at life than the rest of us. Something like that. Their drinks had arrived before Tess had completed her reflections.

Meanwhile, Lucas had begun to chat them up. *Better pay attention before I end up like Patty did.* She re-engaged before they had missed her.

Lucas was consoling Patty on the loss of her mother. He was keeping it very non-specific. Like he hadn't ever been to the house, let alone seen her crumpled body at the foot of the stairs. Good. Their respective stories wouldn't get tangled. No conflicts.

"Still got your bike?" Patty asked. The implication was clear. She was putting the moves on him.

"Tess is the one with the Harley now," he deflected smoothly.

"Really?" Patty seemed surprised. Could she have forgotten? The next natural act would be for her to look at Tess, to discuss this wonder. But Patty's eyes never left Lucas. *Busted, you little minx!*

"We should go for a ride sometime," Tess offered. "The weather's perfect."

"Love to." Lucas accepted the offer intended for Patty.

Ambushed!

"I wasn't talking to you, Deputy Wise-Ass."

"I'm semi-crushed, Tess." He obviously wasn't. His smile confirmed that.

"I'd like that," Patty told Tess. "How about soon? Like before housecleaning robs me of the will to live?"

"Can you last until tomorrow afternoon?"

"What should I wear?"

"Blue jeans, top, light jacket. Real shoes as opposed to sandals."

"Got all that."

"Be ready by 5:30 then. We'll check the weather first, of course."

By then, Lucas had returned the glances of several other young ladies; so he excused himself. "Enjoy the rest of the evening, ladies."

"What a piece of work," Tess commented as he walked away.

"Oh, yeah." Patty agreed enthusiastically.

"I guess I have the privilege of paying for his beer." But Tess held her tongue as to the rest of her thoughts. She didn't see that anything was to be gained by telling Patty that she'd already had her big date with Lucas.

Of all the things to forget!

CHAPTER 70

Cobblers' Knob, Vermont

Thursday, April 21, 2017, 11:04 AM EDT

"Gnawed," said the Sheriff solemnly. He had just gotten off the phone with the Medical Examiner.

"Nod? Like Winken, Blinken and Nod?" Tess asked.

"Guh-nawed. As in canine teeth marks on the bones, especially the long bones where the marrow is — or was." O.K. That made it chillingly clear.

"Post mortem?" Lucas inquired in that lazy manner of his.

"I wish. But nay, young Deputy. Life is not that simple."

"Are you saying they were attacked by wolves, Sheriff?" Deputy Tess asked.

"It's about all that fits, but I'm still hoping for an alternative explanation."

"Still no reported sightings of wolves in the area," Lucas said. "And it would take more than one lone wolf to take out that many people."

"Could be something to those old *Coriloo* legends," Tess suggested. She thought she saw Lucas stiffen for a millisecond, but she wasn't sure.

"How did you hear about them?" Sheriff Roy wondered.

"Lucy Thornton was holding forth on shape shifters one night."

"Figures. She wrote a paper on Wolfman in college."

"It was for a course in gothic literature. Dracula was in it too," Tess explained to Lucas.

"It's amazing what passes for higher education," he responded. Another confirmation that it was a waste of time.

"Well, the *Coriloo* would be an alternative explanation. I'll grant you that," Sheriff Roy conceded. "But they're even scarcer than wolves."

"Even when the Moon is full," Lucas added.

"It wasn't a serious suggestion. Just threw it out there for consideration."

"Could have been an alien picnic," Lucas hypothesized.

"I'm closing the discussion on alternative explanations now." The Sheriff had heard enough on the subject.

"O.K. then. I told Prosecutor Leigh that I'd take the position he offered."

Deputy Lucas looked up from his paper shuffling.

"You'd be crazy not to," Sheriff Roy advised. "Huge career opportunity."

"Even if that's not what I want to do with my life?"

"You're going through four years of college to get your degree. Think of it as post-graduate studies."

"Hadn't thought of it that way," she admitted.

"Maybe you should."

Deputy Lucas entered the discussion with "See how the other half lives, young Tess. Broaden your horizons. Look to the great world that lies beyond Cobblers' Knob."

Both of them looked at him in wonder. Those green

eyes of his sparkled with mischief.

Sheriff Roy concluded that Tess must be the only attractive female in town immune to the charms of Deputy Lucas. That would explain it. This could get interesting. He sat back to enjoy the show.

Tess counter-attacked. "In my brief stay here, Cobblers' Knob has experienced three kidnappings, one probable murder and a state police SWAT team takedown of rogue federal agents, which resulted in a death while resisting arrest. In addition, I have participated in the apparent recovery of a girl who was so traumatized that she could no longer speak. I don't expect to find a comparable variety of stimuli in Burlington."

She's good, the Sheriff decided.

"Furthermore, I have come to appreciate the people of this town in a way I could not have imagined just a month ago. Among them are talents that could shine on bigger stages, but have chosen to be a part of this captivating community in the north woods. Incredibly, I have come to understand that decision, as well. And even if I do become part of a larger reality, I will never forget my time here or the good people of Cobblers' Knob."

She had nailed Lucas to the wall. Except for the intrusion of a few uninvited tears near the end.

"Deputy Tess' Farewell Address," the Sheriff announced. "Write that down for the appropriate time, Tess." She didn't move. "I'm serious. That was rather spectacular."

She was calmer now. *Did I just say that?*

"I don't think we'll forget you either, Tess." It was hard to tell how Deputy Lucas meant that, but she decided to give him the benefit of the doubt.

"I love it when my deputies get along."

CHAPTER 71

Cobblers' Knob, Vermont
Thursday, April 21, 2017, 5:26 PM EDT

Patty's jeans must have been painted on. Her camo tee shirt was cropped to within millimeters of her breasts. The light black jacket was tied around her waist. The shoes appeared to be the offspring of hiking boots and running shoes.

In short, perfect for a biker moll. Roll her in the dirt and knock out a few teeth, she could pass for one of Hell's Angels' own.

Tess had barely stopped when Patty swung aboard. *"Je suis pret!"* She needlessly announced that she was ready.

"Nous allons!" Tess shouted back over the engine noise. Then she gave the bike a little gas, to see if Patty

was as ready as she'd said. It seemed that she was. "Here we go!"

The vintage Harley fishtailed a bit on the gravel where the driveway met the street. Then it caught hold of the pavement and roared off.

In the direction of Necklan's Lake, although that wasn't obvious yet. Tess was still investigating.

As they approached the entrance to Camp Bethany, Patty yelled "Where are you going?" She meant *What the Hell do you think you're doing?*

Tess brought the bike to a stop between the remains of the two stone entrance pillars. "You hot?"

"A bit," Patty admitted. "But I'm not comfortable here."

"Got some icy longnecks in the saddle bags. Thought we might have a few to cut the dust."

"Where?"

"Down by the lake. Might be a breeze there."

"Then we leave?"

"Before dark," Tess assured her. "Long before dark."

"I don't know...."

"We can leave if you get spooked. I just thought it was time you had a good experience here. It is quite beautiful."

"Was this your plan all along?" Patty grew defensive.

"No. When I thought of where we could ride, I realized the road down here was scenic and pretty much free of traffic. Sounded ideal. Having a few beers here came to me later. But we could just go to *Rachel's* instead. Your call."

"What the Hell! Let's go on down to the lake." Spunky.

"That's the spirit!" She revved the engine and headed down the drive.

The sun was reflecting off the surface. The sky was just beginning to turn orange. "It's so peaceful," Patty commented.

"So, you don't hold a grudge?"

"The lake never hurt me," she replied. "It did have some bad associations."

"You said 'did,' not 'does,' Tess observed.

"Hmm. I guess I did."

"See those big rocks over there, in the water?"

"Yeah. What about them?"

"I think you were there, behind one of them, when the rest of the Seniors were attacked."

Patty shivered involuntarily. "Why would I have been way over there? The party was right here."

"Maybe you wanted some privacy." Tess had carefully worked out this wording.

"What? Why would I want...." She stopped cold. And stared at the rocks.

Tess kept silent. It wasn't easy.

"I want to go over there," Patty announced unexpectedly. She began to disrobe.

"What?" Tess was shocked by the reaction. "But the water's freezing."

"You can stay here."

"You might get cramps from the cold," Tess argued. "I can't let you go in there alone."

Patty was stripped down already. "Then come on. I want to see those rocks while it's still light."

This wasn't part of the plan. But Tess looked around to confirm they were alone. Then she began to remove her clothes. Patty went to the water's edge to test the temperature, and give Tess some privacy. She apparently didn't relish being watched while she stripped. At least not by another woman.

There was an involuntary scream, as Patty raced headlong into the lake. Tess followed, and echoed the scream.

Frigid didn't begin to describe it.

As soon as she could think about something besides freezing, Tess began to swim after Patty in the direction of the rocks.

"Rochers!" Patty exclaimed as she arrived.

Tess' brain slowly translated that into 'rocks.' She vowed never to encourage anyone to speak a foreign language again.

Patty was standing at the base of the largest rock. "Was I here?"

"Try putting your back against it," Tess suggested. "Since you didn't see what was happening on shore," she added. Of course, it wasn't just that.

Patty complied, saying "It's smooth, but very cold. About the same temperature as the water, I'd guess."

"Sounds right."

"For some reason, it feels --- familiar is the best word I can come up with."

"Anything else?"

"Comfortable. No, scratch that. It feels good. Really good. But I'm freezing; so how can that be?"

"Maybe you have some pleasant associations with this place, too," Tess suggested.

"Or, it could be the ice forming on my body."

"Ready to get out so soon?" Tess taunted.

"Damn right. But don't let me spoil your fun. Stay as long as you like," she said. "I'll be on the shore, watching you turn blue. Taking photos with my cell phone. I don't think YouTube has a topless Smurf yet."

That was when Tess dunked Patty. Just before she swam toward shore. Vigorously.

Lacking towels, they donned their clothes to conserve body heat.

"Do they make heated bras?" Patty asked, as she reached that stage of dressing.

"If they do," Tess replied "put me down for one."

The sun was setting. It was getting colder. *"Il fait froid!"* Patty remarked.

Tess agreed. It was cold.

Time to leave Necklan's Lake.

CHAPTER 72

Cobblers' Knob, Vermont
Friday, April 22, 2017, 12:07 PM EDT

Rachel's was filling up with the lunch crowd. It was the day set aside each week to celebrate bacon & pepper jack cheeseburgers, at bargain prices yet. Patty rushed over to the booth Tess had secured. "Sorry, I'm late."

"As long as you didn't run over too many people on the way."

"No. I seem to have retained my driving skills," Patty assured her. "Parallel parking is another matter."

"I just arrived myself," Tess admitted. "Ever notice how nobody has anything to say until you get up to leave?" It was rhetorical.

"I just left Earl. He was surprised to see me."

"I'll bet."

"He's going to help bring my computer skills up to date."

"I hear there's this new thing out called Windows."

"Windows? That's not …." Patty stopped mid-sentence. "Nicely done, Tess. I was about to expound on the history of computers."

"Something to do with apples, I believe. Some fruit that grows on trees."

"And the birds sit in those trees and tweet. Two can play this game."

"What about smart phones? Are they on the curriculum?"

"Yes, indeed," Patty responded. "He practically laughed when he saw my flip phone."

"But he didn't."

"No. He wouldn't. He wants me around, I guess."

"Sounds like a good guess, you little heartbreaker."

"That's me," she admitted gleefully. "But I'm not leading him on or anything."

"Understood. Some guys don't need much encouragement for their fantasies."

"I'll bet you have the guys at Dartmouth chasing

you all over."

Tess sighed. "It's never the one you want, is it?"

"Goes without saying."

"So what else is new?"

Just then the waitress appeared. Patty talked Tess into trying the special. They both ordered raspberry iced tea to drink.

"Well," Patty said in a sly way, indicating what she had to say was somewhat of a bombshell, "Earl asked me about an old Harley-Davidson with straight pipes."

That got Tess' attention. "And?' She was trying really hard to sound only mildly interested. Besides, it wasn't the appropriate venue for placing Patty in a hammerlock and applying painful pressure until she talked. One had to be considerate of the other patrons.

"It didn't register at first, and I'm still not sure...."

I could probably get away with a vicious kick to her shin under the table.

"But?"

"I think he might have been talking about Deputy Lucas' bike," Patty finally disclosed. "Have you ever seen it?"

"No. I heard that he wrecked it. Sheriff told me," Tess said. "Why would Earl ask you?"

"That's the interesting thing. Earl thinks I left the Senior Prom on a bike with straight pipes."

"But you didn't?"

"My brain left the prom when the vodka punch kicked in. No idea what happened after that." But she clearly enjoyed the idea of having driven off into the night with Lucas on his motorcycle. *Oh, yeah.*

Tess thought she could feel the heat radiating from Patty at the very thought of it. She wanted to change the subject, but couldn't bring herself to do it. Instead, she heard her mouth say "Patty, have you ever dreamed about that?"

"Going off with Lucas?"

"On his Harley in the night, to be precise."

"Dreams don't mean anything."

She hadn't even attempted to answer the question, Tess noted. Time to lighten the mood. "I had a psych professor who called them brain farts," Tess said with a whimsical smile.

"Really?"

"Yeah. The Psychology Department was kind of divided over the significance of dreams.' Patty's face scrunched up a bit at that; so she continued. "Actually, it was more like religious tribes warring over an obscure interpretation of a passage in the *Quran*."

"Why did you study psychology?"

"Required courses for the degree. A few, like Logic and Philosophy, were pretty interesting though." Then she struck. "So, you dreamed about Lucas."

Patty blushed. "Not as much as Leonardo DiCaprio," she said, defensively.

"That's not the point," Tess said. "Have you dreamed of yourself with Lucas in the water?"

Silence. Tangible silence.

"O.K.," Tess said. "Here come our burgers. *Bon Appétit.*"

They both dug into their food like they hadn't seen any for days. Neither spoke. The homemade potato chips disappeared, as well. Then Patty put her burger down like she was finished, like she'd never eat another bite of any burger anywhere. She glared at Tess.

"Sorry, Patty. None of my business."

That seemed to help, a little. Patty sipped her iced tea thoughtfully.

"Correct. None of your business." Patty agreed.

Tess nodded, but remained silent.

"Wasn't just a dream, was it?" Patty asked her.

"Good question," Tess answered. "Could have been a hybrid, part dream and part memory. I really don't know, Patty."

"It's the same every time."

"Don't know that that would prove anything. I've had similar dreams before."

"Identical." She said it as though it required a conclusion.

"Out by the rocks?"

"My back up against that big rock --- like last night. It was exactly like my dreams."

"Sounds like a pretty good dream," Tess speculated.

"Until the screams started."

"Then what happened?"

"Not real clear on that part. It's blurry. But I'm cold and alone in the water at the end."

"So it's a one-night-stand dream."

"Definitely."

"You ever hear that song *Lovin' for Dessert?*©"

"Country duet, right?"

"That's the one. If you listen long enough, there's this great line sung by the lady.

> *I just don't see the point of hit and run.*
>
> *Romance should survive the rising sun.*©

Sort of nails it."

"I'm an idiot," Patty proclaimed unexpectedly. "It's not a dream, is it?"

"What else could it be?"

"A memory. The hazy memory of a drunken girl."

"You don't know that, Patty." *But I think I do.*

"I'm such an idiot!"

"I seriously doubt that. In fact, I think you're rather intelligent. And now that you've got your life back, I'll bet you do amazing things with it."

"Like what?"

"Stop worrying about the past and move on."

"Away from Cobblers' Knob?"

"That wasn't exactly what I meant, but it wouldn't

hurt for you to get out in the world for a while, at least. Cobblers' Knob will still be here if you want to come back. That's what Lucy Thornton did. It's not a bad place."

"Now that it finally has cable."

"That helps," Tess admitted.

"Maybe I will, after I get mom's estate taken care of."

"No rush."

"I'm not so sure about that. The way my life's been going lately."

"No *big* rush, then," Tess amended.

CHAPTER 73

Cobblers' Knob, Vermont

Saturday, April 23, 2017, 8:00 PM EDT

The members of the Senior Class meandered around the decorated gymnasium. The theme, apparently, was crepe paper. In abundance. Some Seniors had the look of cattle that had just entered the feed lot, equal parts curiosity and apprehension. Each and every student was well aware that this was a special event in his young life, but not one of them had a clue how to modify his behavior accordingly. The country rock band, imported all the way from Montpelier, was tuning up. Sheriff Roy was standing next to Lucy as she greeted those arriving a bit late. The message was clear, the smiling welcoming committee consisted of the very persons who could throw you out of school and could put you in jail. That tended to mute the enthusiasm of some of those being welcomed, although the only serious criminal activity being contemplated that evening was spiking the punch. Not exactly a capital offense.

Sheriff Roy looked rather dapper in a Navy blazer over khaki trousers. He even sported shiny cordovan loafers — without tassels. Lucy rocked a little black suit and three-inch heels. It was time for the Seniors to see her in a different light. But it was Tess that had the boys sneaking glances, despite her demure attire. There was something exotic about an older woman from another place. Tess would have been surprised to be described that way. But she didn't appear to notice.

Tess was focused on her job, which to her included getting to see how the Senior Prom actually worked. The brief and occasionally conflicting descriptions of it had been, at the very least, inadequate. This was her chance to understand the dynamics involved --- such as they might be. Tess admitted to herself that she might be overthinking this, but plunged ahead anyway.

Tess was standing by the snacks table talking with Janet, the librarian who had helped her find information about Patty in the year books. Aside from Lucy, Janet was the only member of the teaching staff she knew.

"So did you ever solve the mystery of Necklan's Lake?" she asked.

"Not really," Tess confessed. "But I did spend enough time thinking about it that I've come to call it Nekkid Lake, just like the kids do."

Janet laughed. "Actually, that's pretty easy to do. The difficult thing is to *not* call it Nekkid Lake. And to not hesitate, because everyone knows you're trying to remember the real name."

"Been there myself."

Janet looked around and then softly inquired "Were you involved in that kidnapping?"

Tess realized that she didn't even know which kidnapping Janet was referring to. "Only peripherally. I didn't solve it or anything." She hoped that would end the inquiry.

"That must have been exciting," Janet suggested. Tess recalled Janet's earlier comment about being stuck in the north woods, bored out of her skull.

"As opposed to writing parking tickets, definitely."

Tess had never written a parking ticket, but she was confident that the adrenalin level was substantially lower than a midnight rescue on horseback and finding a mass grave. The realization that she had participated in a number of discoveries that might never be revealed briefly overcame her.

"Are you feeling all right?" Janet asked.

"Oh. Yes, thank you. I'm thirsty. Maybe a bit dehydrated."

"There's a drinking fountain by the door. Let's have some water." She began to walk that way. "The punch is full of sugar."

The band could have struck up a tune. But it didn't. Instead, the lead singer shouted

Shot through the heart!

And you're to blame!

You give lu-hu-huv

a ba-ad name!

To the accompaniment of rim shots on the snare drum. No sooner was the last word yelled into the microphone, than two electric guitars assaulted the eardrums in a coordinated attack. The Seniors scrambled to the area of the basketball court that had been reserved for dancing. Some didn't bother to bring partners. They just danced.

"It's going to be a long night," Sheriff Roy predicted.

"NASA used less energy to send men to the Moon," Lucy remarked.

"I don't think I can do that," he admitted.

"Don't even think about it. You'd pull a long-forgotten muscle."

"I love it when you talk dirty."

She laughed. "Randy old coot!"

He chuckled at her retort.

Lucy offered hope. "I've bribed the band to play a few old standards later. God knows what that will sound like."

"Old standards," the Sheriff mused. "Like *Smokin' in the Boys Room?*"

"Heaven forbid!"

Shortly before the band's intermission, Sheriff Roy and Principal Thornton showed the Seniors how civilized people danced — or at least used to. The kids actually applauded after the two ended their set with a spirited swing number. They held their heads high as they returned to the sidelines.

"At least we have a year to recover," Lucy noted.

But it was not to be. Tess grabbed the Sheriff before he had a chance to sit, and returned him to the floor. Sensing the excitement of the crowd at this development, the band struck up an encore of *In the Mood* --- a big band song ingeniously updated for guitars and keyboards. Kind of the opposite of playing *Hotel California* on trombones. So Tess gave the Sheriff a break by doing most of the work, twirling around until she was dizzy. Lucy had a cup of water ready for Sheriff Roy when the song ended. Then he and Tess patrolled the perimeter of the school to discourage the Seniors from smoking, drinking and making out. Those activities would have to wait until after the prom. The idea was to prevent hurling inside the gym. Although no one tried to explain a causal relationship between making out and vomiting.

"I've thwarted two attempts to spike the punch," Tess announced.

"Congratulations, but its only halftime. Sooner or

later they realize it needs to be spiked *before* it reaches the punch bowl."

"You have experience in these matters."

"Years of it. The best way to stay ahead of them is to make sure the bowl is kept filled to the top with the real, unadulterated product. Then, even if they do get some of the spiked punch in, it's diluted to the point of being harmless."

If anything, the music was even more frenetic after the intermission. The gymnasium doors were propped open in an attempt to bring in some fresh air. But it appeared that the Seniors didn't require oxygen to dance. Finding that suspicious, Tess sampled the punch. It exploded in her throat. She actually felt her eyes pop. Nearby, a clump of Seniors began to giggle as she tried not to cough.

Sneaky little devils!

And then it was ending. The band began to play wildly. The lead singer shouted "Watch it now! Watch it now!" by way of introduction.

Matty told Hatty

About a thing she saw.

Had two big horns,

and a wooly jaw

Wooly bull-eee,

Wooly bully!

The Seniors immediately recognized this as the traditional closing number for all proms since *Fast Times at Ridgemont High,* a motion picture that predated the birth of them all. Tired or not, everyone danced. Tess and Janet dragged Lucy and the Sheriff off their chairs to join in.

When the band finally stopped, the gym was steaming. The Seniors began to file outside, where the cool night air revived them. They began to get into their cars and pickups. An impromptu convoy was forming in the parking lot. Tess and Janet joined them in the moonlight.

"Where are they going?" Tess asked.

"Necklan's Lake, probably. It's a tradition, and it's not like there's much else to do around here."

"Did you go?"

"I take the Fifth."

"Janet, you are not good at deception."

"I can't handle the punch either," she admitted. The librarian was a bit tipsy.

It took a few moments for Tess to realize what was troubling her.

The Moon was red.

Lucas had said the moonlight was red.

Tess pointed to the Moon "What is that?" She asked Janet.

"Oh. That's a Blood Moon. They happen every so often. It's a type of lunar eclipse where sunlight still reaches the Moon by coming around the edges of the Earth. The Earth's atmosphere turns that light red. There are all sorts of religious...."

"Can you get into the library?"

"Now?"

"Right this second!"

"Sure. I've always got the key with me." Tess had pulled her back into the gym by the time she'd finished the sentence. Now Tess was running toward the library. Janet picked up her pace to follow. "What are we doing?"

"Open the door. We need information."

Janet jammed the key into the lock and twisted it. Tess pushed the door open.

"Now what?" she asked, caught up in the urgency.

"We need the internet. Turn on the computer first."

Janet went to a computer terminal and opened it with her password. She turned to face Tess, awaiting instructions.

"What was the date of the 2014 Senior Prom?"

"Should be in the yearbook." She scurried off to find it. After a minute, she came back holding it open. May 16th. A Friday."

"Now check to see if there was a Blood Moon that night."

"You're not buying that superstitious nonsense, are you?"

"That may depend on the answer. Where there's smoke, there's fire."

"Oh." Janet was typing away furiously, like someone who had actually taken a typing class at one time.

"Anything?"

"Oh, lots of stuff. Prophesies based on Bible verses.

Predictions of doom. Wait! I found a site that actually lists the dates for Blood Moons."

"Good. Was there one in 2014?"

"Yes, there was. Actually there were four, which is unusual."

"Any on May 16th?" Janet's tendency to explain everything in detail was wearing on Tess.

"Yes, there was! Visible in New England, too."

"Thanks, Janet. I've got to run." In fact, she already was.

"But...," Janet looked at Tess racing down the hall. "I'll ask Tess what that was about next time I see her."

Tess sprinted past the Sheriff. "Necklan's Lake. Now!"

She thanked God that she hadn't worn high heels, as she plunged into her Beetle and got it started. She didn't look back to see Sheriff Roy waving his hands in the air. Tess ripped out of the lot and sped down the road, towards Necklan's Lake.

Everything was bathed in a soft red glow.

CHAPTER 74

Necklan's Lake, Vermont

Saturday, April 23, 2017, 11:39 PM EDT

"Here I am, going off to do battle against deadly forces. Dressed for dancing and completely unarmed. Some cop I am." Tess scanned the rear view mirror yet another time, hoping to see the flashing lights atop the Sheriff's Jeep. Only darkness. Reddish darkness.

Then there was traffic coming toward her. As a convertible passed, she recognized the occupants as Seniors — still mostly dressed up for the prom. Except for the topless girl with the beer bottle in her hand. She was processing this information when she saw a flashing red light ahead. On a vehicle astride the entrance to Camp Bethany. Someone was turning away the Seniors!

Her first thought was that the Sheriff knew a great

shortcut. But then she realized the official Jeep had flashing blue lights too. It was Lucas' car with the portable red light on the dashboard. She pulled up behind it and jumped out.

"Hey, Lucas! Great work, heading off the Seniors." She couldn't see him, as she walked through the ruined entrance and down the road toward Necklan's Lake. She'd gone about fifty yards.

"Don't turn around, Tess." Her heart skipped a beat. She hadn't detected him right behind her. He'd done it again. *How does he do that?*

She involuntarily began to do just that. It was a reflex. Both her arms were gripped from behind so hard it caused her to cry out. "What the Hell are you doing Lucas?"

"Trying to save your life, Tess." His voice was different. Kind of raspy.

"Like you saved Patty's --- by jumping her?"

"No. And that's not how I saved Patty."

That confused her. "Let me go and we'll talk about it."

"No time to talk, Tess."

"Tell me what you did to save Patty, and I'll go."

Lucas made a low growling sound that she mistook for impatience. But then he said "I left her."

"You left her?" Tess was incredulous. "That's how you saved her?"

"Yes. Now go! Run as fast as you can! Your life is in danger."

"How did leaving her alone save her?" Tess was nothing, if not tenacious.

"Wrong question, And you're out of time."

"And you aren't?" It had just dawned on her that he wasn't worried about himself.

"Listen. I am *Coriloo*. That night was my first time to hunt. But I didn't know it until it began to happen. I fled to avoid hurting Patty."

"My God! Did you kill the Seniors?"

"Now, Tess! You have to run. Don't look back. I'll run the opposite direction to give you as much time as possible. But once I change, I'll hunt you down and kill you. And I'm not alone. Run for your life. Now!"

His grip relaxed, allowing her to break free. She bolted for her car. In the distance, she heard the sounds of frenzied animals. Wolves. A pack of them headed in her direction. She ran faster.

Then the sound was behind her. Lucas! He was gaining. He must be right behind her.

Claws raked down her back, through her clothes. Ripping into her flesh. She screamed.

It was no longer a race to her car. She'd already lost that one. All she sought was another few seconds before she was ripped apart. Somehow she upped her speed, instinctively knowing she'd have no use for energy once she was hauled down by the creature hunting her.

Another swipe of the claws caught her, scouring parallel lines an inch deep into her back. The blow propelled her forward, stumbling and bleeding profusely now.

She forced herself to stagger one more step toward her car --- her unattainable refuge in the ghastly moonlight. Now she was parallel to the ground, launching her body desperately at the goal.

Another claw tore across her exposed legs, ripping her left calf. She fell into the cool grass, crippled.

Tess could no longer run. There would be no

escape. She would be mauled to death. Wolf-like creatures would consume her flesh, even as she still struggled.

She rolled on her back to face her destiny. Which sensed her defeat, approaching her slowly. It wasn't a wolf. But it sure as Hell wasn't human either. She'd expected fur. Not the case, though. Lucy would have told her that was just Hollywood. The fingers were webbed, with large curving claws at the tips --- red with her blood, she realized. The jaws were extended, like a canine. The nose was flattened. The ears curled forward. The eyes looked human, but pierced her soul. Its teeth were designed to pull flesh from bone efficiently. It was unafraid. It was unwary. The beast regarded her as if selecting the choicest piece of meat.

Tess began to tremble. The creature noticed, took in her fear. Relished it even. Then it crouched, ready to leap on her. To begin the process of tearing her apart. Of consuming her organs, drinking her blood. And she was helpless to stop it.

"Lucas!" she screamed. The beast eyed her curiously --- with Lucas' green eyes.

She heard the other beasts approaching. Since

Lucas had driven away the Seniors, she might be the only prey tonight. Maybe the creatures would descend upon her to share the meal that she had become. Wolves sometimes did that. That would explain why the beast hesitated.

She prayed that she would die from blood loss before they began to consume her. It didn't seem much to ask.

A siren!

The beast heard it too. It had raised its head at the sound. But it didn't appear to be concerned. It was still too far away to help her.

Suddenly, the creature was bathed in light. It spun to look. Headlights. The car was skidding to a stop. It stood up from its crouched position, analyzing this new development. But it did not flee.

The car shot forward, driving the beast under the bumper. The sound of breaking bone cracked in the night. The car shot backwards, over the beast again. It no longer moved. It was no longer a threat.

The driver's door opened. "Tess!" It was Patty. "I remembered the red Moon!"

"Stay in the car!" Tess yelled to her.

The howling increased. The other beasts began to close in on them.

Patty got out. "Can you get into the car?" She opened the left back door, then helped Tess to stand. There was a growl from behind her. She pushed Tess onto the back seat, and climbed in on top of her, closing the door as she did. Then she climbed into the front seat passenger seat as another beast surveyed the open driver's door, watching her intently.

"Tess!" she cried out. Tess found an umbrella on the floor and poked it over the seat back at the beast. All this accomplished was to distract it momentarily from Patty. In desperation, Tess pressed the button that caused the umbrella to burst open in the beast's face. Intelligent or not, this was a new experience for the creature. It was confused, a trifle spooked.

But it didn't run away. It probed at the fabric with a claw, soon concluding it posed no threat. The beast advanced on Patty. She put her arm up to fend it off. It bit into her flesh and twisted.

Then a creature leaped onto the hood. Seconds

later, it disappeared in a shotgun blast. The Sheriff had arrived. The beasts outside took flight. But the one inside the car remained focused upon its next meal. It moved in for Patty's throat. The side window exploded. The beast blew backward with it.

Sheriff Roy quickly pumped another round into the shotgun, as he asked through the destroyed window "Patty? Tess? You two all right?"

"Not by a long shot, Sheriff. We need medical attention," Patty replied. "Tess has lost a lot of blood." She looked at her own bloody arm. "Make that both of us."

"Still bleeding?" he asked.

"Not as much as before, but still too much," Patty answered.

"My leg's pretty bad. I can't tell about my back," Tess yelled.

The siren stopped. The door of the Jeep opened. Lucy Thornton stepped out cautiously. "Is she O.K.?" Lucy asked.

"She'll make it. Patty, too," he answered, as Lucy appeared beside him. "Got to call Doc." He pushed buttons on his cell phone. "Have him meet us at his office for transfusions and tourniquets."

Lucy didn't understand why Patty was there. "Patty? What's she...."

"Lucy?" Tess called from the back seat of Patty's car.

Lucy raced around to assist Tess. She never made it. She tripped over something.

As she fell, her outcry morphed from surprise to terror, as she found herself face to face with what was left of Deputy Lucas. His arms closed around her, imprisoning her. Sheriff Roy was there. He slammed the stock of the shotgun into Lucas' ear. Lucas' arms immediately fell to his side.

Lucy rolled off him, gasping for breath. The Sheriff pulled her up by her arms, embracing her. She buried her face in his shoulder and sobbed. Then Sheriff Roy recognized the mangled form on the ground as his deputy. That form was now entirely human, but not normal. One leg was unnaturally askew. His clothing was ripped and torn, but there was little blood. His injuries appeared to be from multiple impacts.

"What the Hell happened to Deputy Lucas?"

"You killed him!" Patty shouted her accusation at the bewildered Sheriff. She knelt beside him, feeling his neck for a pulse. "I think he's dead!" Patty lowered her head to Lucas' broken chest and wept.

Neither Lucy nor Sheriff Roy could speak, as they held each other tightly. They just stared at the bizarre sight before them by the eerie light of the Blood Moon. It was obvious that a single blow to the side of the head had not inflicted the horrific damage to Lucas' brutalized body. But what had?

The other creatures had moved on, but their howls carried through the night on the cold wind.

Tess managed to extract herself from the back seat. Using the car door for support, she stood up and worked her way to the hood. Her clothes were soaked in her own blood. Her eyes were unfocused. Leaning over the hood of Patty's car, she pointed to the Moon. Her shaky voice announced "Solved your cold case, Sheriff."

Then she slid down the fender and passed out.

CHAPTER 75

St. Johnsbury, Vermont
Sunday, April 24, 2017, 10:28 AM EDT

"Had enough beauty rest?" the nurse inquired as Tess tentatively opened her eyes. Sunlight was streaming through the window.

"Where am I?" Tess asked.

"St. Johnsbury Regional. You got cut pretty badly, but they patched you up. You're here now mostly for observation. Those are antibiotics in the IV. Don't want those wounds to get infected. You're also on some pretty heavy-duty painkillers; so don't try to get up."

That explained the fuzzy cortex.

"And you're going to need crutches for awhile. Nasty tear on your calf. It's in a kind of cast now."

It wasn't like in the books. Her memory didn't

come flooding back. If anything, it was seeping back.

"You shouldn't play with strange dogs. Especially big ones. What kind was it?"

"Large and angry," Tess replied, uncertain of what the staff had been told.

"I'd kind of figured that much out already." She was checking instruments and fluid levels as she talked.

"Is Patty Martin here too?"

"Yes, but still out like a light. They had to operate on her in the middle of the night to reattach some tendons in her arm. She went under the knife right after they finished with you. I heard she stuck her arm in the dog's mouth to save you. Terrible trauma, but she should regain full use of it. Probably leave some scars though."

"What did they do to me?"

"Saved your leg." She realized that could be taken several ways. "I don't mean they might have amputated. But they had to reassemble parts of it before it would work again."

Tess realized she had stopped breathing at the word "amputated."

"You all right?"

"I guess I will be."

"Doctor McAdams stayed here all night. He even scrubbed for both surgeries and advised. That's a dedicated physician. Either of you related to him?"

"No. But it feels like it sometimes."

"And the Sheriff and his wife were here all night too. They finally left when Doctor McAdams did. Nice folks."

"Really nice," Tess agreed. The nurse must have thought Lucy was his wife.

"You two are our most popular patients right now."

"That's Patty's specialty. I'm just part of her entourage."

"Well, the man that came by this morning asked about you first. Of course, neither of you could be disturbed. I told him you were both doing fine and a full recovery was expected. He seemed relieved to hear that, and left."

"Who was he?"

"If he's your boyfriend, you're one lucky girl."

"Did he give you his name?"

"Corey something. Said the last name was too long,

to call him Corey L."

"Corey L." Tess said it aloud, as if that would identify him.

"You'd remember him. Believe me. Must be the pain killers."

Tess concentrated as much as the meds would permit. She focused on the name that meant nothing to her.

Corey. No. *Corey L. Coriloo? Impossible!*

"Green eyes?"

"Oh, yeah. Piercing green," she confirmed. "Wolf eyes."

EPILOGUE

Cobblers' Knob
Wednesday, April 27, 2017, 5:30 PM EDT

"The guest of honor traditionally arrives late," Pastor Matt said to Tess by way of greeting. He opened the door wide to allow her to limp through on one crutch. "No Harley tonight, I see."

She hopped into a chair, leaning the crutch against the arm. "The Beetle is challenging enough for me right now."

"That's your clutch leg, too."

"The cast rubs against the frame every time I engage it. I'm beginning to appreciate automatic transmissions."

"I imagine so. But it will pass," he predicted. "Before the other celebrants arrive, I have question for you. I want you to think it over before you answer."

"Shoot."

"What is your opinion of Deputy Lucas at this time?"

"Whoa! Didn't see that one coming."

He smiled at her response. "I suspect not. While you're considering your response, let me tell you a bit about the *Coriloo*."

Tess' eyes went wide at that.

"They came here from the French Alps. They may have originated somewhere else, but that is unknown. There is speculation that they are a parallel form of mankind, but it's more likely that they represent a successful mutation — meaning it is passed on genetically. But when a *Coliloo* and a normal human produce offspring, there doesn't appear to be any way to determine if those genes have been passed on. Furthermore, if they have been, they may be recessive. Are you following?"

"I think so. If they're recessive, the effects of the gene may not manifest in every succeeding generation. So even if the person suspects he may have those genes, he doesn't know if he will ... become a shape shifter?" Her sentence ended in uncertainty.

"Exactly. Which doesn't seem to happen the first time until maturity. Even then, a person could be in his late thirties the first time it occurs. And many have no clue that they even have the gene."

"Must be a shock when it happens."

"Indeed," Matt agreed. "Difficult to imagine the horror of that first time to someone unprepared for it."

Tess shuddered at the thought. "I wonder where the others are."

"I might have told them to come at 6:00," he said casually, as if he couldn't remember and it wasn't important anyway. "Can you imagine yourself suddenly becoming a shape shifter without knowing it was even possible?"

"No. It's a frightening thought," she admitted.

"Can you imagine being concerned about others while this incredible, impossible thing is happening to you?"

"I can see where you're going with this. But how did you know?"

"I believe I possess those recessive genes. I was

completely ignorant of that part of the family history. But when I first heard about the *Coriloo,* it explained so many family mysteries that I just knew. So I investigated. My father was *Coriloo.* My mother was not. Naturally, I stayed single until I knew for sure that I was not a shape shifter. By then, I was a confirmed bachelor."

"I wondered why you weren't snapped up."

"Your kindness is noted. I tried to come off as the dull, scholarly type. It wasn't that hard to do. I studied the *Coriloo* intensely. I even wrote about them."

"A book?"

"More of a tract. I didn't have enough information for a book."

"Was it published?" Tess was impressed.

"I submitted it to several university presses. Fortunately, it was rejected. Then I figured out that it would be a terrible disservice to the *Coriloo* to expose them to the public like that. Vigilantes would hunt them down. I had been thinking only of myself."

"You're right."

"They don't hunt humans, you know."

"Not so sure about that."

"Let me rephrase that. They don't target humans. If humans wander into their path while they're hunting, then the humans may become prey."

"What triggers the hunt?"

"There are various contributing factors...."

He has no idea.

"But, in New England and Québec, they only hunt during a Blood Moon."

Tess gasped. "Why didn't you say something?"

"What do you mean?"

"There was a Blood Moon last Saturday."

"So?"

"That was the night of the Senior Prom."

"It was scheduled for the following week. I checked."

"It was moved up a week, to the 23rd."

"Oh, my God! What happened?"

"Deputy Lucas stationed himself at the entrance to Camp Bethany. He turned the Seniors away."

"So no one was hurt?" Pastor Matt asked, hopefully.

"Did you notice my crutch?"

"I see," he said. "Sorry."

"So, his tactic wasn't as successful as it might have been," she told him. "But no one died."

"Or disappeared?"

"Well, I haven't seen Deputy Lucas since then...."

"Really? He told me he'd visited you in the hospital, made sure you were O.K."

"You've talked to him?" Tess became excited.

"Yes. He thinks you're angry with him. That's why I asked you what you thought of him. Have you had time to consider your answer?"

"Yes, I have. I think he's an amazing human being."

"For a *Coriloo*," he added.

"He's amazing, period," Tess amended.

"Good. Because I invited him."

"Tonight?"

"Not good?"

"Sheriff Roy might shoot him, is all."

"That could take the edge off the celebration," Pastor Matt predicted. Just then the doorbell rang. "Time to frisk the Sheriff."

Sheriff Roy and Lucy had arrived. The Sheriff

appeared to be unarmed. Doc McAdams was pulling in behind them. Patty Martin was with him, her left arm encased in bandages. When all had been greeted and seated, Pastor Matt announced that there was a small bit of business to attend to prior to embarking upon the festivities.

"You forgot to chill the beer," Sheriff Roy accused. "You're buying time."

"Besides that," Matt said. "You see, we share a secret. And we have to decide what to do about it."

"You're our spiritual guide. What do you suggest?" Doc McAdams knew how to play this game.

"I suggest that we respect the privacy of the ancient beings who dwell among us, while avoiding contact on those rare occasions when they hunt."

"Do we know when they hunt?" Lucy asked.

"When and where. Necklan's Lake during the Blood Moon."

"Why wouldn't we stop them?" Patty wondered.

Tess answered. "Because they can't help themselves, Patty. And they're not after people. They're just hunting."

The Sheriff had another take on it. "It would be like banning guns just because some fool accidently shoots his foot."

"I see now." Everyone still stared at her. "And I agree."

So the Necklan's Lake Massacre remains a mystery," Lucy concluded.

"Along with the Camp Bethany fire," Tess added. When the others looked at her, she added "It occurred during a Blood Moon, too."

The doorbell rang before they'd had time to digest this revelation.

"It appears that our last guest has arrived." Pastor Matt went to the door.

An uncharacteristically reserved Deputy Lucas stepped through the entry, and stopped just inside the door. He wanted to speak first. "I'd like to apologize to everyone here," he announced. "But I'd like to stay, since my best friends are all here."

Sensing reluctance on the part of some, Tess rose, hopped over to him and kissed him on the cheek. "This man saved my life. He's my hero." She read the room.

They weren't convinced. "Patty, don't you have something to say to Lucas?"

Patty approached, but without a clear idea of what to say. "Sorry about the thing with the car, Lucas. Hope you're O.K."

Lucas smiled at her. "Thanks for your concern. I'm fine, Patty. You did what you had to do."

And damned if he wasn't fine. No cuts. No limp. No indication he had been mauled by an automobile a few days before.

How can that be?

Patty gave him a peck on the check, and tried to not sigh too loud.

Sheriff Roy stood, glaring at Lucas like a high noon showdown. The room went still. "Just where is it written that heroes don't have to call in sick?"

Lucas crossed the room to embrace the Sheriff.

"Now cut that out, Lucas. Don't want Lucy to get the wrong idea."

"Don't flatter yourself, you randy old coot," Lucy crowed.

"Don't you just love the mating rituals of the truly

demented?" Doc McAdams asked rhetorically.

"Is he making fun of us?" Sheriff Roy asked Lucy.

"Cut him some slack. He's jealous," she replied.

Lucas assisted Tess back to the couch.

Doc McAdams turned to Matt. "Any truth to the rumor that spirits might be forthcoming, Your Holiness?"

"Now that you mention it, I believe they're overdue. I've heard that you have some expertise in removing the cork from the champagne bottle with nothing but your bare hands."

Doc displayed his hands for all to see. "Indeed I do. Lead the way."

"I'm going to miss you crazy people," Tess declared.

"We're zany," Lucy corrected. "And you're welcome to visit any time. I'd forgotten how big my house was until Patty dropped by. Hardly bumped into her --- except in the kitchen."

"She means the refrigerator," Patty explained.

"Stands there with the door wide open, and forages."

POP! No ricochet.

"Didn't spill a drop," Matt marveled.

Patty and Lucy handed out the champagne flutes, as Doc and Matt entered the living room with the frosty magnum. Once the glasses were filled, Lucy proposed a toast.

"Here's to our new friend Tess, who already feels like an old friend."

To that Sheriff Roy added "To Deputy Tess Chandler, as relentless as she is lovely."

Tess responded. "And here's to all of you, who made me feel so welcome here in Cobblers' Knob."

"Just trying to show the city girl a good time," Lucas said, his green eyes sparkling.

The End.

(La Fin.)

Noah Bond continues to provide us with intellectually stimulating page-turners without foul language, profanity or obscenity. Also by NOAH BOND:

ALL THE TARGETS

After a surprise nuclear attack cripples the West Coast, the new President embarks upon a daring plan to bring peace to Middle East. Enter the amateur terrorist who unwittingly brings turmoil to the highest level of U.S. government. A hijacking over France leads to arson in Sweden. The CIA engages itself in battle. And a comely North Korean girl plays rock 'n roll to get to Kim Jong-il. International intrigue with a twist.

THE LOST TESTIMONY OF BONES LeBEAU

The plot to assassinate President John F. Kennedy from inception through implementation, as explained by a witness whose testimony had been lost. The witness is fictional. The rest is truth. Finally, a coherent explanation of the conspiracy without all the conflicting reports and theories. There is a WGA-registered screen play of this novel.

THE DOORSTEP OF DEPRAVITY

A tale of lawyers, heirs, greed, deceit, lust and death. The young student heiress is not what she appears to be. The one-woman law office representing her takes on the biggest firm in town on her behalf, but there's no getting around the requirement that she must be married to inherit. Negotiations escalate from unorthodox to lethal. People die. Money vanishes. Then the unthinkable happens. There is a WGA-registered screen play of this novel.

NOMAD/Y THE MOON BASE PROJECT

Faced with the probability that a Cosmonaut would walk on the Moon before an Astronaut would, NASA moved the goal posts. The winner of the space race would now be the first to establish a base on the Moon. An international suspense thriller about the greatest cover-up in history and the astonishing events which it generated. Visit *www.moonbaseproject.com* for a free preview. There is a WGA-registered screen play of this novel.

FINE AS FROG HAIR

This is an album of 19 songs released November 8, 2013. Noah wrote the lyrics for all the songs, but one --- for which he wrote a few verses. Consider them as short stories set to music, with the insight and wit common to the novels. (Hand a novelist a guitar and he becomes a songwriter.) The songs are performed by Noah Bond (surprisingly tolerable) and professional vocalist Kathleen Patricia, with guest performances by Nicholas Coppola and Bryan Wilson. The songs feature amazing instrumental performances by Chris Capozza, who also provided the musical arrangements and engineering. *Fine as Frog Hair* was the unanticipated result of an effort by Noah's friend Nicholas Coppola to have Noah's song *Silver Ball on the Roulette Wheel of Life* recorded for posterity. That one session in February, 2013, provoked Noah into a songwriting frenzy that delayed completion of *Nekkid Lake* for two years. A second session followed that May, which included Kathleen Patricia. Five songs were released as downloads. In January, 2013, one of the songs, *I Love You, Keep Reading,* became a music video on YouTube. Later that year the project culminated in a 12-day recording session in June, 2013, that produced 13 new vocal tracks.

Starting with upbeat country, the album moves on to classic rock, progressive rock, and finally eases into bossa novas and other soothing sounds. The songs are available as a compact disc, or they can be downloaded as an album or individually. At this time, they may be previewed and purchased from Amazon.com., iTunes, CD Baby, Spotify, Google, Muve and other sites. The simplest way is to visit *www.noahbond.com.*

If you don't like rap and hip-hop,
if you've had enough disco for this lifetime,
if you find the sound of whining young girls annoying,
if you don't need electric guitars that make your ears bleed,
if you don't need to hear a cowboy lament his lost love(s),

Have a listen.   Have some fun.

**For more information about Noah Bond
novels and songs, visit**

www.noahbond.com.